NEXT
IN
LINE

AMY DAWS

Published by: Amy Daws, LLC

ISBN 13: 978-1-944565-24-4
ISBN 10: 1-944565-24-8

Editing: Jenny Sims with Editing4Indies
Formatting: Champagne Book Design
Cover Design: Amy Daws
Cover Photography: Wander Aguiar
Cover Model: John Michael Dewall

Dedicated to my dad for answering the question:
"Dad, what's a cool place for a book setting that's similar to
the weirdness of a tire shop?"

"A bait shop?"

And then a book was born!

And Dad, sorry to shut down your "Lucy Goosey from
Camp Watoosi" story idea, we'll workshop it next time I'm
home.

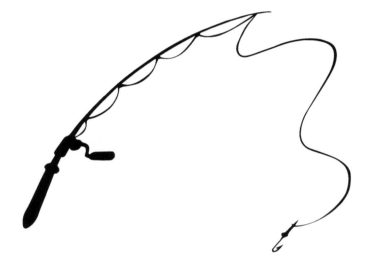

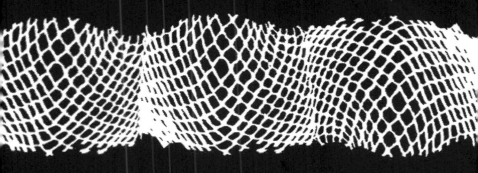

CHAPTER 1

Fish Out Of Water

Sam

"Next in line!" Marv shouts gruffly as he plunges his white-haired arm back into the basin full of fresh chubs.

An older gentleman shoulders past me with his clear plastic tub, ready to collect his bait as though it's the body of Christ being passed out by the pope himself. Several other men press up against my back, all anxiously awaiting their turn because finally...ice fishing season has begun.

Boulder, Colorado, hasn't seen a winter this warm in years. Normally, we're ice fishing before Christmas. But it's already early January, and there haven't been enough cold days in a row to make the ice safe enough to venture out on.

Until now.

I tug at my short beard impatiently as I itch for the smell of my nylon fishing tent. After being ignored for months now, it misses me. I can tell. The smell of the icy lake water permeates my nose as my imagination takes flight. I swear I can even feel the rubbery stiffness of my silicone gloves.

Ice fishing is my escape. It's my sense of freedom. It's something that's only mine.

Marv hollers for the next patron, and I can't help but shake my head at how this eighty-year-old man is still alive and kicking. Every year. Every season. Every weekend. Marv is here.

Marv's Bait and Tackle is an institution in Boulder. Located on a dirt road outside of town and boasting the best bait and burgers within a hundred miles, the restaurant/bar/bait shop is always brimming with die-hard Colorado outdoorsmen from near and far, looking to chew the fat with the infamous Marv.

Marv was a pro fisherman and even had his own television show for a while, but when his father, Marv Senior, passed away, he quit touring and took over the bait shop. Now, he's the go-to guy for the best places to fish around Boulder. He gives advice on the proper bait for the weather, and he's always getting demo rigs in the shop before the big box stores. He's a fishing legend tucked away in this dilapidated old shop.

"I'm next in line," a female voice exclaims as she clicks her heeled boots on the damp concrete floor.

I frown, wondering where this chick came from because there's no way I would have missed the likes of her in a place like this. She doesn't exactly blend in with the old, weathered, smelly fishermen. Myself excluded. I may be out of my twenties now, but my balls aren't sagging to my knees like most of these guys.

The girl is tall and slender with a backside on full display in a pair of tight leggings that cling to her ass. Her very supple ass. An ass that every guy in here is now staring at. She flips her silky black hair over her shoulder, and I catch a glimpse of her profile. Damn, her face is just as beautiful as her ass...which sounds fucking weird, but my dick is doing all my thinking at this point.

Marv spits his toothpick out, letting the wood drop to the floor as he looks the girl up and down. "Next in line for what?" he asks, his voice sounding like he smokes a pack of Marlboro Reds a day...probably because he does.

"I need the fish!" she replies, jutting her chin out defiantly.

"Do you mean bait?" Marv asks, scratching his white whiskers that makes a noise like sandpaper.

"Yes, they are little fish, right? Used for bait?" The girl shifts nervously, fiddling with a piece of hair draped over her shoulder. When she notices the whispering around her, she drops her hair and stands tall.

Marv's face scrunches up like the girl's words just hurt a piece of his soul. "They are chubs, darlin'. And they are used to catch muskies. Big muskies."

"Perfect. That sounds great...I'll take them." The girl crosses her arms and waits expectantly.

Marv shakes his head. "They're heavy."

3

"They don't look heavy," she retorts with a quizzical brow, looking down into the basin of live bait.

"The muskies, not the chubs," Marv corrects, plastering a painfully polite smile on his face.

"Get out of here, little girl!" an older guy shouts from behind me. "Go back to the mall or whatever nail salon you fell out of. We're actual anglers here, not playing make-believe."

The girl turns on her heel to eye the man behind me, and I get a full-on assault of just how beautiful she is. She has a heart-shaped face and the most vibrant blue eyes I've ever seen. Dark hair and light eyes are like catnip to me. And my dick agrees.

The girl licks her lush, peach-tinted lips before replying to the man. "You can go…" She falters for a second, glancing around at her audience once before adding, "Fuck yourself!" She blanches at the sound of that word leaving her lips.

The men behind me erupt into shocked laughter, and I watch Marv wince and dry his hands off on his dirty apron. "Young lady, that language."

"What?" she exclaims, turning back to Marv. "This is a bait shop. Are you telling me you've never heard that word before?"

Marv shakes his head. "Not from a young lady."

"So because I'm a female I can't curse? What kind of sense does that make in this decade? Please, I've been driving for a long time, and all I want to do is go ice fishing. I've got cash, so just sell me a bucket of fish and I'll be on my way. Easy peasy."

"When?" Marv asks quietly, twisting his face in discomfort as if it's been years since he's been around estrogen.

"When what?" the girl asks.

"When are you going ice fishing?"

"Right now, of course!" she retorts, putting her hands on her hips. "I'll need a pole and a fishing hook as well, please. And whatever you use to break the ice."

Marv looks down the girl's body, slowly shaking his head back and forth. "Do you have more clothes than what you're wearing?"

"I have gloves," the girl replies, digging into her pockets and producing a pair of fingerless gloves. They look like children's gloves, gold sparkles and all. She puts them on and waves her fingertips to Marv, who does not look impressed.

"Darlin', I can't let you go ice fishing in that getup. You'll freeze to death, and my old heart can't be worrying over you out there all alone in a spring jacket."

"This has down feathers!" she exclaims, pulling her black jacket tight around her body. "It's really warm. It just has the illusion of being lightweight."

He tsks. "Those boots there are worse than a pair of summer waders. Your feet would get cold in those if you were fishing from the shore in the spring, darlin'. I'm sorry. I won't be selling you bait and tackle today. You look more like a warm weather darling anyways."

The girl lets out a strange noise from her throat. "Oh, come on. I'm trying to step out of my comfort zone here and I am so tired of being labeled, I could just scream."

"I'd like to hear her scream when I'm balls deep in her," a man old enough to be her father mutters not so quietly from behind me.

My teeth crack as I clench my jaw and turn around just as his buddy high-fives him. Toothless smiles greet me as if they think I'm joining in on the joke. I open my mouth to say something but am pummeled in the shoulder by the young girl as she launches herself at the two men.

Everyone erupts into shouts as she shoves the big guy with all her might, but she only ends up knocking his camo hat off. Big guy looks scary pissed, so I quickly wrap my arms around the girl's waist and lift her off the ground to yank her back away from him. He leers at her, almost perversely turned on by her attack.

"Easy, sparky," I murmur into her ear as a whiff of her floral shampoo invades my nostrils.

"Say that to my face, you old pervert!" the girl shouts, flailing her arms as if she's going to claw the man's face off. One benefit of her fingerless gloves, I guess.

The two assholes blink slowly at her, clearly feigning innocence as I struggle to hold her back. She's a wiry one, for sure. A lot tougher than she looks.

"Come with me," I urge, pulling her away from the group of men who clearly just want to entertain themselves with this spectacle. I move around to face her with my back to the guys. I grab her shoulders and look her square in the eyes. "They're fucking dicks and not worth it. Your actions are just encouraging them, so I'm asking you to please come with me."

Her eyes resemble burning sapphires as they connect with mine for a split second before I hear the man say in a deep tone, "I'd kill to see her come on my cock."

As soon as she hears his words, the girl stills beneath my hands, her bright irises fading right before me. She curls into herself as she looks around, taking in our audience. Her eyes begin to water around the edges—and a familiar sense of unease creeps up in my belly.

I have three sisters.

I know that fucking look.

And I don't like it.

Clenching my jaw, I release her shoulders, turn on my heel...and deck the ass-fuck square in the jaw.

The satisfying punch propels him into his buddy, and they both topple to the floor, clearly not expecting my swing. My pulse thunders in my veins as men begin pushing in on us to break up the fight. What they don't know is there won't be a fight. I knocked that fucker out.

Without a word, I do a one-eighty, grab the shocked girl around the waist, and practically carry her away from the swarm of men all grappling for a look at the fallen prick.

I suck in deep, cleansing breaths, trying my hardest to lower my blood pressure so I don't turn around and knock out his high-fiving loser of a friend as well. It's been a decade since I hit someone. Apparently, it's like riding a bicycle...you never truly forget. I'd worry about someone calling the cops, but I'm ninety percent certain everyone in that bait shop wanted to deck the fucker too. Something tells me no one is calling anyone.

I guide the girl through the tackle shop and into the small attached diner. It's decrepit like the rest of the place, and full of old folks slumped into the worn booths and wobbly, mismatched chairs. Thankfully, the smell of grease and musty vinyl is calming, and I need to be calmed right now.

The girl appears to be in shock as she slides into the red corner booth out of sight from the rest of the bait shop. I picked this spot on purpose because I definitely don't need that fuckwad eyeing her or me while I try to figure out what the hell to do with this spark plug.

Looking down at her, I watch her pick at her nails nervously, her hair sheeting her face so I can't see her expression. She's clearly freaked out, and I can't say I blame her. That scene was ugly.

However, I've been to Marv's hundreds of times, and I know it's a safe place. What happened today was not the norm around here. But since it did happen, there's no way I'm letting this chick out of my sight until things blow over.

I pull off my Carhartt winter coat and wool hat, running a hand through my copper hair before hanging them on the hook alongside the booth. I silently offer to take her coat, and without looking up at me, she quickly slips out of it and hands it over. Her jacket feels as light as air as I hang it on the hook with mine. Marv's assessment was probably spot-on about not letting her go out in this thing.

I slide into the booth across from her and do my best not to check out her tits beneath her fitted gray sweater. "Are you okay?" I ask, my voice deep from the spike of adrenaline coursing through my veins.

She nods woodenly as she tucks her hair behind her ears.

"Are you sure?" I ask again, noting the tremble of her gloved hand. Her fingertips look cold as ice. "That guy was a fucking dick, so I wouldn't blame you if you weren't."

She swallows slowly and stares down at my hand fisted on the table. My knuckles have some faint red splotches where my fist connected with his face. Nothing I haven't seen before.

"I'm fine," she mumbles and wrings her hands together.

I exhale heavily. I just knocked a guy out right in front of her. Of course, she's going to be scared of me. "I'm sorry for what I did. And I'm doubly sorry for what he said."

She looks up at me with narrowed eyes. "Do you know that guy or something?"

"Fuck no," I reply, jerking back. "I'm just apologizing for all mankind, I guess. We can be dicks. But I want you to know the other guys who frequent Marv's here are nothing like those two fuckwads. I've never seen them before, so I know damn sure they're not from around here."

She half smiles and looks around the cozy diner, her eyes sliding from one old fisherman to the next. "It looks like a retirement community in here."

I follow her gaze to the elderly man in a wheelchair who's playing cards with few other blue-hairs. "I think you mean a nursing home for Colorado's finest," I murmur out of the side of my mouth. When I hear a small huff of laughter come from her, I'm somewhat relieved to see she's not totally shook up from everything.

The wheelchair man catches us looking at him and gives us a big toothless smile with a delicate wrist flick of a wave. I find myself smiling back at the sweet old guy. Looking at her, I see she's smiling too. It's a genuine smile that's so sweet it could give me a toothache. And somehow, with just that one look, I can tell this girl is good people. She may seem a touch crazy today, but deep down, she's a decent person.

She turns her head to face me, her eyes lingering on my whiskered chin. "I've never had a man punch anyone for me before," she states curiously. "Let alone a stranger."

I cross my arms over my chest and lower my chin. "Are you about to yell at me for interfering in your business?"

"No," she retorts, her brows knitting together in the middle. "I think I probably owe you a thank you."

"I'm shocked," I reply, shooting her a lopsided grin. "I have three older sisters who would have my head if I meddled in their business and freaked out like that."

She huffs out a laugh. "Three older sisters? How did you end up so…?"

"Masculine? Virile? Rugged and courageous?" I waggle my brows at her and puff out my chest.

She pulls her lips between her teeth as she attempts to conceal her laughter, and a deep dimple emerges on her left cheek. "So what, you just go around knocking assholes out to impress girls?"

"No," I reply simply with a shrug. "Impressing girls is just a fringe benefit."

"Seriously, though, how's your hand?" she asks, whipping off her gloves and reaching for my hand.

When her skin touches mine, the connection can only be described as electrifying. Like feeling the pins and needles sensation in your hand after it's fallen asleep. She quickly grabs a paper napkin and fishes some ice out of the cup sitting on our table to put inside it.

"That water was from whoever sat here before us," I state, my tone flat.

Her nose wrinkles, but then she shrugs one shoulder. "Oh, please. If you can handle fish guts, you can handle some secondhand ice."

She holds the ice to my knuckles, and I prop my chin on my free hand, watching her with rapt attention as she tends to my battle wound. She catches me staring at her and shoots me a mischievous smirk. "I feel like I know you."

I lift my brows at that. "Did you grow up in Boulder?"

She shakes her head. "No, but I have this...I don't know...comfortable feeling around you. Like you remind me of someone I know really well. Do you ever meet people, and feel like you knew them in a past life?"

"I don't know if I believe in past lives," I reply honestly. "I think you just hit it off with some people, and others you don't. You're just totally hitting it off with me because I'm so incredibly charming."

She rolls her eyes and tosses my hand away, causing the ice to fall out of the napkin in the process. Hitting me with a serious look, she says, "I hope you realize I'm not going to fall for a bearded ginger knight in shining armor type."

I bark out a laugh at that description. "Oh, I know! If you don't fall for Marv's charm, then you certainly won't fall for mine." I reach up and stroke my chin. "And this is called 'tangerine toughness' by the way."

When she giggles, it makes her look young, which she clearly is, but if I had to guess, I'd say she's at least twenty-one.

"I wouldn't call your beard tangerine…more like a dark red kidney bean. But regardless, you gingers are lucky that Prince Harry brought you back in style," she says with a smirk as she chews her lower lip in a way that makes me think she is flirting with me.

"Pffft," I tut with a roll of my eyes while grabbing the menus from behind the napkin dispenser. "Gingers never went out of style. We're like a fine wine that just needs to age a bit before you can fully appreciate us."

I hand her a menu and prop mine in front of my face, peering over it at her as she looks down at hers. She definitely seems calmer than she did before, so that's good. But she's clearly not the outdoorsy type who hangs out in a bait shop. She looks more like a former cheerleader or a pageant girl. The kind who gets a manicure every other week, not the type who would dig her hand into a bucket of minnows.

So what the fuck is she doing here?

Barb, the elderly waitress who's always working, interrupts my shameless ogling. "What can I get you two?" she asks as she clears the dishes, wipes the table, and gives us fresh glasses of water.

Once I've recovered from my creeper caught in action heart attack, I order a burger and fries. The girl nods and orders the same, once again surprising me when she doesn't order a salad.

When Barb leaves, I decide to cut to the chase. "Look, what those assholes said back there was total bullshit. But I have to tell you, you really are a fish out of water around here," I state, pun intended. "What are you doing here?"

She looks back at me with a frown. "Why am I a fish out of water? Because I'm a girl and I look a certain way?"

"Partly," I reply with an unapologetic shrug. "Sorry if that's sexist, but we don't get many females who look like you at Marv's Bait and Tackle. Barb is the only estrogen these guys around here get, and I'm pretty sure she's gone through," I pause to cup my hand to my mouth and whisper, "'the change' already."

The girl bursts out laughing, covering her face as her cheeks flame red. "You did not just refer to menopause as 'the change!'"

I duck my head and look around nervously, in case someone heard us. It may not be a normal thing for a guy to discuss, but I watched my mother go through it last summer, so I know how much it changes a woman. Mostly because she and my sisters talk about every-fucking-thing that happens to their bodies. Honestly, I've been subjected to some really uncomfortable conversations about pantyliners and night sweats. It was all very upsetting.

But the guys at Marv's don't see a hot-blooded girl like this...ever, so it's no wonder she caused a ruckus. I lean across the table and speak in a low voice. "No need to shout about womanly issues. I'm just saying, these guys aren't used to girls in here, and the fact that you marched in wearing those boots and threadbare leggings when it's fifty fucking below outside means you'll be the center of attention. Going ice fishing in that getup has the makings for some serious frostbite, sparky."

She scoffs at me. "Well...that's for me to worry about... not that Marv guy."

"Marv is a protective old man who was only trying to look out for you because you seem like a nice girl when you're not lunging at assholes." My hands clench on the table, itching to touch hers again for some strange reason.

"Girl?" she scoffs again, her eyes rolling upward with a smile. "I'm a twenty-two-year-old college graduate, all right? I think it's safe to call me a woman."

"You got it," I reply, holding my hands back. I know better than to argue with a female about her label. "So, *woman*, what are you trying to do here today? It's clear you've never been fishing a day in your life."

"I've fished!" she replies defiantly, her jaw setting into a scowl. "Just never been ice fishing."

I shake my head knowingly. "Okay...well, I'll be the second one to tell you that ice fishing is a serious sport. You can't just go out and find a hole. You have to have a drill, a house, and a heat source. Proper clothing. Do you have any of those items?"

"No," she murmurs, fiddling with her fingers in her lap.

"Then what on earth made you decide to go ice fishing today?"

She leans back in the booth and looks up at the ceiling. "You're going to laugh."

"I won't laugh."

"Yes, you will."

"Try me."

She sighs heavily and folds her hands on the table in front of her. "I'm on a road trip of self-discovery."

"Not at all what I expected," I stammer because hell, it's the truth. I ruffle the strands of hair on my head, trying to hide my confused reaction. "And your self-discovery led you to Marv's of all places?"

"Pretty much." She shrugs and then leans forward on the table, with a tiny glimmer of a smile. "What happened was, I was driving down the highway, no music, no phone, no nothing. Just me and my thoughts. Did you know that we're getting so reliant on technology and keeping our brain entertained that we never just sink into our own thoughts?"

"Oh yeah, I totally knew that actually."

"You did?" she exclaims, her eyes bright and excited.

"No, I don't know what the fuck you're talking about," I deadpan. She rolls her eyes in annoyance, and that might turn me on a little bit.

"Well, it's becoming a major issue because now our brains aren't accessing the deep-thinking folds anymore. Just all this surface-level shit of social media and social, social, social bullshit," she sputters and then shakes her head to refocus. "It's more scientific than that, but you get the idea. So I'm trying to access this part of my brain that's been lost to technology when I look over and see this tiny house on the ice. The inside glows from a light, and smoke drifts out of a little chimney. It looked so peaceful. Like something out of a magazine for deep thinking! And I thought to myself, I need something like that in my life."

"I can't argue with that," I reply because honestly, I get it. There is a peacefulness when you're sitting in a small ice shack with frigid temperatures all around you. It makes you feel really connected to yourself—which sounds super fucking lame, but damnit, it's true.

"So yeah, I want to learn how to ice fish," she says with a serious look. "Or try some outdoorsy nature adventures so that maybe, just maybe, I can find a better version of myself."

My brow furrows at that last remark. "What makes you think this version isn't good enough?"

She splays her hands out on the table and shakes her head slowly, her eyes downcast the entire time. "Lots of things. Too many to mention. But the place I'm staying at had a brochure for Marv's Bait and Tackle, so here I am. I assumed Marv would be more helpful than he was. The pamphlet said Marv was some famous fish whisperer or something, I thought."

I bite back a laugh. "I don't think fish whisperer is a thing…but yes, Marv knows his shit. He's a pro. But you came right at the start of ice fishing season, so everyone wants to talk to Marv this weekend. He's like the Buddha whose belly everyone wants to rub so we can find the fishing sweet spots."

"Is that why the bait area is full of waiting assholes?" she asks, glaring around the restaurant.

"They aren't all assholes," I correct.

She rolls her eyes. "Present company excluded... seemingly."

"Seemingly?" I quirk a brow at her.

"Well, I just met you and watched you knock a guy out, so I can't fully determine if you're one of them or not." She eyes me with an amused expression on her face that makes me think she's joking. Yet somehow, I can't be fully sure.

I nod slowly and lick my lips. "How about we introduce ourselves before we judge. What's your name?"

"My friends call me Maggie," she replies with a shrug.

"Well, Maggie, I'm Sam...and I will prove to you that I'm not a brawling asshole by offering to be your ice fishing guide this afternoon." I smile, offering my hand to her, and her answering expression lights up her entire face.

"Seriously?" she asks, her voice high and excited as she slides her long, slender fingers into mine.

I nod and swallow slowly. "Seriously. And before you worry about being alone out in the wilderness with me, I'm going to introduce you to Marv so he can vouch for me. He's known me since I was a kid, and I've done some fishing guide work for him on occasion. You can trust his assessment of me."

She looks at me with an adorable smile that I know I like a little too much. "You've thought of everything, haven't you?"

"Well, if you're on a journey of self-discovery, you don't need any roadblocks getting in your way." I pause and flick my gaze down to her chest. "Oh, and you'd better have a credit card with you because you'll need to buy some seriously expensive gear today."

Squealing with excitement, she nods eagerly just as Barb arrives with our burgers. "And you'd better eat all that. You're going to need sustenance to keep you warm out there."

She licks her lips and pops a fry into her mouth. "I can't wait."

I give her a dubious sort of smile because I'm sure she has no clue what she's in for...and maybe neither do I.

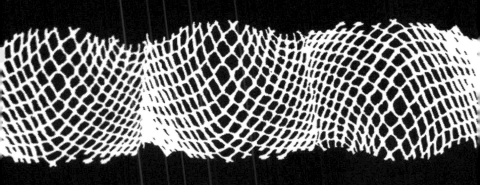

CHAPTER 2

Ice Breaker

Maggie

S am is an interesting and unexpected twist to my day. Oh, who am I kidding? Nothing about this day has been expected. So really, Sam is just par for the course at this point. But if I had to pick a guy out of a lineup to swoop in and save me, I would have never picked this guy.

He's not hard on the eyes by any means. In fact, he's got something going for him that I can't quite put my finger on. His hair isn't fully red, more dirty blond with reddish streaks throughout. And it's cut in that messy, "I just rolled out of bed and stuffed my head into a slouchy knit cap" sort of way. His beard is freshly trimmed but long enough to show off its dark auburn tint.

And if I'm looking at him objectively, he clearly has a

decent body. When he grabbed me around the waist, I felt how firm he was under those winter layers. He's tall and broad-shouldered, and his chest and biceps fill out that white thermal shirt really nicely. Something tells me his workouts are more like chopping his own firewood and shoveling his own driveaway than working with a personal trainer and doing squats at a gym.

Yet still, I wouldn't think he'd be the type to take charge in a crisis, so I'm pleasantly surprised. I wonder how old he is? Judging from those creases on the sides of his eyes and the crinkle between his brows, he's got a good five years on me. He probably spends all his time outside in the sun. I could see him being a ranch hand for a farm maybe. Like a baseball cap-wearing cowboy.

But as I said, he's not handsome in the traditional sense. Yet something interesting happens when he smiles. It's like this shy grin that immediately embarrasses him when it spreads across his face. He even looks away when he does it. It's kind of sexy.

But it doesn't matter because he's definitely not my type. He's just someone proving to be very helpful at a time when I could use a friend. Because no one can know I'm here. No one can know what's going on in my life right now. I want things to appear to be business as usual, and this guy could help me pass the time.

Marv gives me the seal of approval for Sam to be my fishing guide so now I'm making the most of this bait shop waiting room meet cute. Not that this is an actual "meet cute." A meet cute between a couple involves feelings during the act of meeting. An attraction. An instant spark or even love at first sight—at least that's how the romance novels I've read make it seem.

With Sam, it's just a friendly exchange of services with no spark whatsoever. Of course, objectively when he marches me through the shopping area to look at snowsuits, I do have to appreciate the largeness of his frame and how it just seems sturdy and solid. When he walks across the room, you have the urge to either get the heck out of his way or cling to his arm for the ride. And his eyes have this warm, smiling affection to them as if he's a man with very few worries. I like that. It feels safe. But thankfully, I just have a platonic appreciation for him being in the right place at the right time.

Let's do some ice fishing!

I wrench open the ragged shower curtain that Marv calls a dressing room and do a spin for Sam, who I belatedly realize is literally asleep on the log bench that lines the nearby wall. His head is propped against a cork board and his mouth is hanging open as he breathes deeply in and out.

Talk about anticlimactic.

He sent me in here with a mound of clothes like I was Julia Roberts from *Pretty Woman* on a shopping spree, and I guess I just expected him to applaud or something when I came out. Maybe a little ogling. But no, Mr. Fisherman is out cold with his mouth hanging open so wide, I can see his molars!

I clomp over to him in my new snow boots and clap my silicone gloves together in front of his face. He jumps out of his chair and lets out a weird gurgle of a shout. "He said we could fish here!"

"What the heck?" I exclaim, covering my mouth as I giggle. "Were you dreaming?"

"Don't wake me like that," he growls, clearly agitated as he runs his hand through his beard to wipe away his drool.

"How am I supposed to know how to wake you? I just met you!"

"Wake me like a normal, functioning human, maybe."

"Maybe you should stop falling asleep in public places, gramps."

He frowns at that last word. "Well hell, you've been in there changing for over twenty minutes. I got bored."

"You try getting this stuff on! It's not easy, and I can barely move in it." I put my hands on my waist and spread my legs, trying to test out my range of motion in this giant red and white snowsuit. It's not much.

Sam finally takes me in and nods thoughtfully. "You look prepared, though. This is appropriate apparel for winter sports." Standing to his full height, he's a good five inches taller than me, which is saying a lot because I'm five foot nine. He reaches out and flicks the big red ball on top of my stocking cap.

"Do I look like a fisherwoman?" I ask, unable to hide my beaming smile.

"Definitely." He nods, looking down my body with an interesting look I can't quite place.

"Were you seriously dreaming about fishing there just a second ago?" I ask, my giggle bubbling up through my lips again.

"No," he barks back with a frown. Turning on his heel, he calls over his shoulder, "Let's go…we're losing daylight."

I move to follow him and then freeze. He turns when he doesn't hear me behind him. "What is it?"

My face contorts in dread. "I have to pee."

Twelve and a half minutes later, I'm redressed, have purchased my fishing license and gear, and am outside looking around for Sam's truck. Bearded guys always drive trucks, right? He's like the ginger-bearded Brawny man, for goodness' sake. Honestly, I wouldn't be surprised if he drove a tow truck.

"Where's your truck?" I ask, my breath puffing out in front of my lips as I find Sam propped against the side of the bait shop.

"No truck," he replies and points at the parking spot behind me.

I turn around. "Oh my gosh, a snowmobile? Bonus!" I crunch over the packed snow to awkwardly throw my foot over the seat and climb aboard. I grab the handlebars and smile at him. "Do you drive this out on the ice?"

He nods and strides over to the back of the sled. "It's a lot safer than a truck." He double checks the items he has strapped down on the back of the bench and then straightens to eye me one more time. "This is your last chance to back out. You feel how cold it is, right?"

"I'm not backing out!" I exclaim and grip the handles even tighter as I picture us gliding across a frozen lake. What freedom, what a rush! Wide-open air and smooth, cold ice. I bite my lip and look over my shoulder at Sam. "Can I drive?"

"Hell no," he replies and hands me a shiny black helmet that he just ripped the tag off of.

"Did you just buy this?" I ask, looking down at the clearly brand new helmet.

He nods. "While you were changing for nineteen hours."

"Was this before or after your grandpa nap?" I mumble under my breath as I pull my stocking cap off and replace it with the helmet. My voice is muffled when I state proudly, "Now I really feel like a fisherwoman."

"You don't need a helmet to fish there, sparky," he states, then hooks his thumb to silently command me to slide back on the bench as he folds himself in front of me.

I instantly wrap my arms around his waist. This bizarre sense of comfort with Sam is interesting and annoying because I can't put my finger on it. I'm sure he just reminds me of someone I know, but I can't figure out who. Hopefully, it'll come to me while we're ice fishing.

Sam fires up the engine, and a few seconds later, we take off on our adventure. He steers us down into ditches and cuts across various snow-covered roads until we reach a tranquil forest with several other snowmobile tracks. We even pass other sledders on the way, and I can't help but marvel at this whole other culture of society out here.

Outdoorsy types, carving their ways through forests in search of their next thrill. It's exhilarating!

About fifteen minutes later, my cheeks are frozen inside my helmet as we drive past Boulder Junction Lake that's full of fellow ice fishers. I thought we were going there at first, but Sam continued past it, clearly knowing something they don't.

We end up at Partridge Lake, a spot that's a good deal smaller than the one we passed and more secluded because it's surrounded by snow-covered trees. A single lonely house is out on the ice already with a puff of smoke billowing out the top. It's like a postcard and exactly what inspired me to try this out.

I squeal in excitement as Sam ventures down a snow-covered boat ramp, and we hit the open ice. This entire day has already been ten times more thrilling than I ever could have imagined, which is much appreciated after the Christmas I had. Two days ago, I was supposed to be on a plane to the East Coast, but somehow, I ended up here in Boulder. Life is funny sometimes.

When Sam finds the spot he wants, he stops the sled and kills the engine. "Ready to help, sparky?" he asks as he removes his helmet and hops off the snowmobile, readjusting his knit hat so just a tiny bit of his reddish blond hair sticks out beneath it.

I smile at his nickname for me, which only cements the fact that I had to have known him in a past life. We begin setting up camp, and Sam guides me through the entire process. His fishing shelter is a small, cube-shaped pop-up tent made of what appears to be an insulated thick nylon material using collapsible tent poles for framing. The sides have two plastic windows and two flaps at the top for some sort of airflow.

I have to admit that I sigh with relief when he mentions the flaps are for a heater because holy shit, my nipples could cut glass right now. But there is no way in hell I am telling Sam I'm cold. I'm not going to be Basic Maggie today. I'm going to be Adventurous Maggie. However, I'm still kicking myself for not investing in some thermal undergarments to go beneath my two-hundred-dollar snowsuit. Rookie mistake that won't happen again!

I'm on my hands and knees, brushing a square of snow off the ice for the tent when Sam comes over with a giant, scary looking drill. I watch him position the sharp tip on the ice.

"That thing looks vicious," I state, watching with great fascination.

"Want to try?" he asks, eyeing me over his shoulder.

"Yes!" I exclaim and nearly biff it in my attempt to hurry over to him.

He stands behind me and positions my hands where they need to be for the manual crank ice auger. His body feels warm against mine as he presses up against me, but I'm ignoring that pleasantness because this trip isn't about boy hunting. This is about un-basicing. That's a thing, right? A verb? If not, I'm making it one. I'm un-basicing myself, and that apparently means becoming an ice fisherwoman. Which also means I can't be attracted to the first fisherman

I lay eyes on.

Sam helps me crank the handle, and we drill a small six-inch hole through the ice for what feels like ages. But when it finally plunges through to the arctic water below, I can't help but feel an immense sense of accomplishment.

I begin to ladle out the slushy ice inside the hole as Sam quickly drills two more holes. Once we've got them ready to go, we position the tent over the cleared space and shove snow around the bottom edges to seal it off. He unzips the door and begins handing me things I've never seen before in my life. At least I recognize the propane heater! Score one for Basic Maggie.

Sam works quietly inside the hut, propped on his knees, his eyes intensely focused as he slips something into the middle hole and plugs in a video monitor.

"Holy shit, is that a video camera?" I exclaim, dropping to my knees beside him and seeing something sway in the water below. "Was that a fish?"

He chuckles. "Yes, it was a fish, and yes, this a video fish locator. My auger is small, so you can't see what you have going on down there. And this lake is almost a hundred feet deep in some areas, so you need this to see what's going on beneath the ice."

"Fascinating," I say with a sigh. Because it is.

He rigs up two fishing poles next, one of which is the brand new one I just purchased from Marv. There really was no way in hell I could have done this all on my own today. Sam's doing special knots and shit, and I wasn't even a Girl Scout growing up! I was…a cheerleader. And cheer squad has not prepared me for today's events whatsoever.

Sam takes a match and lights the heater at last. As soon as the warmth touches the tip of my frozen nose, I want to kiss him. Well, maybe not kiss him but thank him profusely. But honestly, under normal circumstances and if I were fishing with a boyfriend instead of a complete stranger, this glorious heat would be worthy of sexual favors.

He props up two little stools for us, and in seconds, we're sitting shoulder to shoulder with our poles in the icy water.

Then it begins.

The…ice fishing.

Which I realize now is mostly just sitting in silence and staring at a hole.

Guys really do this for fun?

I shake my head, forcing myself to live in the moment and enjoy the nature all around me. To allow myself to do some deep thinking and embrace something new and different for a change.

So I wait.

And wait.

And wait.

I glance at my watch and am gutted when I see it's only been four minutes. It feels like we've been at this for at least an hour. Is my watch broken?

More minutes tick by.

Or is it seconds?

Is there a weird wrinkle in time here on this lake where everything slows down? And flipping heck, why is it so quiet? This silence is excruciating. All I hear is the cold wind outside and the faint crackle of the propane heater every once in a while. No city or traffic sounds...nothing!

We're all alone out here. The only other ice house is on the other side of the lake and probably wouldn't even hear my cries over the wind.

"Let some—"

"Ahh!" I scream, my eyes going wide in horror as I realize Sam's voice just made me jump like the dumb girl in all horror films.

"Jesus hell, what's wrong?" Sam asks, turning to gawk at me with worry.

I shake my head aggressively. "Nothing."

"You scream like that when nothing's wrong?" he asks. I can feel his eyes on me, but I can't bring myself to look at them.

"Your voice just...surprised me," I chirp.

He's staring at me now. He's staring at me in that silent, easy way he has about him. "Were you doing some deep thinking there, sparky?"

"No," I balk defensively, and then my brows lift. "Or maybe I was!" I look at him with wide, excited eyes. "I mean, my imagination was certainly taking flight. Do you think that's deep thinking?"

"I have no fucking idea," Sam replies with a laugh and a shake of his head. "But I know screaming like that is going to scare all the fish away...so maybe, try to deep think a little more shallow."

I smile at that remark because at least he didn't accuse

me of being basic. After another moment of silence, I finally ask, "So this is it?"

Sam jiggles his line a bit, letting more slack down into the hole. "This is it."

"You just…sit out here and wait?"

He nods. "They'll come."

"How do you know?"

"I don't know…Marv knows. If Marv says they'll come, they'll come."

"Is this like a fishing *Field of Dreams* moment or something?" I ask curiously and then lower the timbre of my voice to sound deep and soulful. "If you fish it, they will come."

Sam angles his shoulders to face me and watches me with a twinkle of amusement in his eyes. He licks his lips as though he's about to say something but then just as quickly turns back to his pole and remains silent. He's so good at the silent.

I exhale heavily and try to figure out why I'm not good at silence. I wanted to come out here to be alone with my thoughts and reflect, so I shouldn't need to fill the silence like this. What's that say about me?

"A nice cold glass of Chardonnay would be really good right about now. I'm sure most fishermen drink beer, but I hate beer, and I don't see why you couldn't have wine too. It's not a highbrow beverage like some people think. A gas station by my parents' house sells really good Chardonnay three for ten bucks. And it comes with a twist-off top so you could drink it right out of the bottle if you wanted! And with how cool it is out here? You wouldn't even need a bottle chiller. Just stuff it in some snow, and you're all set. I feel like wine should be the official drink of ice fishing!"

I laugh awkwardly and turn my face away from Sam in mortification. My inane rambling needs to stop like immediately. Maybe if I turn the attention to Sam, that'll help me shut the heck up.

"So why do you like ice fishing so much, Sam?" I ask, turning to him.

"Do you hate it already?" he replies with a smirk.

"No!" I exclaim, my chest rising defensively. "I'm just trying to learn more about the appeal, that's all."

He shrugs. "I grew up ice fishing with my dad. I was the only son, so it was kind of our thing to get away from all the estrogen in our house."

"Does your dad still come out here with you?"

He pauses, his brows furrowing for a moment. "No, he doesn't."

Oookay, I think to myself. He clearly doesn't want to elaborate on that subject. "Do your sisters ever come out here with you?"

He shakes his head with a laugh. "Definitely not. This isn't their thing at all."

Suddenly, Sam's eyes go wide, and I follow his gaze to the video monitor. "You're getting a bite, Maggie."

"I am?" I squeal, my hands squeezing my fishing reel so tight, I feel like I could break the thin metal.

"Shhh, just stay calm…watch."

The fish darts at my rig once, and a chunk of the bait

floats away from it as if he got just a taste. Then it comes back and opens its mouth wide and…

"Set it!" Sam exclaims loudly.

"Set what?" I exclaim back.

"The hook!"

"What?" I cry out, completely confused. "What are you talking about?"

Sam drops his pole and quickly wraps his arms around me, his body snug against mine. "You have to set the hook in the fish's mouth. Just give the pole a good jerk."

He yanks the pole upward, and as soon as he does, I feel a heavy weight pulling down the tip of my pole. "Holy heck, is this a big fish?"

Sam's warm breath tickles my cheek as he chuckles. "It feels like it."

"Awesome!" I squeal because I can't help it. This is all so thrilling.

Sam helps me through the process of bringing the fish up to the surface. It's deep down there, so it's a lot of pulling up on the pole, reeling it in, and then pulling it up again. It feels like it's taking forever, but when the fish finally gets close to the surface, I see it going bonkers right below the hole.

"Think you can grab it with your hands?" he asks, his voice breathless and excited, just like mine.

"Sure!" I exclaim, biting the fingertips of my gloves and yanking them off my hands.

Sam looks taken aback for a second but then shakes his surprise off and grabs the line with his hand. The fish stills for a second, and as he quickly pulls it through the hole, he says, "Grab it right in the open gill there."

I do it.

I don't think. I just…do it.

It's freezing and wet and kinda sharp around the edges, but I hold this big ole squirming fish in my bare hand. Flipping heck, I'm holding a fish! I squeal with delight, and my smile is ear to ear as Sam watches me with an equally pleased expression.

"This is way cool. I can't believe I'm holding a fish right now."

He laughs hard. "Honestly, me neither."

"Right?" I exclaim and waggle my brows at him. "What do I do with it now?"

Sam's shrugs. "Do you want to release it or eat it?"

"Release it," I reply instantly. "Definitely release it."

Sam takes the fish from my hand and gently extracts the hook from the fish's mouth. It looks like a strong fish. Like a fish who probably had his whole life figured out before this hook came out of nowhere and completely derailed him.

I know that feeling.

I'm all too familiar with that sense of contentment when you're confident in your next step. When you feel yourself climbing this perfect staircase, but then suddenly, someone comes out of nowhere and shoves you straight backward.

Sam looks at me with earnest eyes. "It's your catch, so you have to be the one to release it. Just grab it with two hands here at the tail and submerge it halfway into the water. Careful of his dorsal fin, it's sharp. Wait until he swims out of your hand, okay? Don't just drop him back in there if he doesn't seem ready. He needs to take off on his own."

Good god. The metaphors in my mind right now are out of control!

I nod slowly and grip the fish's slimy scales firmly as I immerse his head into the water. It takes a minute—the poor guy must be in shock still—before he begins writhing in my hands, his tail flipping side to side viciously as I hold on for dear life.

I look at Sam for confirmation. When he nods his approval...I let Flipper go. Okay, I know I didn't catch a dolphin. Let me try again.

I let Nemo go.

Wait, I feel like since I'm a bit lost right now, this fish's name should actually be Dory.

I let Dory go.

I watch her swim away in the video monitor as if her life depends on it...because let's face it, it does. She was living her best life, got hooked by some delicious bait that was meant to taste good and make her belly full and satisfied, and then she was completely sideswiped by a right hook.

Dory is my spirit animal.

Adrenaline surges through me as I watch her swim fast and free. Like a magnificent creature that can't be held back by anything.

I hear Sam say, "That was a nice, strong release. You want them to really take off out of your hand because then you know they'll survive next time."

"Next time?" I ask, my high buzzing in my head so

loudly, I can barely take in his words.

He shrugs. "The next time they're caught."

"Caught again," I repeat to myself because the life of a fish is both tragic and beautiful. Beautiful because they have moments of complete freedom. Moments when they take the bait and see a new part of the world. And moments when they are released and allowed to live their lives. But tragic because ultimately, they are at the mercy of a fisherman. Someone to catch and release them. Or worse yet, consume them until nothing is left to show for themselves.

I swallow against the growing pit in my belly because I won't be consumed. I won't be caught. In this hut, at this moment, I am not a fish. I am not Dory waiting for the bait. I am a fisherwoman, and I take what I want.

What happens next can only be described as an out-of-body experience or a demonic possession of some sort because it is so unlike anything I've ever done before. And when I realize my lips are locked on Sam's, I have no other choice but to embrace it.

Sam grunts when my body rams into his with all the grace of a flailing fish. Or a girl in a fishing hut is maybe a more suitable analogy for this particular scene. Either way, it's a foreign physical movement for me because I've never made the first move on a guy before, especially not in a bulky snowsuit.

Sam's beard is rough against my mouth as I grab the lapels of his jacket and arch my neck up to flatten my lips to his. When he realizes what's happening, he goes stiff as a board for a minute, and I fear that he's going to out

35

fisherman me and release me back into the wild.

But then, his shoulders drop. His hand releases the fishing pole he was in the middle of re-rigging and cinches tightly around my waist as he pulls me up on my knees. Now we're both kneeling in front of each other, sucking face like a couple of largemouth bass at the bottom of the lake. Our snowsuit-covered bodies are flush against each other, the thick fabric rubbing against all my sensitive nerve-endings that have come alive under this surprising and unexpected embrace. Sam's tongue parts my lips and sweeps inside with an unwavering confidence he wants me to feel. And man do I feel it. I think I even whimper a little when he yanks off his gloves, and his warm, dry hands cup my face. His palms are rough, but his touch is tender as his thumbs caress my cheekbones.

I may have started this kiss, but he's completely taken over now, and his deft touch makes me feel like an inexperienced, never-been-kissed teenager. Oh my heck, is this what it's like to kiss an older man? Someone with experience? Someone who's rugged and rough around the edges? Who's clearly not only lived life but also made life his bitch? Because if so, I had no idea what I'd been missing out on by dating college boys. Preppy college boys have nothing on this...fisherman.

But this fisherman is also a complete stranger. A familiar stranger but still a stranger I'm kissing in the middle of nowhere after recently getting dumped. I am an idiot.

As if the ghost that possessed me earlier has left my

body, I jerk back, then press my hands flat against his chest to put some space between us. Our breaths are foggy and ragged as I lick my lips that are now raw from his beard and burning in a way that I basically love.

"I really didn't mean to do that," I pant, looking up at him with blazing eyes.

He smolders back at me, his gaze holding a wicked promise as he pulls his lower lip into his mouth. "It's seriously okay."

I bite back a groan. "No…but like, I really didn't mean to do that." I move away from him, extracting my body from his and shaking my head from side to side as I reposition myself on my stool a solid two feet away from him. It suddenly feels horribly hot and cramped in here. Did the heater get turned up?

"I'm not complaining," Sam replies, his voice still deep with arousal. He moves to his own stool, and I swear I see a bulge in his snow pants. *Holy shit! How big is he if he has a bulge showing through thick snow pants?*

"Going ice fishing wasn't a ploy to get a new guy, you know," I state firmly as I begin tugging at the chest of my snowsuit to get some air to my clammy skin underneath. I'm literally sweating! How can I be sweating on a frozen flipping lake? The heater isn't that warm. "I'm supposed to be finding myself. There's more to me than just my hormones. I graduated a semester early and at the top of my class in college, ya know?"

Sam chuckles as I fiddle with the zipper under my chin. "I thought you were interesting the moment I heard your voice today, sparky."

I look over at him, and he's staring back at me with complete, unhindered attraction. I swear his green eyes have somehow darkened with desire. *Oh my heck, maybe I should dunk my head in the lake because I get a really funny feeling between my legs when he looks at me like that.*

"I just don't want you to judge me," I mumble because if I was judging myself right now, I'd say I'm a silly girl who can't handle a simple life change without going off the rails and deciding on a whim to become an ice fisherwoman. "Why is it so hot in here?" I ask, unzipping my snowsuit and trying to stop this hot flash from taking over my body. Gosh, maybe I'm going through "the change" like Sam's mom! Is that possible at my age?

Sam's silence has me looking over to find him staring at my chest with a downright sinful expression on his face. I look to see what he's seeing, and my eyes go wide. "Shit!" I exclaim, grabbing the edges of the snowsuit and closing it up quickly. "Motherfetcher, what was I thinking?"

Sam's laughter is shaking his entire body. "You're typically supposed to wear clothes under your snowsuit." He turns his head to try to hide the fact that he's laughing so hard, and I hate that he looks so cute doing it.

"Ugh!" I exclaim, covering my face in horror because I know Sam got a good eyefull of the hot pink bra I'm wearing under my snowsuit. I had wondered if I was supposed to leave my clothes on underneath it, but it was such a process to get it on that I couldn't stomach the idea of doing it again just to put my sweater on. And I figured, who would know?

Sam would know.

Because I'm an idiot.

I shake my head, and mumble, "I'm a mess."

Sam's still laughing. "Hey, you're a hot mess at least."

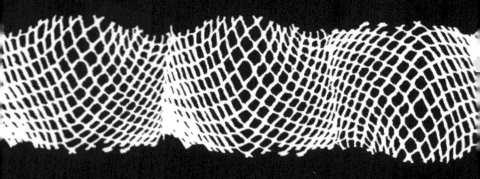

CHAPTER 3

Nibbler

Sam

Most chicks would have bitched about the cold. Most chicks would have bitched about spending $474 on something other than a pair of designer shoes. Most chicks wouldn't have touched a fish with their bare hands.

This chick…wasn't like most chicks.

The following Monday, I'm back at work at Tire Depot, but my mind is most definitely not on tires. It's on all things Maggie, which is actually really fucking embarrassing because I'm thirty years old and the sales manager of a successful company I'll be taking over soon. I shouldn't be obsessing over some young chick who happened to look really hot in a snowsuit. And also out of the snowsuit as it turns out.

I could have forgotten about the kiss we shared a lot easier if it wasn't for the little peep show she gave me as a bonus. For the next two hours we spent fishing together, I had to threaten to dunk my cock into the icy lake every time he got a mind of his own and puffed up a little.

But all these Maggie thoughts are pointless right now because I have responsibilities I need to focus on. Like how I can bring Tire Depot to the next level and set myself up for early retirement just like my uncle.

Tire Depot is a huge car care center that my uncle Terry owns in Boulder. I've been working here since I was a kid, back when he and my dad used to run it together. Until they didn't. Regardless, I have fond memories of coming here after school. I'd always get a soda and a cookie and mosey into the garage to gawk at the nudey calendars posted at the guys' stations.

Now my uncle is prepping me to take the reins so he can retire and cruise up to Canada on his Harley. The guy is sixty-four years old and ready to drift off into his golden years like the lone wolf he's always been.

"Sammy!" Uncle Terry bellows my name from his office in the back so loud that I can hear it all the way up in the reception area where I'm working at the high-top customer counter. "Come back here for a sec."

I save my work and turn to make my way down the small hallway to his office. The walls are papered with classic car posters, various tire awards, and vacation pictures he's taken throughout the years. Piles of papers that need to be filed cover his desk, but he never makes the time to do it.

I stare down at what he's holding in his hands, and my blood runs cold when I see my three-ring binder opened in front of him. "This is your business plan?" he asks, scratching his white beard as he flips a few pages.

"Um...yes," I reply, rubbing the back of my neck and shifting nervously. "But I wasn't ready for you to see it yet. I'm not quite done."

He looks up to me with a serious look in his eyes. "Well, this is a much bigger idea than the customer comfort center."

"Yes, it is," I acknowledge his reference to the first proposal I presented to him almost ten years ago.

I was fresh out of college with all these business classes swirling through my head, and I got the idea that providing complimentary beverages and snacks to our staff and customers would cultivate a positive company culture. Enter the customer comfort center, which resulted in a huge boost for business.

"So when do you want to go through this with me?" Terry asks, eyeing me seriously. "I'm not going to be around much longer, you know."

I nod somberly. "Yeah, I know. Give me another week or two, and I'll be ready."

"Good," he replies, closing the binder and handing it to me. "I look forward to it, Sammy."

When he stands up and pats me on the back before making his way toward the shop, I exhale with relief that he didn't totally flip out on me about this. I've been buying my uncle out of Tire Depot for the past five years, with plans for me to take over. But the contents inside this binder are a much bigger venture.

Tire Depot is the perfect future for me. I fucking love this place. The smell of tires and grease, complimentary coffee and baked goods, plus decent, hardworking guys earning an honest living for their families. It's a good gig. I've come to really care about my employees and their families, and there is nowhere else I'd rather be. But I have dreams that would take us to the next level, and if I can get Terry's blessing before he leaves, I'll feel a lot better about things.

I exit his office and make my way back to the counter when a female voice interrupts my thoughts. I look over and see my best friend's girlfriend strolling into the tire shop as if she owns the place.

"Michael! Did Shelly finish my book yet?" Kate asks with a big smile for my top salesman as she rests her elbow on a short stack of display tires.

"She did! And you were right...I totally got lucky." Michael high-fives Kate.

Kate laughs and nods knowingly. "I told you! She's gotta take a break from those self-help books and read something dirty. It's life changing!"

Chuck steps out from behind the counter and approaches Kate next. "Hey, Kate...next time you're here, can you bring me a signed copy of one of your books? My girlfriend's birthday is coming up."

"Definitely, Chuck! I have a cool book sleeve I'll give you that matches it. It'll be the perfect gift."

"Awesome," Chuck replies with a relieved grin.

Kate takes her time greeting my other two salesmen, and I can't help but marvel at how she has completely fucking charmed my entire staff now. A romance novelist and a tire shop…it's a fucking weird combination, but hell if it doesn't just work.

Kate's journey with Tire Depot is a funny one. This past summer, Kate was suffering from a case of writer's block and started sneaking into our waiting area to write because that was where she got her best words in. My buddy, Miles, happened to catch her in the act, and they've been inseparable ever since. Kate's been living with Miles for a few months, and the two of them come into Tire Depot together almost every day. Miles works in the garage, and Kate works in the customer comfort center. It's so fucking cute, I could puke.

Kate finally reaches me at the end of the counter. "Hey, Sam," she chirps happily as she adjusts her laptop bag on her shoulder to free the red hair trapped beneath the strap. "What's going on?"

"Nothing much, Kate. How are you?"

"I'm good," she replies and hooks her thumb over her shoulder. "I stopped in the garage to look for Miles, but I didn't see him."

"Our shuttle driver was sick, so he ran someone back to work," I reply, gesturing to where our courtesy van is usually parked. "He should be back any minute."

"Cool," she says, dropping a set of keys on the counter. "I have my girlfriend, Lynsey's car here. It needs an oil change."

I nod and begin to punch Lynsey's name into the computer. "Are you ever going to stop bringing other people's cars in for a service?" I ask with a shake of the head.

Her brow furrows. "Why on earth would I do that?"

"Because I told you that my uncle doesn't care that you write your books in our waiting area. You post about us every time you're here, and we've seen an increase in business since you started writing here. I charted it out." I lean across the counter and grab the keys from her to clip them to the service order I've just printed. "And we aren't doing any new advertising, so I know you're the reason for the boost. You're essentially a micro-influencer for Tire Depot, and you don't even know it…which makes it that much more authentic. Authentic advertising is what sells. And you sell, girl."

"That's awesome!" she exclaims with a big smile. "Do you think your uncle will give me more of those koozies for my readers then? They flip over those things."

I drop my head down and laugh. "You kill me. You want to be paid in koozies?"

"And complimentary beverages and cookies, of course."

I shake my head. "Whatever you want, Kate. Honestly, though, we should probably be paying you. You're a marketing dream come true."

Kate scoffs. "No way are you paying me! This is good karma I'm working on, Sam. Don't you ever just do something nice for someone just because?"

My brows lift as I instantly think of taking Maggie ice fishing. I've never taken anyone ice fishing with me before. Not even Miles, and we do tons of stuff like that together. But ice fishing is different. It's a thing I've always done on my own ever since I quit going with my dad. I hadn't even thought about what a big deal it was to take Maggie out there with me until right this second.

"Earth to Sam? Come in, Sam!" Kate states, waving her hands in front of my glazed eyes.

I look up and shake my head. "Sorry, I was just thinking about this order I need to place."

"You were?" she replies, leaning across the counter and eyeing me in speculation. "Because from the looks of it, I'd say you were daydreaming. I'm a writer, Sam...that makes me highly qualified to spot a daydreaming moment."

Suddenly, the door by the comfort center opens, and Miles's big, tall frame fills the entrance. "Babe! What took you so long to get here?" he asks, striding over to Kate with a furrowed brow. "I dropped you off at Lynsey's over an hour ago."

She rolls her eyes. "Lyns and I just got to talking...no need to worry."

Miles growls in his chest. "When your best friend is neighbors with your douchebag of an ex...I worry."

Kate shakes her head and stands on her tippy toes to kiss Miles on the cheek. "Relax, I didn't even see Dippy Dryston over there. Lynsey is just having some boy problems she needed to talk out."

"Mmmkay," Miles grumbles as he drapes a possessive arm around his girl. "It's not you I don't trust. It's that asshat of an ex you have."

Kate turns accusing eyes on me. "Seriously, Sam, I've told you Miles can't have caffeine after nine, or he gets all caveman-y."

I hold my hands up. "I'm not his keeper! You're the one living with him now, so that makes him your problem."

The truth is, Miles and I haven't seen much of each other these past few months. He's in the honeymoon stage of his relationship, and I'm not about to begrudge him of it…even if it's not something I ever want for myself.

Kate narrows her eyes at me and then looks up at Miles. "I'm going to go write now unless you were planning to club me over the head and drag me away."

"Don't tempt me," Miles says, waggling his brows at her.

I can't help but groan out loud. "Seriously, you two… get a room."

Kate giggles, shoving Miles as she strides toward the customer comfort center with her laptop bag in tow.

Miles props his elbow on the counter and watches her leave. "I wasn't even worried. I just love getting a rise out of her."

"You guys are gross," I mumble as I punch some numbers into the computer. "You've been living together for months. I thought the gross stage would be over by now."

"Not even fucking close," Miles murmurs. I have to swallow the bile that bubbles up my throat as he asks, "So what's up, man? How was your weekend?"

"Good actually. How about yours?"

"Mine was good too, but that's normal for me." He winks like a creep. "Why was yours good? I thought you were just working and ice fishing. Did you catch a shitload or something?"

AMY DAWS

I rub my lips together and nod slowly. "Something like that."

Miles eyes me carefully. "I know that look."

"What look?" I ask, and I can't hide the shit-eating grin on my face.

He smacks his hand on the counter. "Don't hold back on me now, man. You and I have chased our fair share of girls around Boulder, and you're giving me the 'I just got laid' face!"

I press my lips together and remain silent. Miles and I did have some fun times together after he broke up with his ex. We made a regular thing of beers after work and girls after dark. But since I've started working on taking over Tire Depot and he's started spending time with Kate, we haven't talked as much as we used to.

Miles lifts his brows, his blue eyes expectant as he says, "Oh come on, give me some details. I haven't been out with you for months. I know nothing about your love life anymore."

I freeze and stare at him.

He stares back. "I'm really embarrassed that just came out of my mouth."

"No shit," I reply.

He rolls his eyes. "It's not my fault, man. I'm living with a romance novelist. She has me like...verbalizing shit now."

"Do you get to verbalize dirty shit too, I hope?" This is a question only a true wingman can ask. It's my responsibility to make sure my buddy's balls stay intact.

"Oh yeaaah," he answers with a creepy leer. "But come

48

on, I feel like a dick because I haven't talked to you in a while. Give me some details."

"Like what?"

He leans across the counter, and says softly, "Like what positions?"

"Come on, man," I groan.

"What?" he balks. "It can't be any crazier than the shit my girl writes in her books."

I exhale heavily and prepare for the assault that's to come when I tell him the truth. "We didn't hook up...we just kissed."

Miles slow blinks at me. "You're smiling like that over just a kiss?"

I touch my jaw because I hadn't even realized I was smiling. "It was an epic kiss, I guess."

He blinks again, clearly unable to process my response. "Okay, so where'd you meet this epic kisser?"

My smile grows. "Marv's."

Miles face contorts. "The bait shop?"

"Yep."

"Did she have all her teeth?"

"Fuck you, man. She was hot. Like smoking hot."

Miles chuckles disbelievingly. "Okay, so what happened after this epic kiss?"

"Well...not much, but I'm hoping it's just the start."

"Huh, interesting," Miles replies, his brow furrowed deep in thought.

"Why interesting?"

"Well, you never take anyone seriously."

"Who said I'm taking this one seriously?" I scoff, feeling my shoulders rise defensively.

"The way you're telling this story, it's clear this chick is different than your typical one-night stands. I'm not judging either. I think that's awesome. You turn thirty-one on Saturday, so you're no young buck anymore."

"It doesn't matter how old I am, asshat. You know I'm not doing serious. I have enough women who depend on me already. I don't need another one...even if she is an epic kisser," I state firmly because it's the truth. If I'm not doing stuff for my mom around the house, I'm helping my recently divorced sister with her kids or running interference between all of them because a household full of women is never short on drama. "You're just pushing a relationship on me because you're prepping to pop the question to your ball and chain."

Miles's face falls, and he leans forward to shush me. "Shut the fuck up, man. She's right around the corner," he says, pointing at the comfort center.

"She can't hear me from in there...but hey, did you find a good hiding place for the ring? I can still hold it if you want," I state, lowering my voice to calm him down. I may not want a relationship myself, but it doesn't mean I don't fully support his. Kate's the best thing that's ever happened to Miles.

Miles grins. "I put it in my toolbox. She never goes in there."

"Perfect. But you're still holding off on popping the question?"

"Yeah, I don't want to rush this. Things are perfect with us right now. Living together is great. I just couldn't see that ring and not buy it, ya know?"

"I get it, man. Your chick is into tires, and a circular diamond is a rare find."

"Just like her," Miles says, getting a dreamy look in his eyes that makes me want to nut punch him. Shaking away his thoughts, he asks, "So when are you going to see this chick again?"

"Maybe this weekend...at least, I hope."

"Cool. Well, keep me posted if she turns into more than another one-nighter, all right?"

"She won't."

"She could. But even if she doesn't, I still want the dirty details...I'm not married yet." Suddenly, Miles's phone lights up. "Oh hey, I gotta take this call. I'll check you later."

He walks away, and I shake my head. Miles is so wrapped up in his own world these days that it'll be weeks before he even asks about my spark plug again. And I'm cool with that. Just because I don't believe in long term doesn't mean I don't understand why things between us have shifted a bit.

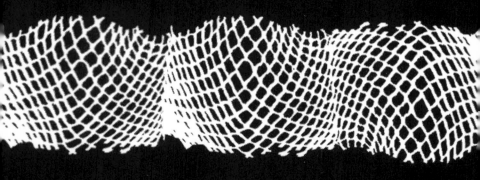

CHAPTER 4

Catch And Release

Maggie

A big yellow rotary telephone trills from the bedside table, and with a pained groan, I throw my arm across the bed to pick it up. "Hello?" I answer, trying not to sound like I was asleep but failing miserably.

"Hello, Miss Hudson, this is Claire from the front desk." Claire's waspy voice is like a feather on my cheek, annoying and soothing at the same time.

"Hi, Claire…yes, I'm coming down for breakfast. Sorry, I overslept again." I shove the quilt off my body, allowing the cool air from the weak radiator heating of the Briar Rose Bed and Breakfast where I'm staying help me wake up.

"Oh, it's perfectly okay. I was calling to remind you about your room."

"My room?" I sit up and shove the hair out of my face to look around the adorable suite I've been calling home for a week now.

"I told you we had a group of travelers checking in today, so we'll need to turn over your room as soon as possible."

"Oh, right. Yes, of course," I reply, trying to hide the urge to weep into the receiver. "I'll just finish packing, then I'll be on my way."

"You're welcome to stay for breakfast, of course. And if you need to stay in the living area for the day, that's okay too. We can hold your luggage," Claire adds helpfully. She really is a sweet old lady.

Nodding, I look at the clock to see it's ten a.m. already. "It's okay, Claire. I have somewhere else I can go." I inhale deeply and shake my head. "I've avoided my brother for far too long as it is."

I can almost hear Claire's awkward smile. "All right, dear. We'll see you down here for breakfast then."

I hang up and drag myself to the en suite bathroom for a shower, but it does nothing to dampen my anxiety over finally having to face my brother today.

After Christmas and everything in my life went to shit, I jumped into my car and drove eight hours to cry in the arms of my brother who lived in Boulder. Then, just before I reached town, I happened upon the Briar Rose Bed and Breakfast, an idyllic little place that reminded me of a Nora Roberts romance novel. She always has the swooniest happily ever afters, and that's just what I was after. So I pulled

53

in and have been holed up eating Claire's baked goods and avoiding my brother ever since.

And let's face it...also thinking about that incredible kiss with Sam the fisherman.

Kissing Sam was a mistake. A huge, monumental mistake. I was nursing a broken heart and got caught up in the moment. Simple as that. It didn't help that his lips tasted like freedom and his unyielding grip around my body felt like delicious confinement that I never wanted to end. But it meant nothing, and it was certainly not going to distract me from my goals.

I throw on a knit sweater and jeans, leaving my dark wet hair hanging loose down my back as I head downstairs. When I noisily drag my suitcase through the living room and into the beautiful formal dining room where I've spent all of my mornings, I halt in place as a group of five men are seated at the table with forks frozen halfway to their mouths.

"Hi," I state, awkwardly waving at the group of gawking men.

They all murmur their hellos and then resume shoveling the food down their throats. Claire emerges from the kitchen with wide eyes. "Oh hello, Miss Hudson, have a seat. I have your plate right here."

She walks slowly over to me, her old age slowing her down, but her smile as bright as the day I checked in a week ago. She sets the food in front of me and affectionately rubs my shoulder just as my mom would.

"Boys, this is Maggie...Maggie, these nice boys who

have just checked in are from *Backwoods Magazine.* They are here working on a piece about ice climbing on grain silos. It all sounds very exciting," she tuts while looking down at everyone's plates. "Oh look, you need fresh coffee. I'll be back in a jiffy."

She disappears through the double doors into the kitchen so I force a smile and say the first thing that comes to mind. "Why is there ice climbing on grain silos? Is it some kind of weather anomaly?" I spoon a big bite of cinnamon oatmeal into my mouth.

The guys all fail to conceal their amusement as the one closest to me responds. "No, it's a sport...like ice climbing but instead of a mountain, we're climbing a man-made iced silo. Definitely not a weather anomaly." He chuckles around a sip of his coffee.

"Interesting," I reply politely. "Why do you guys do it?"

"Because it's fucking awesome," the younger guy from across the table answers with a laugh. "It's the hardest climb you'll ever do because it's eighty feet of straight vertical. No natural slopes like you'd get on a mountain. It's a rush."

"Sounds like it." My eyes widen with interest. "How do they make the ice?"

"They dribble the water down the silo slowly during freezing temperatures. It takes several weeks before you get a good enough base to climb."

"I see," I reply and briefly wonder if this extreme sort of stuff is a Colorado thing, or if they do this back home. I was such a girlie-girl growing up that I would have never even noticed. My brother did a lot of outdoorsy things, but the only sporty thing I ever did was ski down the bunny hills for school trips. I was even too chicken to try snowboarding with my friends.

"I just went ice fishing for the first time last weekend," I state proudly because this feels like something these guys would appreciate. "So yeahhh..." My voice trails off as I realize these guys have zero interest in ice fishing. "I thought that was pretty adventurous," I add so they understand why I brought it up because they all continue to stare blankly back at me.

"Hardly," replies the guy with dreadlocks pulled back into a ponytail on the other side of me. "With ice fishing, you just sit there. There's no physical exertion. No sense of danger or adrenaline. You're missing the best parts of a rush. If you're looking for an adventure, you should come check out the silo we're climbing tomorrow. Experience isn't required, and that's where the real adventure awaits." He digs into his pocket and fishes out a small business card. "This is the card to the farmstead where the silos are located." He pauses and grabs a pen out of his pocket and scribbles something on the back. "And here's my personal number if you'd like some personal coaching. My name is Ezekiel." He looks up and winks at me, his dark eyes sparkling with obvious flirtation as he passes the card over to me.

I turn it over and finger the logo of the farmstead with a website and address. "Okay then."

"I really hope to see you there tomorrow," Ezekiel adds as he stuffs a bite of eggs into his mouth, then he mumbles, "I guarantee it'll change your life."

My eyes light up at those last words. Ice climbing on grain silos sounds like the total opposite of Basic Maggie. Ice climbing on grain silos would catapult me to Adventure Maggie for sure.

And you know what else? Adventure Maggie could probably ice fish on her own now too! I don't need an oddly cute bearded ginger with kissable lips to be my guide. And since I can do it all on my own, it also means I get to avoid heading to my brother's for a few more hours...double bonus. Maybe this is just the sort of risk-taking I need to turn everything around.

Sam

It's a frigid and sunny Saturday afternoon as I make my way out to Marv's Bait and Tackle. Normally, I'm a morning fisher. I like to get there early before all the out-of-towners make it in. But today, I held off for one very obvious, very gorgeous reason.

Maggie.

Fuck, I don't even know her last name yet. We had our hands so full of fish and each other, we really didn't get to talk a whole lot. And when we parted ways outside Marv's, I could tell she was acting all twitchy because of our kiss. So young and innocent—hell, it's fucking hot. And I did nothing to calm her nerves either. I just let her fumble her way back to her car without saying a word. Asking for a chick's number is against my rules. I prefer to just let nature take its course. If I see her again, so be it. If I don't, I won't lose any sleep over it.

But I really hope I see her again.

When I maneuver my snowmobile into the parking lot of Marv's, I'm grateful that the helmet I'm wearing is covering the way-too-fucking-happy smile on my face.

Sitting right outside of Marv's on the curb in her puffy red and white snowsuit, Maggie wears an adorably sullen look on her face. Her black hair is hanging out the bottom of her red stocking cap, and she's punching away at her phone so aggressively, she doesn't even notice me pull up in front of her.

When she finally looks up and sees me climbing off my sled, she rolls her eyes like I'm the cherry on top of her clearly shit-tastic day. I stride over to her and slip my helmet off, noticing a heap of something by her feet that looks like the corpse of a fishing hut on the ground.

"Don't say anything, all right?" she barks, looking away from me with a firm shake of her head and cold air puffing out between her ruddy lips.

I halt in front of her and close my mouth.

"I can already guess what you're going to say," she snaps again, kicking her booted feet out in front of her to shove the offensive pile farther away from her.

Again, I say nothing. My mother always said I was like a Labrador—great at following commands.

"You're going to say that I'm still a rookie, and I shouldn't

think I can do this all on my own after only one session."
She stares up at me, and her vibrant blue eyes sparkle in the
sunlight.

I cross my arms over my chest.

"And you're going to say I wasted money on this fishing
hut because it's a pile of crap, and if I had asked you for advice, you could have suggested something more suitable for
a beginner."

I exhale, my hand coming up to stroke the hair on my
chin slowly as I listen.

She stares up at me and flicks her hand in my direction.
"But honestly, after I assaulted you last weekend, I just didn't
think I could face you again."

A small huff escapes my lips because that kiss was no big
deal. Don't get me wrong, it was a great kiss. Really great. But
it wasn't going to scare me off her.

She rolls her eyes at my expression. "Well, say something, won't you?"

My shoulders lift once as I ask, "Wanna go ice fishing?"

An hour later, she's apologized no less than nineteen times
about that kiss, and she's sworn twenty-four times that it
won't happen again. I've reassured her eight times that it's
no big deal. And once that conversation is done, we're on
my sled and heading back to the same spot we fished last
weekend.

The heater in my hut has just finally taken the nip out of the air when I decide to fish for some details from the chick who swears on her life she won't be kissing me ever again.

"So what's the real reason you're so determined to be an avid ice fisher?" I flick my line roller up and release some slack out of my pole, allowing my rig to fall deeper just as a small school of muskies ventures closer to where we've dropped.

Maggie exhales heavily and mimics my actions. "I hate to say it's because of a guy…"

"But it's because of a guy," I finish.

She nods. "It's stupid, and I'm certain you don't want to hear all the hairy details."

I clench my jaw, trying to determine if I should write her off because she's on the rebound. Normally, rebound girls are like catnip to me. They're horny and emotionally unavailable…just my style. But it's one thing to be recently rejected. It's a whole other thing if they're still hung up on the guy. If Maggie is going to these lengths for a guy, she's clearly not ready for a rebound.

"I don't need to know all the details, but I'm curious what kind of guy would inspire a person to take up ice fishing?"

"He's a quarterback." She states those two words as if they're supposed to impress me. When I have no reaction, she quickly adds, "And he's being drafted by the NFL this spring."

"Okay," I reply noncommittally, trying to conceal what I'm really thinking.

Now look, I don't consider myself a judgmental prick most days, but growing up in Boulder, there were two kinds of guys: athletes and adventurists. And since I always preferred the rush of snowboarding down a black diamond hill or rock climbing a 5.15 mountain over shooting hoops and playing catch, I definitely ran in a different crowd than the athletes. I even tried ice swimming once when I was drunk. *My poor balls have never forgiven me.*

The point is, I'm an adrenaline junkie who loves the outdoors more than a "hey man, let's play catch or get tickets to a game" type. So I never really understood why girls put athletes on a pedestal. I'm not condemning them for it, girls can be attracted to whoever they want. But part of me feels a pang of disappointment when I find out Maggie is one of those girls. I knew we were opposites when I met her, but after she held that fish, I had hoped she was different.

I guess I was wrong.

"I suppose you think I'm a lame cliché, right?" Maggie states, her voice wobbling with insecurity at the end. "You've probably never done anything to impress the opposite sex."

I shake my head and remain silent as I watch the school of muskie swim away on the video monitor, almost as if they couldn't bear to hear this sob story either.

"But Sterling and I had plans, okay?" she states firmly, spinning on her stool to face me. "I met him this summer at a party, and it was love at first sight, which is exactly how my parents met, and they've been married forever. It's like the stuff my mom and I have been reading about in romance novels for like our entire lives! Sterling and I fell so hard and so fast. We were talking about marriage, kids, and our future together on our third date."

"You were planning your future together after only a few dates?" I ask incredulously, doing nothing to hide the shock in my voice.

"Yes, don't judge!" she snaps back, and the fire in her eyes has me biting my tongue. "Haven't you ever been so madly in love that you can look at a person and see your whole future with them?"

I bark out a laugh. "No fucking way."

"Well, how have you felt when you're in love then?"

"I've felt nothing because I've never been in love," I assert. "I've never even been in a relationship before. But I don't have to experience commitment to know that talking about a future together after only three dates is fucking crazy."

"But you're old," she retorts, looking me up and down as if she's going to find a fucking deformity to be the cause of my lack of emotional commitment. "Surely, you've had at least one serious girlfriend."

"I'm not that old," I grind out because fucking hell, today is my birthday, and I don't need to be reminded that I'm getting older.

"You're pretty old. Come on, how old are you?" she asks, latching on to this topic change like a dog with a bone.

I glare at her for a second and then lean forward so we're nose to nose. "I'm thirty-one today as a matter of fact."

She jerks back, her challenging eyes softening instantly. "Today is your birthday?" she asks, her voice high pitched and overly sweet. "Happy Birthday!"

"Yeah, yeah," I grind out, rolling my eyes. "Since you think I'm such an old fuck, you'd better run on ahead and save me a seat with the blue-hairs at Marv's. I've been dying to take Arthur in Old Maid for weeks."

A laugh escapes her lips at my deadpanned expression, and I sit back, adjusting my pole in the water again and shaking my head at this girl. She really seems young now all of a sudden. Either that or I really am just an old fuck. "Finish your story. What happened with this love at first sight guy?"

She exhales heavily and begins toying with her pole. "Well, we were planning our future together, right? My parents loved him, and my brother even took to him, which is a shock because he hates all the guys I've ever dated. So we started making plans for after graduation because I was finishing in December and the NFL draft is in April. Anyway, he asked me not to look for jobs until he knew what team he was going to play for. And I thought taking a few months off to spend time with family sounded nice. No big deal because we were clearly on the road to forever, right? The former cheerleader and the future NFL star. The beginning of a fairy-tale romance. Then Christmas morning came…we were visiting my parents, and he was acting weird, which made me think, 'Oh my god, he's going to propose!' Well, I was ridiculously wrong because he was actually preparing to dump me."

"Wait, what?" I ask, lowering my pole and turning to face her again. "You got dumped on Christmas morning?"

She nods, her lips jutting out into an angry duck face. "Yep," she replies with extra emphasis on the p. "At my parents' house before the sun came up over homemade cinnamon rolls and coffee."

"Fuck," I drawl, shaking my head from side to side. "Getting dumped on a holiday...that's cold."

"Colder than this lake," she adds, sliding her boot on the glossy ice beneath us. "But the real kicker wasn't that I got dumped...it was what he said when he dumped me."

I wince because this douchebag already seems like half the idiots I got into fights with in high school. "I don't even know if I can bring myself to ask."

"Oh, don't worry, I'll tell you." Maggie sets her pole down and leans closer to me, her dark hair framing her angry face perfectly. Her lake blue eyes lock on mine in a threatening way that actually somehow makes her even hotter. "He said I was too basic."

"Basic?" I repeat with a shake of my head. "Like...girl, that outfit is so basic?" I ask, regurgitating shit that I hear my sisters say to each other all the time even though they are all in their thirties.

"Exactly," Maggie confirms.

"What kind of guy uses that word?"

"Exactly!" she exclaims, pleased with my small show of solidarity. "And he said I was really pretty and smart and an obvious match for him, but he wanted someone who brought more adventure into his life."

"What a dick." I scoff, squeezing my pole hard and thinking this guy deserves to get knocked the fuck out.

"Yet for some sick reason, I'm the asshole out here trying to find a sense of adventure." She shrugs helplessly. "I was even texting him pictures of me trying to set up that ice hut today, thinking it might impress him. I'm so pathetic."

"Is this how you think you're going to win him back?" I ask while reeling my pole in a little.

She winces and begins tugging at her silky black hair. "I think trying out some outdoorsy adventure stuff could change how Sterling sees me. Make me seem less…basic." She looks over at me with big, sad eyes and a pouty lip that have my body reacting carnally. "Does that make me a silly girl?"

I shake my head and fight the urge to throw her over my shoulder, take her back to my place, and show her she doesn't need to change for some guy. She's great just the way she is.

Instead, I inhale deeply and stare back at her, gentling my voice before I reply. "I think you're silly for thinking that taking up extreme sports is going to make you look better to some guy. Especially since he sounds like an asshole."

Her eyes flare. "You don't even know him."

"I know his type," I grind out and jig my pole in frustration. "And the fact he thinks you need to change to be enough for him confirms my assessment. He's blind because…well, hell…you're clearly fucking awesome."

As soon as my words are out, a heavy silence falls over us in the tent. I look over and see a faint puff of white air in front of Maggie's lips as she exhales a breath and stares back at me with an intensity that's hard to look away from.

Her eyes dart down to my lips. Slowly sliding my tongue across them, I do everything I can not to think of the last time we were here together. Of our bodies pressed together. Our tongues massaging each other and wishing they were licking something much more fleshy than just another fucking tongue.

I shouldn't be thinking about this, though. Because if I think too hard, I'll want it again. And this is something I shouldn't want.

My gaze moves from her lips to her eyes, flashing back and forth, conflicted with which one I want to stare at more because both of them are making the crotch of my pants feel really fucking tight.

Damnit all to hell. Now I'm the one wanting to strip off my snowsuit because this potent energy pulsing between us is smothering my poor ball sack. And my dick wants to be suffocated by something else entirely.

I make a small move toward her, and she gasps, her eyes flying wide. "Are you getting a bite?" she exclaims, her voice all froggy and weird sounding.

My gaze snaps to my pole, then I look at the monitor and see nothing but an empty lake below. "There's nothing there," I reply. Settling back on my stool, I stare for a moment longer, expecting to see something show up.

She clears her throat. "Oh, sorry...I swore I saw your line move."

Depends on which line she's referring to. Because if it's the thick one between my legs, then there was definite movement. "Yeah, maybe it'll come back," I state with a hopefulness to my tone that I can't hide.

Goddamnit, I want to fuck this girl. I want to fuck her right here and right now. But she just told me she's trying to win her ex back so that should be a deal breaker. That should have me running in the opposite direction because I don't do girls with baggage. That's a hard pass for me, normally. But for some ridiculous reason, her innocent idealism keeps drawing me back to her.

I clear my throat and ask the first thing that pops into my head. "So what kind of crazy stuff did you want to try to get your ex back?" I turn to look at her with a forced smile. "'Cuz I'm sorry to be the one to tell you, but ice fishing is not what I would call super adventurous."

"I know," she grumbles, and her eyes light up as she points at the monitor as that school of fish reappear. "It was just the first thing I tried, and I have to admit, I kind of like it."

I smile at that because it makes the fact that I took a chance by inviting her out here all the more worth it.

She wiggles her pole a little. "But I'm going to try something more daring because, deep down, I think Sterling might be right," she adds, tucking her hair behind her ears. "My whole life has been safe and easy. I make plans, and I stick to them. I don't handle change very well. So now is the perfect time for me to break some of my own rules."

A grin splits my face as I check out this stunning, very girlie chick sitting on a hard stool in the middle of a frozen lake. "Breaking some rules can be fun," I reply and drag a deep, cleansing breath in as I wish she'd break some rules with me right now. I clear my throat harshly, struggling to get my mind out of the gutter. "And as much as it pains me to say this, I actually think it's pretty cool that you're going to such lengths for a guy. Not many girls would bother."

At that moment, she gets a bite, and without any guidance from me, she sets the hook like a fucking pro. "I got one!" she squeals and begins cranking her reel. "I got it on my own this time!"

I smile and drop down onto my knees while feeling really weirded out that this is turning me on so much. I steady my thoughts, and say, "Let's see if you can reel it in on your own, too."

"Okay," she beams, sticking her tongue out as she concentrates.

I watch her with great fascination because even though everything she said sounded like everything I'd run the fuck away from, something about her keeps reeling me back in.

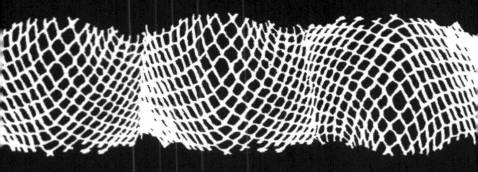

CHAPTER 5

Little Fish...Big Problem

Sam

"Happy Birthday!" my mom cheers as my three sisters finish singing to me in perfect harmony.

I lean over to blow out the candles with my eight-year-old niece, Kinsley, propped on one knee, and my six-year-old nephew, Zion, propped on the other. They both stare at me with sad puppy dog eyes.

"You guys don't think I can blow all these candles out myself, do you?" I waggle my brows and watch their faces transform into pure joy as they lean in and basically spit all over my birthday cake.

It'll still taste delicious.

Sliding off my lap, they rush over to my mom when she drags the cake to where she's sitting beside me. "Who wants

Uncle Sammy's face?"

"Me, Grandma!" Kinsley squeals. Making a fist around her plastic fork, she growls, "I want to murder Sammy's face!"

Everyone's smile falls as we stare at her in disturbed horror. I look at my oldest sister, Tracey, who's horrified eyes are locked on her daughter. "Kinsley, what did Mommy say about murder?"

"Come again?" I croak, rapidly blinking up at her from where she stands on the other side of me.

Kinsley's voice sounds sad. "Don't repeat what you hear in Mommy's car."

Tracey laughs awkwardly and looks around at all of us with crazy eyes. "I'm so sorry. She heard a tiny little bit of My Favorite Murder podcast, and now she's all weird and murdery. We're working on it."

My other two sisters, Erin and Holly, do nothing to conceal their looks of judgment as they both balance a toddler on their hips.

"Work harder maybe," Holly states, grabbing Tracey's arm seriously.

"Shut up, Holly! Like you're one to talk. Isaiah fell out of his crib last week."

"That situation is under control!" she growls back through clenched teeth while clutching her one-year-old tightly to her chest.

"So is mine," Tracey harrumphs.

"Girls…my darling grandchildren clearly don't need to watch you two have a catfight, so please, sit down and eat your feelings like normal mothers."

My three sisters all sullenly take their seats as my mom dishes everyone a giant piece of white sheet cake. Between my three older sisters, I'm the proud uncle to three nephews and, apparently, one murder-loving niece. Holly's having her second child any day now to even the playing field a little for the girls.

My sisters all look just like my mom with fair skin, freckles, and shades of auburn hair. However, the truth is, my mom looks more like their oldest sister than their mother because the woman hasn't aged a day since I was old enough to notice.

Debrah O'Connor is an RN at the hospital in Boulder and a favorite with all her patients. She works way too fucking hard, but you can't stop her. She'll work a twelve-hour shift, bake a birthday cake, and still offer to babysit all her grandkids without hesitation. She is like the Energizer Bunny.

And even though she doesn't have a single gray strand in her short, auburn hair, I know working so hard wears on her. Occasionally, when she thinks no one is looking, I see her wincing when she's crawling on the floor with her grandkids. She's only sixty-years-old, but all those years of working on the hospital floors have taken a toll. I can tell her she's pushing herself too hard, and I frequently ride her ass about retiring but she just shushes me and says she has a plan and she can't afford to quit now.

It kills me because I want to fix it for her. She deserves that.

"I'm glad you could come over for some cake, Sammy," Mom says, smiling at me with that motherly twinkle in her eye.

"Well, I had to fix your garage door, so I figured I could choke down some cake too." I wink playfully at her because she knows I'll always be parked at this old kitchen table on my birthday eating her homemade sheet cake with my face printed on it.

"I told you the garage door could wait," she tuts, the corners of her mouth turning down.

I stare at her for a beat. "Mom, it's twenty below out there. You don't need to be parking your car outside."

"I don't mind!"

"Speaking of fixing stuff," Tracey interrupts and looks straight at me. "My water softener has been really loud lately, Sammy. What do you think that means?"

"Is it still cycling salt through?" I ask, pushing my bite of cake to the corner of my mouth.

Tracey looks at me with blank eyes. "How would I know?"

"When's the last time you put salt in the tank?"

Her lips twist into a grimace. "Matt was probably the last one to do it."

I nod and inhale when she mentions her ex-husband who was about as handy as a toddler. "I'll come look at it tomorrow."

"Thank you!" she rushes out in gratitude. "Did you hear that, guys? Uncle Sammy is coming over tomorrow for Sunday Funday."

"Yes!" Zion exclaims. "We're going to play *Madden*, and I am going to destroy you...again."

I roll my eyes. "You'd better watch it, twerp, or I'll bring in my secret weapon."

"Which is?" Zion stares back at me with a challenge in his eyes.

I point at my niece who smiles with a decidedly murdery smile. Zion's face falls. "No fair...Kinsley is good at everything."

I laugh and shake my head. "Every dog has his day, man. Don't give up."

The kids finish their cake and take off upstairs to where my mom has redecorated all our old childhood bedrooms into themed playrooms for the kids. Whenever we're all here, they always play upstairs and make an epic mess. They love it.

"So Sammy, what are your birthday plans tonight?" Mom asks, slipping a forkful of white cake into her mouth.

"You're looking at it," I reply, lopping one more bite of cake off the cardboard tray.

Erin's eyes narrow on me. "You're not going out for your birthday?"

"Nah. What's so special about thirty-one? It's just one year closer to forty. Plus, I have some business proposals I need to finish for Uncle Terry. I want him to approve them before he takes off in six months."

"Sammy," my mom says in her scolding voice. "It's your birthday. You should go do something fun. You work too hard."

"I went ice fishing today. That was fun." I shrug.

My sisters all look at me with sad eyes, but Tracey is the one who speaks up. "I hate how you ice fish alone all the time. And you're alone in that log cabin you bought in the country, too. It's depressing."

"And a little pathetic," Erin adds.

"You're turning into a hermit," Holly chimes in at the end. "Or one of those rural weirdos from Tracey's murder podcasts."

My eyes nearly bug out of my head. "I like my acreage, and I like my cabin. People who live in town can be lonely and murdery too…it's not the country that makes someone homicidal. And for your information, I wasn't alone when I went ice fishing today, so get off my back!"

"You weren't alone?" Mom asks, looking at me with fear in her eyes. "Who were you with? It wasn't *him*, was it?"

"No," I reply with an annoyed growl. "God, no. It wasn't him…it was just a girl."

"What girl?" Holly chirps.

"Just a chick who's new to ice fishing and needed some help."

"You took someone who wasn't Dad out ice fishing?" Tracey asks, her jaw dropped.

"Yes," I reply, my shoulders tensing at their overreaction. "It wasn't that big of a deal."

"You never take anyone ice fishing," Holly states, and I swear I can see the anger rising up to her eyeballs. "I've asked you to take me hundreds of times, and you always say no."

"Well, it wasn't a planned thing," I argue and fork my last bite into my mouth. "It just sort of…happened…twice."

"Twice?" my sisters all exclaim at once.

Just then the doorbell rings. In a flash, I splay my hands out on the table and push my chair back loudly. "Please, for the love of all things holy, let me get that."

I hear my sisters gossiping behind me as I stride down the hallway to the front door. When I open it, I'm shocked to see Miles on the other side with a big, toothy smile. "Happy Birthday, dick stain."

I squint against the setting sun behind him. "Thanks? What are you doing here, man?"

Miles punches me in the shoulder playfully. "You weren't at your place, so I figured you were here. Come on, I'm taking you out."

"Where's Kate?" I ask, looking behind him at his empty truck.

"She's saving us seats at Pearl Street Pub. We got a table."

"Damn, I haven't been there in forever," I state, rubbing my jaw excitedly. Miles and I used to frequent the bar after work until I got busy with Tire Depot and he got busy with Kate.

"You'd better not even think about going there with someone else," he retorts seriously. "I know I've been distracted, but Pearl Street Pub is our place, and I'll fuck up anyone who tries to go there with you and take my place."

I stare at Miles with a slow shake of my head. "Come on, man."

He closes his eyes and presses his hand to his face. "I

know. Goddamnit, I'm just going to give you my man card now because I'm sure that's not going to be the last cheesy thing that comes out of my mouth tonight. Living with a romance novelist is ruining me."

I laugh and yank Miles inside to say hello to my family while I run upstairs to give my nephews and niece a hug goodbye. After buttoning a couple more buttons on my green flannel shirt, I ask, "Am I dressed okay?"

Miles looks me up and down. "You're wearing boots, jeans, and a flannel…that's basically the Boulder dress code, bro. You look fine. Let's go."

I leave my SUV in the driveway and hop into Miles's truck. I hold my hands up to the heat vents, still feeling a nip on my skin from fishing earlier today.

"So did you see her?" Miles asks as he maneuvers out of the neighborhood.

"See who?" I ask, eyeing him curiously.

"The ice fishing hottie."

I huff out a laugh. "Oh, I saw her all right."

Miles hits the steering wheel. "Yeah, you did! Did you get birthday sex already? I was prepared to wingman you tonight."

My brow furrows. "I did not get birthday sex."

"So what happened?"

"Nothing, technically, but goddamn, I don't know, man. This girl makes me fucking crazy. She's young but not necessarily immature, just like idealistic or some shit. And she's crazy hot. I got a glimpse of her tits, and they are like two water balloons that I know would fit perfectly in my hands."

"Nice," Miles replies with a knowing nod. "Gotta love a good handful."

"Right," I reply. "She's like no one I've ever hooked up with before, which I think is why I can't seem to stay away from her. And every once in a while, she gets a spark in her eye that makes me want to…"

"What?" Miles asks, his tongue nearly hanging out of his mouth as he listens intently. "Fuck her in a tent in the woods so people in the next campsite over can hear you and give you a mental high five?"

I eye him curiously. "I was thinking more like throw her up against a wall, but sure, your tent idea sounds pretty nice too."

"Damn right, it does." He fist-bumps me.

I stare out the window at the fresh snow that's begun falling. I love fresh snow. It's so…untainted. "This might actually be the first girl I break some rules for, Miles."

"Shock, awe, stupor, aghast, agog."

"What are you doing?" I ask, turning to Miles as he continues watching the road.

"I'm giving you adjectives for the word shock because I'm in major shock right now."

"Why are you giving me adjectives?"

"It's just something I do with Kate when she's looking for a better word in her book. I thought I could make it a thing between you and me too." His face looks so hopeful. I almost feel bad for crushing it.

Almost.

"Nah, man. I'm going to have to pass on that one."

Miles rolls his eyes. "Whatever. I'm just saying I'm amazed you're breaking any rules for this chick. Since the day I met you, you've been playing musical beds with chicks left and right."

"Nothing is changing there," I confirm, eyeing him seriously so he fully hears me. "I'm not getting into a relationship with the chick. She has serious baggage that I'm not interested in saddling myself with. You know I don't do serious after watching what my dad did to my mom. I'm never going down that path. I just exchanged phone numbers with her, so musical beds is an option. That's all."

"Fair enough," Miles replies, nodding thoughtfully as we stop at a red light on Pearl Street. "Still, though, exchanging numbers is not something you've done before."

"I know," I reply with a deep breath. "This one makes me do weird things."

He huffs out a laugh and reaches over to fist bump me. "Hell, you met her at a bait shop—it's already weird. And since I met my girl in a tire shop, I can tell you with one hundred percent certainty that weird can be hot."

"Hot and temporary," I add for good measure. "Just because you're Mr. Monogamy doesn't mean I have to be."

Miles pulls his hand back and nods seriously. "I hear you, man. Musical beds, it is."

"Exactly," I reply with a relaxed smile.

Minutes later, we pull up in front of Pearl Street Pub and Cellar. Miles and I started hanging out at this low-key bar when he first moved to town. It's sort of a hole-in-the-wall type of place with a chill staff and awesome grub. Plus, as one of the only places on Pearl Street not packed with college kids or tourists, it's a favorite of mine.

We walk into the low-lit, wainscoted pub, and once my eyes adjust, I see Kate's fiery red hair piled on top of her head back by the pool tables. We make our way over to where she's sitting, and I see her friends Lynsey and Dean are beside her with several of the guys from Tire Depot and a couple of my buddies from college who have gotten to know Miles since he moved here a couple of years ago.

My top mechanic hands me a beer out of the bucket of ice as I see a big tire-decorated frosted cookie cake sitting right in the middle of the table. "You guys didn't have to do all this," I state, shaking my head. I hate being the focus of everyone's attention right now.

"Yes, we did," Miles says, clapping his hand on my shoulder. "You've been working hard lately, and you deserve to have some fun."

I roll my eyes, moving around the table to say hello to everyone else. Kate yanks me her way, and says, "Sam, you remember my friends Lynsey and Dean, right?"

"Happy Birthday, Sam!" Lynsey exclaims and reaches over to clink bottles with me. Lynsey's a little on the kooky side, but so is Kate, so I can see why their friendship is so strong. Kate's guy friend Dean, on the other hand...I'm still a little leery of him, but I paste on a smile for him and do my best not to smirk at his plaid blazer.

Suddenly, I hear Miles bellow, "There you are, Megan! Come over here and meet my best buddy, Sam! He's technically my boss at Tire Depot, but I don't like to remind him, or he gets a big head."

I turn to shake hands with whoever Miles is talking to, and suddenly, I feel like I've been kicked in the nuts.

Or actually...the taint.

Yeah, this feeling right here...it's too deep for a nut kick. This panic-seizing, gut-twisting, body-tremoring attack overwhelming all my senses has a taint kick written all over it.

Because I'm staring into the stunning blue eyes of my ice fishing companion from the past two weekends.

"Sam, this is my baby sister, Megan, visiting us all the way from Utah. Megan, this is my best friend, Sam." Maggie's smile falters with recognition as Miles, her...*brother—oh fucking fuck, her brother*—drapes his arm over her shoulder and smiles back at me.

Like a moron, I instantly bring my beer to my lips and take three slow glugs. Whatever I can do to avoid touching her outstretched hand right now because I'm convinced the second I touch her in front of her brother, Miles will know I've thought about her naked no less than nineteen times.

And now I'm thinking about her naked again.

I nod stupidly and continue to chug my beer like a damn college frat boy as Miles and Maggie watch me curiously. Finally, I pry the cold glass from my lips long enough to give her a head nod.

A fucking head nod.

Only douchebags who call a girl basic would give a fucking head nod.

I look down at where she's still holding her hand out

for me to shake, and God help me, my traitorous eyes scan the rest of her body at the same time. Her perfect round tits are covered beneath this short black lace dress. It's way too fucking dressy for the likes of Pearl's, but hell if she doesn't look sexy. She's wearing black plaid tights and little ankle boots with a big ass heel that bring her up to my chin. I'd gotten used to her being at my chest in her snow boots. *The same boots she was wearing when I kissed my best friend's little sister in my fucking fishing hut.*

My mind instantly begins trying to remember everything I said to Miles about his sister in his truck earlier. *Jesus Christ, this is bad.*

Suddenly, Maggie reaches out and forcefully grabs my hand to shake. "Hi Sam, my friends call me Maggie. Miles is the only one who still calls me Megan…even my parents say Maggie. It's nice to *meet* you…for the first time."

She's talking slow, and I feel myself nodding with buggy eyes as I attempt to swallow back the cotton in my mouth and ignore the sparks shooting up my hand from her touch. "Nice to meet you for the first time, too. How long have you been in town visiting?" *Jesus hell, I sound like a robot on acid.*

Her dimple flashes when she realizes I'm not going to spill the beans. "I just arrived a couple of hours ago."

I unclench my jaw and belatedly realize we're still shaking hands. "Today?" I can't help but say it as a question because where the fuck has she been staying for the past week if Miles thinks she just got into town today?

"Yes, I was visiting my boyfriend in his hometown on

the East Coast and decided to stay in Boulder for a few weeks before heading back to Utah."

My eyes are blinking, and I can't stop them because my mind is completely jumbled up right now. I can't differentiate the lie from the truth. Is she still with her boyfriend and was lying to me? Or did she tell me the truth, and she's lying to Miles?

This is why you don't break your own rules, Sammy. Girls with baggage are never easy.

Finally, I find my voice, and say, "Well, I hope you have a pleasant visit." I quickly yank my hand from hers and wave my empty beer bottle to Miles as he settles on the stool next to Kate. "I'm getting the next round. Nobody argue."

I turn on my heel and hightail it over to the bar for some space to think. Propping myself on a stool, I thread my hands through my hair, reeling over what's just happened. How the fuck did I not figure out that Maggie was Miles's sister, Megan? They totally look related.

Does this mean I'm attracted to my best friend?

I shake that thought off instantly because Miles doesn't have water balloon tits. Call me a barbarian but breasts are a must for me, I'm afraid. The bartender asks me what I'd like, and I reply, "Another bucket of Coors to stick my head into."

He harrumphs and sets to work when a voice scares the shit out of me. "You can't tell Miles about us."

"What?" I exclaim, my head snapping over to find Maggie standing right next to me.

"You and me," she repeats, leaning in so close her breast brushes against my arm. "You can't tell Miles we know each other."

"No shit," I growl and yank my arm away from those glorious specimens that have turned me into a fucking pervert. *Fucking fuck. Did I describe her tits to Miles earlier? Goddamnit, I'm a moron!* "Miles is going to rip off my nuts and hang them on the trailer hitch of his truck like those assholes who drive around with bull testicles."

"What?" she asks, her blue eyes blinking with confusion.

I shake my head. "Never mind."

"So we're in agreement? He doesn't need to know that you and I have…met before."

She stares at me with a pleading look on her face, and my adulterous gaze drops down to the swell of cleavage beneath the lace overlay of her dress. I swallow hard and quickly turn back to face forward. *Just stare at the liquor bottles on the shelf, Sam. Just stare at the liquor bottles on the shelf!* "We're in agreement."

She exhales heavily and slides onto the stool next to me. I do a jerky look over my shoulder to make sure no one is watching us. Everyone appears to be happily listening to Kate tell a story, all their eyes alight with amusement.

Through clenched teeth, I ask, "Are you going to tell me why Miles thinks you still have a boyfriend?"

She winces and looks like she's swallowing razor blades. "I can't tell my family that Sterling dumped me."

"Why not?" I ask, my brow furrowing. "Miles always said his family is cool. Super supportive and shit. He calls his mom every Sunday!"

"Our family is cool," she groans, bringing her hand up to pinch the bridge of her nose. "They are perfect, and they are everything to me. If I tell them Sterling dumped me out of the blue on Christmas morning, they will all hate him."

"So what?" I grind out, staring down at her hunched frame. "I think the fucker deserves to be hated."

She turns to look at me with glassy eyes. "I can't have them hating the man I want to marry."

In one day, I've been taint-kicked and gut-punched... happy fucking birthday, Sammy. "You really want to marry him?" I groan and scrub my hand over my jaw.

She nods glumly.

The bartender hands me a bucket of beer, and with a heavy sigh, I murmur under my breath, "It's your life, sparky."

I stand and gesture with my head that we should go back to the group before anyone gets suspicious. We rejoin the group, and I decide that going beer for beer with Miles, who has a good three inches and thirty pounds of muscle over me, is a good idea. We clink bottles, and I do my best to forget what Maggie said at the bar and definitely forget about playing musical beds with her.

For tonight, I push aside why all of this bothers me so much. It definitely surprises me that she wants to marry that asshat. In the brief time we hung out over the past week, I got the impression she was better than that. I know I told her it was cool she was trying something different to win him back, but now knowing that she's not just trying to get her dimwit of a football player back but plans to marry the guy—it scares me for her. And it makes me doubt everything I thought about her.

But hell, she's not my little sister. She's Miles's. *My best friend*...in case I need reminding. And apparently, I do need reminding because I can't stop checking her out all night. At one point, I have to squeeze past her to get around the table. Our fronts end up rubbing together, and I swear to fuck, I get a half-boner. My buddy's little sister has turned me into a goddamned teenager, so I have a strong desire to slam my forehead into the wall until I black out.

I head downstairs to use the bathroom located in the dingy basement of Pearl's. I'm getting drunk because this is fucking painful. The one girl I contemplate breaking my rules for ends up being the one girl I cannot touch.

On my way back up the steps, my eyes land on a sexy pair of legs covered in tights that could easily take my mind off my fishing buddy. But when I raise my gaze to her face, I'm junk punched by the stunning raven-haired, blue-eyed beauty who shares the DNA of my best friend.

"Hey," I state, propping myself up against the wall opposite the railing to give her a wide berth. I pretend to tip a fucking hat that I'm not even wearing at her and then consider eight different ways I could dick punch myself for being so uncool.

"Heyyy," she says slowly, pausing on the staircase and pressing her back to the wall opposite me.

Don't stop and talk to me right now. Keep walking. The less I look at you tonight, the better.

"Listen," she says, biting her lip and tucking her hair behind her ear. "Thanks again for not saying anything to Miles."

I lift my palms and shrug. "There's nothing really to say. I mean…nothing happened, and I know nothing."

"Right," Maggie says, nodding curiously as she stares over at me. "Are you drunk, Sam?"

"No," I scoff and buzz my lips like a moron.

She giggles and brings her hands up to finger the necklace at her chest. *And now I'm staring at her tits. Way to fucking go, Sammy.*

"You seem drunk, which kind of surprises me. I would have pegged you for a guy who's always in control." She narrows her stunning eyes at me, and my brows lift.

"Wellllll," I sing out in a weird, high-pitched voice, screwing my face up as I attempt to find the best words to convey my message. "When you realize the girl you went ice fishing with who has exquisite tits is the younger sister of your best buddy, alcohol just seems like the only thing to make that all less horrifying."

She blinks at me, clearly taken off guard by my honest response. "Did you just say my tits are exquisite?"

"So not the point, sparky!" I groan, pinching the bridge of my nose and throwing my head back on the wall behind me in frustration. "Maybe just keep a ten-foot radius from me for the rest of the night. It's my birthday, and I can't be trusted."

She smiles, seemingly flattered by this ridiculous request. She takes a step down toward that bathroom and then looks over her shoulder. "I guess at least I now know why you seem so familiar to me. You and Miles are a lot alike."

I nod and exhale heavily, feeling weird that she just told me I'm like her brother. "Yeah, he's good people."

"I completely agree," she confirms, and then pauses for a moment, eyeing me like she wants to say something more, but then she gives up and turns on her heel to make her way down to the restrooms.

And like a fucking pervert, I stand there and check out her sexy legs in those tights for her entire walk down.

It's midnight before everyone clears out, and I'm a little drunker than I should be. Miles throws his arm around me and walks me through the bar, going on about how much he loves me, and how he can't wait until we're running Tire Depot together, side by side. Kate and Maggie are just ahead of us, talking quietly like old friends, and I pray to fuck Miles doesn't notice me checking out his sister's ass.

"So Sam, are you going to call your fishing goddess?" Miles slurs, touching my ear with his lips and making me cringe.

"Huh?" I mumble, unabashedly pushing his face away from me. God, this fucker is a close talker when he's drunk.

"Your fishing buddy. The one you're going to break all your rules for." He leans in close and whispers loudly. "Water balloon tits."

"What's that?" Kate asks, looking over her shoulder with wide, curious eyes.

"Nothing!" I exclaim and slam my palm over Miles's

loud fucking mouth just as Maggie looks back. I avoid eye contact, and add, "Nothing at all."

They both turn away, and when I release Miles's mouth, he gasps for air. "Jesus man, you were plugging my nose too!"

I wind back my elbow and jab him in the ribs. "Well, shut the fuck up then!"

"What?" he slurs, rubbing his ribs halfheartedly, clearly too drunk to feel any pain. "Kate won't judge. She loves this shit. It's all book material for her."

"Your sister is right there," I grind out into his ear as we step outside onto the sidewalk. "Just shut up, man. I'm serious."

"Meg doesn't care either. Meg is going to marry a quarterback who plays for the Broncos, and then we can get tickets to all the games we want!" Miles throws his hands up into a touchdown formation, and I begin to wonder how we ever became friends. "I only met him once, and I think he could be douchey, but I'm trying to stop being overprotective of my baby sister because apparently I'm 'ruining her life.'" Miles imitates Maggie's voice at the end, and I have to bite back a laugh because it's so uncanny, it's freaking me out.

"Okay, big guy…let's get you in the car," Kate says, tucking herself under Miles's giant arm to take over. She ushers him to the curb while I peer over at Maggie through the corner of my eye. Kate grabs the keys out of Miles's pocket and winks at him while opening his truck door. "I'm driving."

He bops her on the nose. "Yes, you are, my future wifey."

"Come again?" Kate asks, quirking a curious brow.

"I called you my future wifey because—" Miles's next words have me clumsily barreling over to step between them. If my best friend proposes to his girlfriend while drunk, he will never forgive himself.

"He calls people who take care of him when he's drunk wifey. It's a thing he does." My words are slurred, but they seem really solid. "He's called me wifey more times than I can count." I laugh a little too hard and turn on my heel to shove Miles into the truck with a severe look before he says something even stupider. "In you go, hubby," I add through clenched teeth.

"Aww, thanks, wifey." Miles giggles, then reaches out and slowly drags all five of his fingertips from my forehead to my chin. It's a weird, affectionate embrace that I'm embarrassed to admit felt really nice.

I shake my head at that and shut the door before turning back to face Kate and Maggie. "He doesn't usually do that face pet thing." I laugh awkwardly, trying to ignore the puzzled look on both of their faces. I pull my phone up to my face. "I'm just going to call an Uber."

"Megan's car is here," Kate states, placing her hand over my phone to stop me. "She's sober, so I'm sure she can take you. You don't mind, do you, Meg?"

Maggie looks at Kate with wide, nervous eyes. "Um… sure?"

"Perfect," Kate exclaims with a clap of her hands. "I feel like I need to get Miles to bed before he ends up proposing to Sam." Kate reaches out to give me a hug. "Happy

Birthday, Sam. We'll have you out to the house for dinner soon, okay?" She turns to Maggie. "See you at home in a bit!"

"See ya!" Maggie calls back with a weak wave.

Seconds later, I'm left on the curb of Pearl Street Pub with my best friend's little sister...who I most definitely want to fuck.

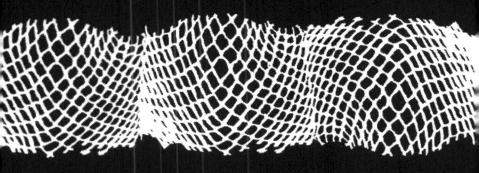

CHAPTER 6

A Reel Expert Can Tackle Anything

Maggie

S am and I silently make our way over to the lot behind
the bar where I parked my car. As I walk beside him,
my mind races with everything that's happened in the
past week. I cannot believe the same Sam I've been fishing
with—the same Sam I basically attacked with my tongue—
is my brother's best friend! I went through all of high school
and never looked twice at one of his buddies. I drive eight
hours to Boulder and randomly stumble upon one? How in
the heck?

What's worse, Sam now knows I'm lying about still being in a relationship with Sterling, which is embarrassing on
so many levels. But whatever, it is what it is. Now I need
to make damn sure Sam doesn't tell Miles about that or my

plan to transform myself to win back my ex. If Miles knows what lengths I'm going to for this guy, that tiny bit of freedom he's given me will be ripped away, and he'll do that annoying big brother overprotective thing all over again. And I'm certain I can fix this on my own.

I glance over my shoulder and lock eyes with Sam, who quickly looks away. He's been doing that all night, and I hate the way it makes my tummy flip. This would all be a lot easier if he wasn't so attractive. That reddish beard with a faint smattering of freckles over his nose all bundled up in that cozy plaid shirt make him definitely majorly cute. He looks like the kind of guy you want to lie on a couch with and dry hump during a movie.

Dry hump? Oh my heck, Maggie…get a grip!

I click the key fob to my little white Malibu and jump into the car quickly. Sam folds himself into the passenger seat, and his knees instantly hit the dash. *Good Lord, he's big.* I reach over to pull the lever under his seat so his chair will slide back, but at the same time, he spreads his legs farther to do it himself, and somehow…because apparently, the world decides I can still be more pathetic…my hand ends up at the apex of his groin.

Oh crap, I'm touching his dick! I'm totally touching his dick, and I think it just moved!

"Whoa there," he mumbles into my hair, his hot breath sending shivers down my spine. "If you wanted to play Bop It, you should have just said so."

"Oh my god," I exclaim, snatching my hand back and squeaking out a weird noise from deep inside my throat.

"That was an accident!"

Fumbling with the key, I pray like heck I don't look over and see Sam's apparently very impressive dick growing inside his snug jeans.

He chuckles, running his hands down his jeans-clad thighs, and says, "No worries, I'm not a fan of the twisting and the bopping anyway. I'm a simple 'pull it' guy all the way."

I groan loudly, in no way amused by this mortifying situation. I just need to drive and focus on something other than Sam in those jeans. What is it with those jeans anyhow? They are a night and day difference from the work jeans he had on at Marv's Bait and Tackle. These are like… man jeans. Is that a thing? If not, it should be because these are what men wear, not boys. They are faded and distressed in all the right places and snug but not like skinny jeans snug. And they're not so long that you can't see his sleek brown ankle boots, proving that Sam actually has some sexy style going on under all that dry-humpable manliness.

Not that I'm checking him out.

I'm not. I'm totally not.

I just appreciate his taste because Sterling always wore baggy jeans. Ones that wrinkled over his shoes and looked sloppy. That's the only reason I noticed Sam's appearance tonight. He dresses like a grown-up, and I appreciate that. End of story!

As I pull out onto the road, I can feel Sam's eyes pinpointed on me as his deep voice echoes in my car. "Don't you need directions?"

I flinch like an idiot because where the hell was I driving to just now? "Yes, directions would be good."

He instructs me through a couple of turns until we're headed toward the west side of town. After a few minutes of silence, he asks, "So tell me this, if Miles thinks you just arrived in town today, where have you been staying since the last time we went ice fishing?"

I exhale heavily, wishing I could get out of answering this question, but I know if anyone deserves the truth, it's Sam. "I was staying at the Briar Rose Bed and Breakfast outside of town."

"Why?" he asks, and I can hear the judgment in his tone already.

"Because I was supposed to spend the week at my boyfriend's in North Carolina, and no one knows we broke up, so I needed a place to hide out essentially."

"A guy who uses the word 'basic' doesn't use social media and update his relationship status on Facebook?"

"I begged him not to," I reply with a groan. "I told him I was going to wait to tell my parents until sometime after the New Year because I didn't want to ruin their holiday."

"And he agreed?"

"Yes."

He harrumphs.

"What?" I ask.

"I'm trying to figure out why he had no problem ruining *your* holiday." His eyes are hooded as he looks at me expectantly, clearly waiting for an answer.

I chew my lip before defending Sterling's actions. "I

think I might have freaked him out at my parents' house."

"Oh?" Sam asks, angling his body to give me his undivided attention.

"Well, he was staying with me at my parents' house before his flight left on Christmas morning to go to his parents' house. We were lying in bed the night before, and jeez, I don't know...I guess you could say I was drunk on Christmas spirit because I may have started naming our kids and talking about what we could give them for presents from Santa."

Sam says nothing, so I continue.

"I could tell I maybe went a little too far because he didn't touch me all night, and normally, he's all about sex. But I hoped he'd get over it, so I got up at three a.m. to make him cinnamon rolls from scratch before his flight."

"Jesus, Maggie," Sam groans, running his hand through his hair with clear frustration.

"What?"

"Fucking cinnamon rolls?"

"Yes. What?" I exclaim and tighten my grip around the wheel. "They are his favorite, and I was just trying to be sweet. He was about to spend Christmas morning at the airport, and I wanted him to feel my love."

"And then he dumped you over cinnamon rolls and coffee," Sam concludes, knowing how the story ended.

"French pressed coffee," I add with a pitiful pout. "And he did it before anyone else was awake. I was obviously a mess when I took him to the airport. I couldn't believe we were ending things like that. But then he kissed me when we were standing on the curb outside the airport. Like seriously kissed me. It didn't feel like a goodbye kiss. It tasted like regret. There was a look in his eye when he waved goodbye that made me feel like we weren't necessarily over for good."

I peek over and see Sam watching me with wary eyes full of drunken judgment and zero understanding. Which makes sense because he's a guy. He doesn't know how to read between the lines. Thankfully, I do.

"When I got back from the airport, I pretended nothing happened." I shrug and drum my fingers along the wheel. "It was really hard because Kate has a really sharp bullshit meter, but if she knew anything was up, she never said a word."

"So what is your grand plan exactly?" he asks, crossing his arms over his chest.

"What do you mean?"

"I mean…this lie," he states with a frustrated huff. "How long are you going to keep it up?"

"As long as it takes to show him that I've changed." I shrug as if it's the most obvious answer in the world.

Sam clearly does not agree because I can see his hands tensing with agitation on his lap. "And you're planning to do that how exactly?"

"My plan is to just hang out in Boulder and test out some adventurous activities in the hopes of winning him back. I think if I send pictures of all the fun stuff I'm doing, he'll be impressed."

"So you guys are still in touch?" he asks, eyeing me seriously.

"Yes, we text. Just friendly texting, but it's something."

"Don't you think it's a little naïve to go to such lengths for a guy who broke up with you just because you're certain he wants you back?"

"No," I reply instantly, pursing my lips in determination. "Because I believe that love is worth fighting for."

He exhales heavily at that response, his fingers moving up to pinch the bridge of his nose. After a moment of silence, he slaps his hand on his leg, and asks, "Okay then. Exactly what kind of adventures are you considering?"

I smile broadly. "Tomorrow I'm going ice climbing on a silo."

"You're what?" he snaps, and I swear the alcoholic buzz he had from earlier disappears and is replaced by rage.

Bracing myself, I reply, "It's like a silo that you can ice climb. It's a thing."

"I know it's a thing...but how do you know it's a thing?"

"Some guys who checked into the bed and breakfast told me about it. They said anyone can do it."

"Have you ever even climbed before?"

"Like ice, you mean?" I ask.

"Like anything. A wall...a cliff...a StairMaster?"

"StairMaster...yes!" I exclaim with a big smile. "I slay it on a StairMaster. Do you think that'll help with the iced silo?"

Sam groans and scrubs his hands over his face. "You can't go ice climbing, Maggie. That's like advanced level stuff."

"There are safety harnesses, and the guys said beginners could do it. I'll be fine!" I exclaim, just as Sam directs me to pull into a driveway.

"You won't be fine," he retorts, "so you're not going."

My eyes fly wide as I throw my car into park and eye him fiercely. "The hell I'm not! You're not my keeper, Sam!"

He stares at me through the darkness, the faint blue light of the dash illuminating his face as he inhales and exhales so heavily, his nostrils flare. "What time are you going?"

"Around ten, why?" I snap.

"Where?"

"Peterson Farm, why?" I snap again.

He nods. "I know the place. I'll take you."

I bark out a laugh. "Sam, it's not necessary. Those guys will be there. I'm sure they'll be helpful."

"Exactly why I'm taking you. You don't know those guys from fucking Adam."

"Well, I didn't know you either, but that didn't stop me from going ice fishing with you."

"I was vetted by Marv."

"Oh yes…Marv's word is the gospel apparently."

Sam glares at me. Leaning across the center console, he gets so close I can feel the heat of his breath on my face. "I'm going with you unless you want to tell your brother what you're doing so he can accompany you."

"No!" I reach out and grab Sam's forearm. "I can't tell Miles because then he'll know something is up. I didn't do anything adventurous as a kid. I was more the read a book or go take a dance class type. If he finds out I'm silo climbing, he'll know something is up."

"Then I'm going," Sam states firmly with a casual shrug that makes me want to shake him. "You're my best friend's little sister, and I'm not letting you kill yourself on a frozen silo for a fucking football player."

I bite my lip and turn to face the house. It's a quaint little two story with a garland wreath on the front door. It looks nothing like what I imagined Sam would live in.

Trying to change the subject, I grumble through clenched teeth. "Whose house is this anyway?"

"My mom's," Sam replies, exhaling and sitting back into his seat again.

"You live with your mom?" I ask, feeling disappointment in the little fantasy I have swirling in the dark parts of my mind that I don't want to admit to.

"No, Maggie, I don't live with my mom. I was here having cake with my mom and my sisters when Miles surprised me with this birthday outing. My vehicle is here."

"You're not driving home," I state worriedly, preparing to back out of the driveway and kidnap him if I have to.

"I know I'm not. Don't worry about it, all right? I usually have breakfast at Mom's on Sundays mornings, so I'll crash here."

"Oh," I reply quietly.

"It's nice to know you care, though," he states, and I look over to see a sexy grin on his face.

"Whatever," I reply immaturely but then slowly pull my lower lip into my mouth because with just that one smirk, the whole car has filled with sexual tension.

We're quiet for a moment. The only sounds in the car

are the idling engine and our soft breaths. Today has been a crazy, unexpected day. Boulder seems to be full of the unexpected, and Sam is at the very top of that list. I can feel him looking at me for a beat, and when he lifts his hand, I suck in a sharp breath because I think he's going to reach for me...until he pulls out his phone.

"I'm texting you my address," he says, his voice all business. "Pick me up tomorrow, and I won't tell Miles what you're doing." He opens the door to get out but then pauses to look back at me. "I have to hand it to you, sparky. This sounds like the worst plan I've ever heard, but you're committed, and I kind of like you more for it."

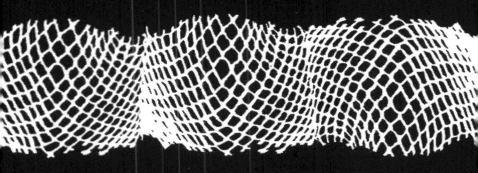

CHAPTER 7

Caught On The Hook

Maggie

"Hey, where ya going?" Kate asks, catching me at the front door as I'm gingerly slipping my feet into my Sorel wedge boots.

I plant a smile on my face as I glance down at her bare legs sticking out of my brother's giant T-shirt. Kate moved into Miles's fixer-upper in Jamestown a few months ago, but this is the first time I've witnessed them cohabitating. It's pretty damn cute if I'm being honest. I've only been here a day, but I already watched them argue over Kate's short dress last night with big, goofy smiles on their faces the entire time. If that's how most of their fights go, then I'm pretty sure I'll be calling Kate a sister sooner rather than later.

I'm just glad Miles found someone worthy of him. Miles

AMY DAWS

had brought Kate back to Utah with him a few months ago so she could meet my parents before they moved in together, and it was love at first sight for all of us. Though admittedly, his ex, Jocelyn, was so vile, Miles could have brought home a blow-up doll, and we would have been over the moon with the step up.

But Kate is creative, funny, kind, and just the right amount of crazy for him. She takes on his overbearing nature like a champ. I wish I had just an ounce of her moxie.

"I'm...um...just going for a drive," I stammer and shove my foot into my other boot as Kate pads barefoot over to me.

She eyes me curiously and crosses her arms over her chest. "A drive to where?"

"The mountains?" I reply, and my face screws up in horror. *Why did I say mountains?* "I mean...shopping. I was going to go shopping."

"The shops around here don't open until noon on Sundays, and you have mountains in Utah," Kate states with a suspicious twinkle to her eye. "Where are you really going?"

I roll my eyes and exhale heavily. "Somewhere that Miles would not approve of."

A Cheshire cat grin spreads across her face as she leans against the wall. "Miles is overprotective, overbearing, and possessive—believe me, I know it," she replies with the chastising click of her teeth. "As his girlfriend, it just so happens to be my favorite parts about him...but I totally understand how having a big brother like that would be hard on a single little sister."

"What are you talking about? I'm not single!" I exclaim, my voice rising in pitch as I lie through my teeth.

Kate's chin drops. "Meg, on Christmas day, you ate an entire bowl of cookie dough without even pausing for a drink of milk. That type of Olympic-style binge-eating can only be the result of a broken heart."

I groan and press my back to the front door, chewing my lip nervously. "Are you going to tell Miles?"

Her eyes flash with interest. "Not as long as you tell me who you're going on a date with."

"What makes you think I'm going on a date?"

"You have a date look," she replies, looking me up and down. "I mean, c'mon, your hair is even curled."

I glance down at my appearance for a moment. My cream sweater has a lace underlayer that drapes over my stretchy faux-leather leggings. Obviously, all of this will be going under the snowsuit currently stashed in my trunk, but I do admit I'm probably a tad overdressed for ice climbing. Maybe I need to invest in some outdoorsy activewear?

I look up and give Kate a serious look. "It's not a date but an outing that Sam has agreed to take me on."

"Sam? I knew it!" Kate exclaims, and I quickly put my hand over her mouth to shush her. "Sorry...but I did know it," she mumbles against my palm.

"There's nothing to know!" I reply, shaking my head and pulling my hand away from Kate's face. "Sam is just being friendly."

"No way," she retorts with narrowed eyes. "I saw how he

watched you last night."

"What do you mean?" I ask, flipping my hair casually and ignoring the butterflies taking flight in my belly.

Kate shakes her head knowingly. "He watched you like a man watches a filet on the grill."

My mouth waters with that analogy, and a strange tingling begins in my fingertips. "I don't think that's true. He was probably looking at me like Miles does. In a brotherly fashion. He's protective just like Miles."

"Think what you want, but I know romance, girl. And that man wasn't looking at you like his little sister."

"We're just friends," I state, knowing I can't give that thought too much headspace or I'll be a total idiot with him today. I reach past Kate and grab my coat off the hook. "Will you tell Miles I went to work out or something? Cover for me…on…all of it? The ex and everything?"

She nods, the grin basically permanent on her face right now. "I will, but eventually, you're going to have to spill the details on the ex, okay?"

"Fine," I reply, rolling my eyes and opening the front door. "I'll see you later."

"Later, loverrrr," she coos, hanging her head out the front door and waving at me coyly.

And with a nervous feeling in my belly, I punch in Sam's address on my phone and head toward Boulder.

It's a sunny morning, but the road is still covered in frost as my GPS takes me west on Boulder Canyon Drive, a curvy blacktop that winds through the mountains. This area reminds me of Salt Lake City, so I can see why Miles feels so at home here. It's an outdoor lover's paradise—if you're the adventure type. I never really was, but I seem to be changing now, which is good.

In high school, I was the girl who did everything but loved nothing. I was class president, captain of the cheer team, and an active member in the drama club. I was even a mathlete for a while because I had a huge crush on a guy in my geometry class. I was never labeled one thing because I did everything.

Miles, on the other hand, was a gearhead through and through. He was always working on cars and motorcycles. He was stir-crazy if he didn't have his hands on something, whereas I was perfectly happy curling up with a book and letting the written word take me on a journey.

But I have to admit, putting myself out there—even with just ice fishing these past couple of weekends—has brought me a sense of pride and accomplishment that I never expected. I can't imagine how I'll feel after climbing a frozen silo.

I turn onto Sam's narrow gravel road that has sharp curves and seems to only go uphill. This has to be dangerous during a storm or in heavy snow. Maybe that's why Sam has a snowmobile? Regardless, it is beautiful back here. The farther I drive in, the more and more stunning the area becomes. It's heavily wooded and full of fresh, untouched snow as far as the eye can see.

I drive uphill a while longer until a small log cabin finally comes into view. It has a high-pitched roof and a large wraparound porch with Adirondack chairs positioned on either side of the bright green double doors. Smoke billows out of the chimney above, which I can only assume is from a wood burning fireplace inside. Talk about rustic. The entire cabin looks like a scenic painting topped with fresh snow and sweeping views of the mountains on all sides. It reminds me of a much larger version of the fish hut I saw out on the lake—secluded, quiet, peaceful.

I pull up alongside the house and get out, eager to take in the sights when I hear the front door open. My gaze swings over to Sam's broad frame as he turns to lock the deadbolt. I swallow slowly as I unabashedly zero in on his ass. Has it always been that...full? I don't remember ever noticing it before. Maybe because he's wearing different pants now? He's wearing some sort of special mountain trek trousers by the looks of the label, and they are tight! His ass looks like two footballs stuffed under a blanket. I sincerely hope there's some stretch in them, or he most certainly isn't going to be climbing any sort of silo today.

He turns on his heel, his eyes cast down as he zips up his black winter coat. He begins descending his front steps, finally looking up, and then pauses on the last step. "What are you wearing?" he asks with an accusing gaze as he stares down my body.

My brows furrow as I tighten my red wool coat around me. "Clothes. What are you wearing, Mr. Tight Pants?" I mumble the last part under my breath.

"I'm wearing winter climbing gear because it's January and cold enough to freeze the balls off a brass monkey. Where's the stuff you bought at Marv's?" He looks damn near angry with me!

"It's in my trunk," I reply. Walking to the back of my car, I pop the trunk and produce the infamous red and white snowsuit. "I couldn't leave my house in this getup in case Miles woke up before I left. I thought I could change here."

Sam exhales heavily and turns to reclimb his front steps. "So this means you're not backing out?" he states with great disappointment as he fumbles through his keys.

I walk up the steps, squeezing my snowsuit and boots to my chest. "I didn't back out of ice fishing, and I'm not backing out of this. I'm excited to get some shots of me in action today. Sterling will flip out when I send him pictures of me on an iced silo!"

He grumbles under his breath as he finally finds the key he was looking for and begins to push open the door. When I move to walk inside, he steps into my path. "Wait, did you call me Mr. Tight Pants down there?"

I bite my lip, a deep flush rushing up from my neck. "Maybe."

His brows lift, and he does that shy smile thing again that he's horrible at hiding. "Were you checking out my ass there, sparky?"

"No," I bark out a bit too aggressively. "I was just watching you, and I couldn't help but notice that you bought your pants a size too small."

"These are professional climbing pants," he states, leaning closer to me. "They are supposed to fit snugly so they don't get hung up on any jagged edges."

I shrug my shoulders dismissively. "I knew that."

He chuckles under his breath and steps back for me to enter, and I do my best to ignore his manly scent as I pass him. When I walk into his foyer, I'm surprised at how grown-up looking Sam's cabin is. For a ginger brawny man bachelor, I guess I expected it to be a mess of mismatched furniture—an old couch from college and maybe a folding table and chairs.

But Sam not only wears man jeans, but he also has a man house on top of it. The entryway opens into the living room with a black sectional sofa and cozy leather armchair. On the far right wall is a natural stone fireplace that still has embers glowing inside it. On the left is a dining room with a long rustic table and unique chairs with industrial piping that make a strong statement. Just past the dining area, I can see a bit of the kitchen. It has knotty white cabinetry and a small island in the middle. This cabin is adorable.

Sam's footsteps march across the pale pine flooring as he directs me to the hallway straight ahead. I follow him closely as he points to the left. "Bathroom is there on the right." He turns around, clearly not expecting me to be standing so close because our bodies brush up against each other, reminding me of the moment at the bar last night and that damn kiss last weekend.

"Sorry," I mumble, stepping back and ignoring my racing heart.

Sam does the same, furrowing his brow as though he's deep in thought. Without a word, he strides back the way he came and disappears into the front of the house.

I close the bathroom door and press my back to it, exhaling the breath that was stuck in my lungs as I take in Sam's cute bathroom. It has an elevated soaker tub in one corner with wide-open views of the mountains. Obviously, you don't have to worry about curtains when you live in the wilderness.

Past the vanity, a pocket door has my curiosity piqued. I set my stuff down on the counter and walk over to slide it open. On the other side is a large bedroom. I look down and see Sam's brown boots from last night on the floor at the foot of his bed and realize it's not just a bedroom, but it's Sam's bedroom.

I take a single step inside and eye the king-size bed against the wall. It has a large barnwood headboard and a taupe duvet with fluffy white pillows scattered at the top. He even took the time to make it, albeit a bit sloppily. Natural light pours in from the large windows that wrap the corner of the room, so you feel like you're sleeping right in the mountains. And I swear if I breathe in deeply, I can smell the faint scent of leather and Irish Spring soap. It smells just like Sam.

I walk over to the long dresser on the opposite wall and see an old photo in a frame. It's a picture of a man, a woman, three girls, and a little boy who looks about twelve years old in this picture. The boy and the man are holding a long board with a row of fish hanging from it. I reach out to finger the old fishing lure he has sitting on the dresser beside it. I get the sinking suspicion that this is personal and I'm crossing a line so I quickly tiptoe back to the bathroom and close the pocket door.

Trying to forget about what I saw, I quickly change into my winter gear that cost me more than my textbooks did for my final semester at the University of Utah. Thankfully, I remember to keep a layer of clothes on underneath this time. I then grab my wool coat and Sorels and make my way out of the bathroom to find Sam.

He's sitting in the big leather chair with his head tipped back and his eyes closed. His chest rises and falls in a deep, rhythmic pattern.

"Are you seriously asleep?" I blurt out, not the least bit worried about the polite way to wake him up. We've been zipped into a tiny hut together for hours on end, so I think manners are optional at this point.

The corners of his mouth curve up as his eyes remain closed. "I could be."

"I got dressed really fast I thought," I reply, tugging out the gloves in my pocket.

He peeks at me through one eye. "Faster than last time, that's for damn sure."

I roll my eyes as he sits up and rubs his hands over his face. "Are you nursing a hangover?" I ask, eyeing him speculatively.

He eyes me right back. "Boys get hangovers. Men get over it."

I smile at the response and watch him stand, towering

over me once again now that I'm out of my heels. He catches me looking, so I swerve my eyes around his living room. "I like your place."

He nods, and a sense of pride casts over his face. "It's been home for a few years now."

"How big is the property?"

"I have almost five acres. It's all timber, but I have room for my big shed out back that stores all my toys."

"What kind of toys?" I ask and cringe when my mind went to someplace dirty.

"Just my quad, snowmobile, motorcycle, and pickup."

"I knew you had a pickup."

His brows lift. "Did you now?"

I sigh deeply. "You're just like my brother. I can't believe I didn't figure it out sooner."

Sam laughs at that. "Well, you're nothing like your brother, so I think I get a break for not realizing who you were when we met."

"What does that mean?" I ask, my voice rising defensively. If he doesn't think I'm like my brother, what does he think I'm like? "Are you going to call me basic too?"

"Hell no," Sam replies quickly, his brow furrowed seriously. "Maggie, you are like a jigsaw puzzle with a million pieces. I think it'd take me years to figure you out."

I smile at that very specific comment, a warmth creeping through my chest that I haven't felt in a long time. To crush the moment full of sexual tension, I quickly punch Sam in the shoulder. "Just as long as we get it all on camera for Sterling!"

Sam's face falls, and I catch a glimpse of a wounded expression as he touches the spot I just hit. "Just don't be so focused on the future that you miss what's happening in the present, all right?"

He turns on his heel and walks out the door, leaving my mind reeling with his parting words.

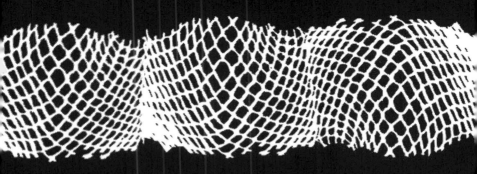

CHAPTER 8

Fish Or Cut Bait

Sam

We arrive at Peterson Farm, just east of Boulder. It's a place I've been to a couple of times with my climbing buddy I met in college. We belayed each other for years until he moved to Denver with his wife. I haven't really done much climbing since, but thankfully, it's like riding a bike. And let's face it, I'm here to make sure Maggie has a trustworthy belayer and doesn't land herself in the Boulder hospital with some crazy injury that her brother would find a way to punish me for.

We pull up to three eighty-foot silos that are iced to perfection with huge curtains of ice gleaming in the sunlight. A couple of climbers are already on one, aggressively swinging their ice axes and slowly moving their way up to ring the bell at the top.

I slide out of my truck and walk to the back, pulling the tailgate open to grab my bag.

Maggie joins me, her eyes wide as I open a bag that probably looks like it's full of murder weapons to her. "I don't have any of that stuff," she says, looking nervously at my gear and then up at the ice climbers. "I didn't know I needed it."

I half smile and shake my head at her. "No worries, they have everything here."

"Maggie!" a voice calls out, and I turn to see a guy with a ponytail running toward us. He's literally running as if getting to her five seconds faster will be worth it. "You actually came."

"Hi..." Maggie falters, clearly searching for his name.

"Ezekiel, remember?" He reaches out and pulls her into a hug, which seems overly friendly for someone whose name she didn't even remember. "And you are?"

He looks at me, and I reflexively puff my chest out. "Sam."

"Ezekiel," Maggie stammers, "this is my friend, Sam. He's apparently an avid climber and has offered to assist me today. Sam, Ezekiel was staying at the same bed and breakfast as I was and is one of the guys from the magazine who recommended I try this out."

"You're an avid climber?" Ezekiel asks, his eyes falling down my body like he doesn't believe it.

"I used to be," I reply through clenched teeth because I can already smell this guy's fucking testosterone, and I don't like it. "I haven't climbed in a couple of years."

"If you don't use it, you lose it, man."

I roll my eyes and sling my bag over my shoulder. "I'm not worried."

"This ain't no waterfall climb," Ezekiel states with narrowed eyes.

I lift my brows and have to hold back my laughter. "No, it certainly is not. But my buddy and I did a lot of bouldering and redpointing…so I think I'm going to be just fine."

Ezekiel's Adam's apple bobs, and I can feel Maggie looking nervously at the two of us as we stare each other down for a beat. This is why Maggie can't just go gallivanting around Boulder looking for adventure. There are way too many potheads around here who think they're God's gift to the world and to women. Maggie doesn't need to be dealing with that bullshit on her own.

We head over to the empty silo, and the guides on staff at the farm get to work setting Maggie up with their rental gear while I strap into my own. Maggie's eyes look wide and wary as she takes in a brief climbing lesson from the female guide named Sherry.

When I finish tightening my harness, a voice sounds off from behind me. "Care to do a little wager?"

I look over and see Ezekiel with his helmet on, looking ready for action. "What are the stakes?"

"Winner gets to be her belayer." His eyes are on Maggie who is only half-listening to her instructor because she's watching us instead.

"No," I reply instantly. "I'm here with Maggie. I'm her belayer."

"C'mon, old man...you scared?" Ezekiel goads me with an annoying tip to his chin that makes me want to punch him. His buddies come walking over with big smiles that I also want to smack right off their faces.

"I'm not fucking scared," I state, feeling adrenaline surge through my veins at their challenge. "Or that old," I mumble to myself mostly.

"Then do it!" one of the guys shouts and then goes quiet when I glare at him.

"What are you worried about?" Ezekiel asks. "If I win, you'll know I'm an experienced climber, so it's not like she'll be in novice hands. My hands are very good at belaying beautiful women."

Damn do I want to punch this cocky fucker. And I want to beat him. Punch him and beat him and shove his face in this snow. All of the above would feel really good right about now.

"Do it," Maggie chimes in, and the instructor Sherry seems to be equally interested in our conversation.

"Why are you all ganging up on me right now?" I ask, looking around at everyone gathering closer, instructors and climbers alike. "I'm just here to belay my friend."

"We have a tradition here that's pretty cool," Sherry states with a big smile. "If you let us film you guys racing live for our social media page, the winning racer gets a free weekend stay at our ski chalet up in the mountains next weekend. It has a private natural hot spring that is life changing, not to mention some pretty awesome snowboarding slopes."

"Yes," Ezekiel cheers with a fist up in the air. "We're doing this."

"We're not," I state firmly.

"Sam," Maggie interrupts. "Just do it. What's the worst that could happen?"

"This fucking idiot belays you poorly, and you get injured."

"Ezekiel has been here all morning," Sherry states, stepping closer to me. "I can assure you he is an excellent belayer."

I exhale heavily and wonder how the fuck this went from me helping Maggie not die to me racing up a damn silo against some asshole with beaded dreadlocks.

"Unless you're scared," Ezekiel states with his hands held back. "I get it. Your bones are brittle, and you wouldn't want to injure yourself."

Maggie giggles softly from beside me, and my inner caveman voice shouts, *Don't let this blond, dreadlock-wearing, granola-eating pothead show you up in front of a girl! You know you can crush him!*

I shake my head at Maggie. "You should be on my side."

"I am!" Maggie exclaims excitedly. "It'll be fun to watch. And it'll help shake off the major anxiety I have over climbing up this thing right now." She gives me a look that is so sweet and innocent, yet somehow sexy and alive…I realize with great embarrassment that I'd probably eat yellow fucking snow for this chick standing before me.

So like an idiot, I turn to Ezekiel, and state, "Fuck it… on belay, man."

Ezekiel and his buddies whoop with joy, and minutes later, we're standing ten feet apart at the bottom of the silo, geared up, helmets on, and cell phone cameras all pointing at us. A video camera and a photographer are catching all this action as well. *I better not get my ass beat.*

"Belayers, are you ready?" Sherry shouts from her position between us.

"On belay!" we both shout back, and I look at the staff member who is belaying for me. Maggie is standing right beside him with a big, bright smile on her face.

"Belay on!" the belayers shout back.

And we're off.

The climb is intense. It's a straight up vertical with no breaks and no ice screws anywhere. Just me, my two ice axes, and the crampons on my boots to hold me up. Because it's a top rope climb, there's a rope that goes from me through an anchor at the top of the silo and then back down to the belayer. The belayer keeps the rope nice and tight as I ascend the wall, giving me slack only when I need it.

The climb is a blur of ice chunks as my ax pierces the firm curtains of sparkling frost and I make my way up the silo. I actually don't even look at the other guy because I know that'll just slow me down. I continue jabbing my toes in foot by foot and make my way toward to top. Maggie's cheering from below grows fainter the higher I ascend. This is definitely a more intense workout than the waterfalls, and my quads and biceps are screaming at me as I push them to their breaking point. Normally, I'm slow and steady, but right now, I'm doing larger grabs and using my muscles to heave my body up this silo as fast as I possibly can.

I finally lay eyes on the guy above me with his cell phone camera pointed right at me. "Come on, man, you're almost here! This is insane!"

I frown, wondering how badly I must be losing for that sort of comment. I didn't think I'd heard a bell ring yet, but maybe Ezekiel rang it a long time ago, and I was too low to hear it?

With one final crunch of my ax into the ice, I yank myself up the last three feet and swing my other ax straight at the brass bell hanging from the top. The ding is loud and echoes along with the cheers from the bystanders below. The guy takes my tools from me so I can hoist myself over the edge of the silo. I lean down, bracing my hands on the railing while sucking in big gulps of air.

"Fucking hell, that was hard," I state halfheartedly to the guy beside me as my heart thunders in my chest.

I look out and steal a few seconds to absorb the scenery from my new vantage point. Hills and hills of snow-covered trees with the Flatirons as the backdrop. It's incredible. "Now I get why you guys climb here."

Maggie's cheers drag my gaze down below, and I give her a wave before looking over to find my racing challenger. I assumed he was up at the top already, but he's nowhere to be seen. The guide at the top has moved to the edge and is pointing his cell phone camera down below again. I walk over and lean forward to find Ezekiel stuck at the halfway point on the silo.

"Holy shit, what happened? Did he drop his ax?" I ask,

assuming a gear malfunction would be the only reason he'd be that far behind me.

"No, man," the guy replies with a laugh. "You fucking flew up this silo like Spiderman. I got hard watching you!" he exclaims and then shakes his head in amazement.

My jaw drops in shock. "He hasn't made it to the top yet?"

"No way...you climbed fast as lightning. None of us could have caught you. This video is going to break the internet."

I stare down at the iced silo with my brow furrowed as I try to determine whether I was really that much faster than normal. It's been too long for me to truly remember my normal pacing, but hell, I don't know...maybe I was just extra motivated not to let this fucker be Maggie's belayer.

I shake that thought off because it feels too sentimental. And my reason behind helping Maggie has nothing to do with feelings. I'm just trying to protect my buddy's little sister. Nothing more.

Ezekiel drops his axes to the ground below and begins repelling back down to the bottom, clearly too butthurt to finish the fucking climb. What a dick. You always finish a climb.

I take in the view for a few more minutes before beginning my own descent. When I reach the bottom, Maggie jumps into my arms like a girl greeting her man home from war. It brings an alarming stirring to my belly as her arms tighten around my neck. "That was incredible! An impossible act to follow but incredible!"

She pulls back, her blue eyes sparkling in amazement as she bites her lip and stares down at my mouth.

Goddamn, she looks...turned on. She looks how she looked that day we kissed. She should not be looking at me like that!

"Thanks," I murmur and step out of her arms to unclip my rope. "It was a fun climb."

The guides all come over and congratulate me as Ezekiel and his buddies disappear off to the warming lodge. Sherry gives me her business card and tells me to call her for the keys to the chalet on Friday. I smile sheepishly, hating all the attention and doing my best to turn it back onto Maggie because she's the reason we're here in the first place.

Sherry begins clipping the ropes on her when Maggie pulls her phone out of her snowsuit pocket. "Do you think you can take a picture of me climbing?" she asks quietly.

Sherry nods eagerly. "Definitely. I'll snap throughout the whole climb, and we have a guy at the top who will get a shot of you when you ring the bell."

"*If* I ring the bell," Maggie corrects, chewing her lip nervously as she buckles the chin strap of her helmet. "If Ezekiel couldn't finish, I probably won't either."

"You'll ring the bell," I state, stepping in closer to her and putting a reassuring hand on her shoulder as she stares up at the ice. "This isn't a race, Maggie. And you are not a quitter. Look at what lengths you're going to, to win back your ex."

Maggie nods woodenly, her lips rubbing together the entire time. "I'm scared."

"That's good," I state, looping her rope through my carabiner. "Fear will drive you. Just go one step at a time, and you'll get to the top. We're not just out here for a picture."

She looks at me, her bright eyes wide and watery in the cold. "Are you sure about that?"

"Yes," I state firmly. "Make this climb for you, not your ex. The best part of climbing is reaching the top. You got this."

I shoot her a wink that draws a smile across her face, and she positions herself at the base of the silo with the ice axes in her hand.

"I'll be down here the entire time," I reassure her, taking my position and anchoring myself in with her rope wound through my belay device.

Maggie nods once and then yells over her shoulder. "On belay?"

I smile at the doubt in her voice and shout back confidently. "Belay on!"

Slowly, she makes her way up the silo.

Like…really slow.

Honestly, it takes her almost an hour. I worried that she might freeze to death before she reached the top, but the girl never even considered quitting. I coached her the entire way, helping her get better ax swings and encouraging her when she needed it. She may not be a fast climber, but I have to admit I find her tenacity impressive. When she finally reaches the top and rings that bell, I'm pretty sure she's full-on crying because she hugs the guy at the top for longer than appropriate, considering he's a complete stranger.

At least she didn't kiss him, I think to myself like an asshole. Hanging out with Maggie is going to become an issue for me if I keep thinking everything she fucking does is a turn-on. I'm not a relationship kind of guy, so falling for my best friend's little sister—someone you most definitely can't have casual sex with—isn't an option.

She makes her way down, and we head over to the warming house. Thankfully, it's cleared out of the granola-eating dreadlock dudes.

Maggie is all smiles as she slips out of the top of her snowsuit and kneels by the fire. "That was so exhilarating!" she exclaims as she rubs her hands together.

I nod and drop down beside her with a dopey smile because it's hard not to get sucked in to her enthusiasm. "I'm seriously impressed that you didn't give up."

"I didn't think I'd make it," she states, rubbing her hands along her arms. "Holy heck, what a workout. My arms are like Jell-O. I thought they were going to give out." She shakes them out and moves a hand to her shoulder blade to rub a tender spot.

"Yeah, you're going to be sore as hell for a few days," I state. Moving my hand to the spot she can't quite reach, I press my thumb gently into the knotted muscle. "I suggest lots of water and ibuprofen around the clock."

She moans loudly when I hit the spot, and my dick twitches. *Goddamn.* Has any woman ever made my dick twitch with just a noise? She drops down on her butt and turns to give me easier access.

"Holy heck, don't stop," she moans, and now my dick is

doing a hell of a lot more than just twitching.

I move my other hand up and rub both her shoulders at the same time. She feels dainty in my hands with small but defined muscles. I have a huge urge to dip my hands beneath her sweater and feel her bare skin on my fingertips.

"You earned that weekend at our chalet," I state, my voice deeper than usual because I'm seriously turned the fuck on right now.

"What do you mean?" she asks, turning her head slightly. "You're the one who won that race. You should have it."

"Nah, I already know how to snowboard. You'll get more use out of it if you're still on this adventure mission."

She goes quiet for a moment while I work on her shoulders to the sounds of the crackling fire. "I don't know how to snowboard, though."

"Oh," I reply dumbly and bite the inside of my cheek because I know the next thing that's going to come out of my mouth. "I could show you if you want?"

She turns to face me. "Seriously?" she exclaims with a big smile on her face.

I shrug. "It's no big deal."

"Eek!" She launches herself at me again, wrapping her arms around my neck. "It's the perfect next adventure! Let's do it!"

She's bouncing and wiggling up against me so much, I can't believe what starts to happen inside my pants. This is fucking embarrassing. I'm sure it's because I lost my wingman, Miles. I've been going through a bit of a dry spell, but still, I'm over thirty. I shouldn't just be popping boners like Pez.

She pulls back, and her eyes are alight with excitement. "I haven't even sent Sterling a picture yet! He's going to flip when he sees me on that silo!"

With that last remark, my boner drops like a cooked noodle. But like a thick noodle. A big ole cannelloni for sure.

"Yeah, you'd better get those sent," I grumble and stand to make my way toward the door. "I'm going to go pack up my shit. I'll see you in the truck."

The door closes behind me, and I feel like I need to shove my own face in the snow for being so stupid just now. She's after her ex, not my fucking noodle. I need to get my shit straight before being locked away in that cabin with her for an entire weekend.

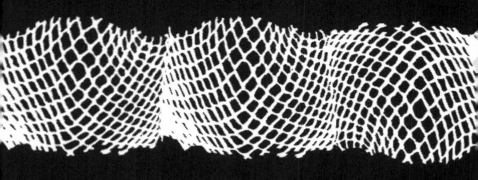

CHAPTER 9

Complimentary Coffee And Advice

Maggie

The next day, I'm seated at Miles and Kate's kitchen table when Miles comes strolling in. "You're up early," he states with a yawn as he reaches into the cupboard and pulls down a box of corn flakes.

"I put on a pot of coffee!" I reply excitedly, doing my best not to seem like the freeloading pain in the neck little sister who showed up unannounced and has no specific departure date in sight.

"Oh, you shouldn't have," Kate's voice croaks from around the corner before she shuffles into the kitchen in fuzzy slippers and another one of Miles's giant T-shirts. "We don't drink coffee at home."

"You don't?"

"*She* doesn't," Miles replies with an eye roll as he dumps some cereal into a bowl and adds milk to the top.

"I'm a purist," Kate replies and offers Miles a sleepy-eyed smile. "I wait for Tire Depot coffee because it's the best."

I nod slowly at that response. "So, do you go to Tire Depot every day then?"

She shrugs. "Not every day. I mean…the days I don't want to shower, I usually stay home and write because I get good words in here too. But today is shower day, so I'll be going in with Miles. You should come with us!"

"To Tire Depot?" I ask as I shovel a bite of cereal into my mouth. "Like where Sam works too?"

My face instantly flames red when my brother frowns at me. "Well, Sam more than works there. He's months away from owning the joint. But yeah, that's where he works. Why do you mention Sam?"

"Oh…well," I begin to stammer. "He, um…"

"Meg gave Sam a ride home after his birthday shindig Saturday," Kate interjects helpfully. "So I'm sure she's just connecting all the Boulder dots."

"Yes," I agree quickly, my eyes feeling wide enough to pop out of my head as I nod a silent thanks to Kate. "I met a lot of people that night. Hard to keep track of everyone."

Miles shrugs and slurps a big bite of cereal while mumbling, "Is your car due for an oil change? I could do it there this morning. Easier to do it there than here."

"Ummm, probably," I reply as I try to figure out if this could be weird with Sam. I mean, we faked it at a bar, so surely we can fake it at Tire Depot, right?

"It's settled then!" Kate states happily. "I'll ride in with Megan. That way you don't have to wait for us to get ready, Miles. Meg, I just want you to know we'll be missing the Danishes most likely."

Her face is so somber, I wait for her to start laughing.

She doesn't.

"Okay then," I reply with equal somberness. "Thanks for letting me know."

"No prob." She nods. "But don't be too sad. The cookies are very scrumptious as well." She beams over at me knowingly, and I know instantly she's not just talking about the cookies.

"Sounds greeeat," I reply slowly and then excuse myself from the table. If I'm going to Tire Depot today, I suppose it's a shower day for me as well.

Before Kate and I leave the house, I send a quick text to Sam to warn him of the plan. He doesn't flipping reply, and that only makes me more anxious about how this all could go.

"Why do you look so nervous?" Kate asks, cutting into my internal freak-out.

"I'm not nervous!" I exclaim, my hands wrapping tightly around the wheel.

Out of the corner of my eye, I see her turn in her seat to face me fully. "Admit it, you're totally smitten with Sam!"

"I am not!" I exclaim and then flinch at my way too

defensive and shrieky tone.

"What the hell happened yesterday then? You got home kind of late, and Miles wouldn't leave us alone. I've been dying for some details, so spill."

"Nothing happened. Sam helped me go silo ice climbing, and he was really sweet and really impressive at climbing. That's all." I say it all in one breath like that's somehow going to make this conversation easier.

I'm wrong.

"Did you say silo ice climbing?" I glance over and see Kate's twisted-up, confused face. Gosh, she's adorable.

"Yes, that's what I said."

"Silo ice climbing is not a thing."

"I thought the same thing at first, and I was wrong." I whip out my phone and show her a selfie of me at the top with the big ole iced silo behind me. "It's a thing."

"Amazing," she states, grabbing my phone and swiping through more of the pictures. "Were you any good at it?"

"God no, but Sam was amazing. Like gladiator good. I couldn't believe my eyes. No one could."

My mind drifts back to watching him scale that wall like a...*man.* It was so unexpectedly sexy that I found myself drooling at one point. Those tight pants and the grunts I could hear every time he swung his ax...*mmm.*

And then he had such a casual look on his face as he finished. He just rang that bell and hoisted himself onto the top of that silo like it was no big deal, win or lose. It was... impressive.

Sterling is the complete opposite of Sam. He's actually

practiced victory dances in front of me to get my opinion on which one I loved more. I never understood it because he's a quarterback and that seems like something receivers do, but regardless, he wanted to have his dance down. He said it was for his future video game endorsement deal.

But Sam...Sam was so mature about it. It made it impossible for me not to hug him the second his feet hit the ground. There's a quiet strength to him that draws me in so easily. And the fact that his ass didn't look bad in those pants yesterday made it all the more confusing.

Kate hands me my phone back with a shit-eating grin on her face. "Did I just hear you compare ginger-bearded Sam to a gladiator?" Her peals of laughter completely yank me out of my delightful memory.

"You're a redhead too. Where's your solidarity?" I snap back defensively.

"I'm totally kidding," she replies and reaches out to touch my arm, making me realize I'm probably overreacting a bit. "But wow, silo climbing? What made you decide to do that of all things? Miles never mentioned you were the outdoorsy type. I thought you were one of my people...a book nerd!"

My brows knit together with that very apt description of me. "I am a book nerd, but I'm trying to win back my ex by showing him how un-basic I am."

"Books aren't basic...books are life," Kate deadpans, and I know she's one hundred percent serious.

"I agree," I reply quickly so she knows I'm not downplaying her amazing abilities. "But Sterling wants someone with some adventure inside her."

"Like becoming a frosty dildo climber," she states, still not laughing.

"And snowboarding."

"When are you going snowboarding?" she asks, her eyes bright and intrigued. "Have you snowboarded before?"

"No, I've only downhill skied a couple of times during trips for school. I was terrible at it. But Sam raced this pot-head climber up the frozen silo and crushed him, so now he won this free weekend at a ski chalet this weekend. Sam said he would take me along and show me how to board."

Kate just blinks back at me, completely stunned into a rare silence. "I have to write this in a book. Please tell me I have permission."

"You do not have permission!" I exclaim, heat flaming my cheeks at just the thought of my pathetic-ness being published in a damn romance novel. "I was hoping you could figure out a way to cover for me with Miles this weekend."

She growls in frustration. "So wait…you're doing all this to win back your ex? What about Sam?"

"Sam is just helping me out! There's nothing going on between us." I state it so defensively that I know Kate isn't going to let it slide.

Kate's lips disappear into her mouth before she replies. "If Sam is hiding this from his best friend, that means something *is* going on. Fess up."

Now it's my turn to groan. For Kate being my brother's girlfriend, she has an uncanny way of irritating me like a nosy sister. "It's nothing, okay? We may have kissed when we first met, but that was an impulsive accident, and we didn't even know each other yet."

"Oh my god," Kate exclaims. "This just keeps getting better and better! How far did it go?"

"Just a kiss. Would you stop? Sam is just a friend. I don't want Miles to know Sterling dumped me because Miles will hate him forever. I'm hoping if I show Sterling that I'm more exciting, he'll want me back, and we can get back together before anyone realizes we ever broke up. I want our original plan. I had our whole life figured out."

"Which was?"

"I don't know, the usual...marriage, babies, seeing the world together. Love at first sight is so rare, and I think it's serendipitous that my parents had it, and now so do I. I already have my wedding toast halfway written in my head."

"Oh Meg," Kate says, reaching over and patting me on the head. "You really are a slightly unhinged hopeless romantic, aren't you?"

"Oh, shut up," I snap, batting her hand away as I pull into the parking lot of Tire Depot and find a front row parking spot. "I'm just focusing on my dream life. There's nothing wrong with that."

I kill the engine, and at the same moment, Miles walks out from the big shop door off to the side. He's rolling a tire over the snow-packed sidewalk toward the front lobby entrance. He's not wearing a coat, and working outside in his jeans and a Tire Depot T-shirt looks damn cold in this frigid temperature.

"I'm living in my dream life," Kate replies slowly, her voice taking on a deep, husky tone. I look over just to see her staring hard at my brother and licking her lips like a tigress getting ready to pounce.

"Ugh, you're going to make me puke." I look away from her just in time to see Sam come out of the garage next, also rolling a tire. His biceps flex beneath the fit of his Tire Depot polo, and I feel a sharp pang of attraction.

"Admit it," Kate states quietly. "You think Sam is super freakin' cute."

I roll my eyes and groan before pressing my forehead to the steering wheel. "Of course, he's cute. I mean…if you like that bearded, mountain man sort of look." I peek up again just as he turns to enter the main part of Tire Depot, and he gives me a shot of his ass in those work jeans of his. "It doesn't matter, though. I have plans with Sterling."

"Blech," Kate mumbles under her breath. "Fine. It's your life, and you're entitled to do what you want. So what do you need from me exactly? You want to go away with your brother's best friend this weekend, and you need to make sure Miles doesn't know?"

"Yesss," I reply slowly, hating that she has to throw the best friend part in my face again.

"Okay, let me think…" Her eyes light up instantly. "You know what? Oddly, Miles has been pushing to go see my parents again sometime soon, so I guess I could finally agree to it. That would get us out of the house for the weekend, and he won't even know you're missing."

"That would be perfect, Kate!" I exclaim, grabbing her

and pulling her into a hug. "He might see if I can come along, but I'll fake an illness or something."

Jiggling her chest into mine, Kate coos, "Oh baby, are you this thankful to Sam, too?"

"Shut up!" I exclaim and shove her away. "You're such a perv!"

"I'm told it's my best quality." She winks and hops out of the car.

With a heavy sigh, I follow her into Tire Depot for some complimentary coffee, cookies, and a free oil change from my brother. Gosh, I'm liking Boulder more and more every day.

When Kate and I walk into Tire Depot, I do a quick scan of the shiny lobby area for Sam. I just need to know where he is. As long as I'm not surprised by him, I can school my features to be cool and collected. Miles is wiping off a display tire that he's hung up on a rack with several other tires when he sees us coming.

"There are two of my favorite girls!" he beams, hitting us with a pearly white smile. "Ready for the Tire Depot experience, Meg?"

"Sure!" I state cheerily and wiggle my keys at him. "Here you go."

Miles gestures for us to follow him over to the counter. "We'll get you checked in here first."

As we approach the counter, someone's head pops up from beneath the bar height countertop, and as soon as I realize it's Sam, I bump into Kate.

"Ouch!" Kate exclaims, turning to rub the back of her ankle. "Walk much, Meg? Or just read about it?" She giggles and winks at me, clearly pleased with her little joke.

Miles looks over at me with concern. "Are you feeling okay, Meg? You look kind of flushed."

He moves over to feel my forehead, and I shake him off as Sam's eyes dance with mirth the entire time. He waggles his brows at me playfully before resting his elbows on the counter to enjoy the show.

"I'm fine, Miles. Can we just get my oil changed, please?"

"Sam?" Miles says.

Sam holds his hands back. "I'm afraid I can't help you today."

My expression falls. Is he about to out us?

Then Sam gestures over at a small girl standing beside him whose chin barely clears the counter. Sam does a quick maneuver, evidently moving his step stool over, and this little strawberry-blond girl climbs on the stool.

"Is this your kid?" I bark out without thinking, sounding even more psychotic than I intended.

Sam does that heart-melting shy smile thing again as he turns his face away from me. "No, this is my niece, Kinsley. Kinsley, these are some of my friends. You know Miles. This is his girlfriend, Kate, and his sister, Maggie."

"What can I do for you?" Kinsley states, pushing her

pink glasses up on her nose. "Are you in need of a rotation today?"

Her serious face has me smiling like a loon as my gaze moves from Sam to her and the adorable little connection they clearly have together as he leans on the counter next to her.

Kate elbows me, and I jump forward, realizing that everyone was waiting for me. "I need an oil change and probably a tire rotation. I've put a lot of miles on my car recently."

"Can do," Kinsley states, her voice deep as though she's playing a character. "What's the make, model, color, and year of your car?"

I giggle and tell her all those things. She takes ages to write it all down in her notebook, but Sam doesn't rush her one bit. He just smiles affectionately down at her as she lowers her face to her notepad and sticks out her tongue in concentration.

When she's finished, she looks at her little watch. "It's going to be about an hour. Will you require a shuttle service today? Or would you like to enjoy our exceptional customer comfort center?"

My smile is permanent now. "Customer comfort center, please!"

Kinsley takes my keys and looks at her uncle briefly before holding her hand up to her mouth and whispering, "Might I suggest an excellent podcast."

"Kins!" Sam barks, and her eyes go wide like she's just been caught with her hand in the cookie jar.

"Or just enjoying complimentary cookies and coffee is

good too!" she rushes out and hops off the step stool. "I'll just go take these keys to the guys in the back, and we'll call you when your car is done."

Kinsley scampers off, and I turn my eyes back to Sam who is smiling so big at his niece, his entire face lights up. When he looks back at me, I ask with a laugh, "What's with the seriously adorable child labor?"

He shakes his head and pushes up off his elbows to his full height. "It's bring your niece to work day."

I frown. "That's not a thing."

"I made it a thing," he says with a wink. "School is off today, and that one has been driving her mom nuts, so I'm just trying to help out."

He smiles sweetly, and our eyes hold for a few seconds before Kate clears her throat behind us.

We both turn quickly to refocus on Miles as he says, "Well, let me show you ladies the comfort center so I can get back to work. My boss is a hard-ass."

I hear Sam grumble under his breath as I follow Miles and Kate to the back. Before I round the corner, I can't help but look over my shoulder, and my smile grows when I catch Sam checking me out. I know it shouldn't make me feel so good because I have a plan, but damn, it kind of does.

Kate shows me the coffee machine, and we both get a cup of our preferred beverage before taking a seat at a high-top table. I look around at all the patrons with their Styrofoam cups, scrolling through their phones, or munching on a cookie. The *Price is Right* is blaring on the TV, but it all seems very cozy as a whole. I can see why Kate likes to hang out in here.

"So Meg, I have one more little tiny thing to say to you, and then I'll drop it and let you go back to living in la-la land."

I roll my eyes and exhale heavily as I wait to hear what craziness comes out of her mouth next. "Let's hear it."

"Okay, so let's say your plan to win your ex back works. You end up married with babies and a crazy football player's wife lifestyle that you're convinced you will love. That's all fine and good, and I hope that for you, you know? But right now, this moment, this weekend...you are a gorgeous twenty-two-year-old single woman with a hot, bearded ginger who's bending over backward to help you out. Why not make your time with Sam really count? Why not make him your last fling before the ring? Sam is the perfect no-strings kind of guy. He doesn't do relationships. Ever. No exceptions. You're going to be locked up in a cozy cabin with him for two days, and I really don't want your muscles to only be sore from snowboarding if you catch my drift."

"Oh my god!" I exclaim and whack her on the arm because this is all so embarrassing. It's one thing to read Kate's dirty books, but it's another thing entirely to have her basically coaching me about sex. "You are so not giving me permission to bone Miles's best friend. You are completely unhinged."

"I'm not unhinged, Meg. I'm a realist. And you're an idealist, which gives you tunnel vision and causes you to miss the *real* adventure opportunity here."

Kate's voice goes quiet as Sam comes striding into the

comfort center with his niece skipping alongside him. Kinsley reaches up and holds his hand like it's completely natural and she does it all the time. They head over to the cookie case, and she picks out a treat and then gives him puppy dog eyes when she asks for two. He gives her a firm no and then turns his back to grab her a napkin.

She quickly grabs a second cookie when he's not looking and stashes it behind her back. He looks over at her with a frown, and her angelic smile turns devilish as he turns her around and busts her with cookie number two. With a bemused smile, he shoves her toward the door, and she goes skipping away merrily with her two cookies.

Before Sam walks out the door, he swerves his eyes to where Kate and I sit watching him. He shoots us a sexy sheepish smile, and then with a wink, he's gone.

Oh my heck, another wink.

Leaning in close, Kate whispers, "Admit it, Meg, you've got it bad."

I realize that my chin is propped in my hands and my mouth is curved up into a swoony smile as I watch Sam disappear around the corner. Covering my face with my hands, I mumble against my palms, "Are you sure he's a no-strings guy?"

"Absolutely positive," Kate responds.

I turn to look at her. "I don't even know him that super well yet."

Kate shrugs and grabs my phone up off the table. "You have a week to get to know him."

I stare at it in confusion.

AMY DAWS

"Text him, Megan." She laughs at my denseness. "You'd be surprised by how powerful the written word is."

I bite my lip and pull Sam's number up on my phone. "What should I say?"

Kate shrugs. "What difference does it make? Tell him a stupid joke or something. Whatever it takes to get the ball rolling."

As my finger hovers over the screen, I eye Kate and say, "You know if my brother knew about any of this, he would murder all three of us, right?"

"You leave your brother to me." She winks and sinks her teeth into a cookie before cracking open her laptop and most likely taking notes about this insane love story that is currently my messed-up life.

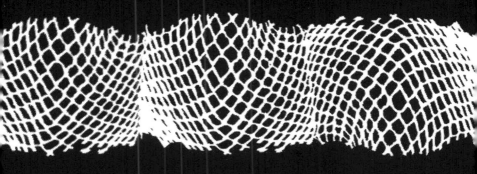

CHAPTER 10

A Reel Expert Can Tackle Anything

Sam

My cell phone rings, and I assume it's Maggie because it's Friday and she's supposed to be here any minute now to ride out in my truck to the ski chalet, but when I look at the screen, I see Miles's name illuminated.

My shoulders tense as I answer the call. "Hello?"

"Hey, man, how's it going?"

"All right," I say slowly, feeling nervous for why he's calling.

"Listen, I was wondering if I could ask you a favor."

"Sure, what's up?"

"Kate and I are headed to Longmont this weekend to visit her folks." The phone muffles as Miles whispers into the line. "I was hoping to ask Kate's father for permission to marry her this weekend. Kate has no clue."

"Okaaay," I reply with a soft laugh. I knew the minute Miles bought that ring it would burn a hole in his pocket.

"Anyway, I assumed Megan would come with us, but she says she isn't feeling well. I feel kinda bad leaving her here all alone since this isn't her town and shit…but I really do need to see Kate's dad in person to do this, ya know?"

"Yeah, I get that."

"So I was wondering if you could check in on Meg?"

My body tenses with his very innocent request. "Check in on her?"

"Yeah, stop by with some soup for her tomorrow maybe. Make sure she doesn't need to see a doctor or something."

"You want me to bring your sister soup?" I ask for clarification because I'm a guilty motherfucker.

"Yeah, man. I wouldn't ask, but she's my baby sister, ya know? I normally watch out for her, but I can't, so I'm hoping you can."

I pull my lips into my mouth and exhale through my nose before replying. "I can watch out for your sister, Miles." I pinch the bridge of my nose, hating that I'm keeping this secret from my best friend, but I also made a promise to Maggie that I can't break. "I'll check in on her tomorrow."

"Awesome, you're the best. We'll be home Sunday afternoon, so depending on how she's feeling, you might need to go back Sunday morning. That cool?"

"That's cool."

"You're a great friend, Sam, you know that? I know I'm a shitty one these days, but you're a great one. I really appreciate it."

My head bows in shame. *You wouldn't think I'm a good friend if you knew what I did last night while picturing your sister.* But of course, I don't say that. Instead, I continue to lie to my friend and don't mention a word about taking his sister to a secluded cabin for the weekend. *I am such a fucker.*

We hang up, and I scroll through the text messages Maggie and I have exchanged this past week. There are easily over a hundred. So many that I had to change her contact name in my phone from Maggie to Sparky because I was terrified she was going to text me at Tire Depot when Miles was around.

Sparky: Why can't you tell a joke while ice fishing?
Me: Because you're sitting beside me, and I don't think you're funny.
Sparky: Eye roll emoji.
Me: Fine…why can't you tell a joke while ice fishing?
Sparky: Because it'll crack you up! Get it?
Me: I got it, sparky.

Sparky: What do fish and women have in common?
Me: This could go so many ways, and most of the ways I have in mind are dirty.
Sparky: They both stop shaking their tail after you catch them!

Me: See? Dirty.
Sparky: That's not dirty.
Me: It is if you're in my head.
@Sparky: ☺

Sparky: Where do football players go shopping in the off-season?
Me: I hope it's not Marv's.
Sparky: The tackle shop.
Me: Oh boy, just when I thought these were getting better.
Sparky: My ex didn't think that was funny either.
Me: In that case, I thought that joke was fucking hilarious. You are a comedy genius, and I think we should go on tour together.

All week, Maggie kept hitting me with stupid fishing jokes she found on the internet. And all week, I couldn't wipe the stupid smile off my face. It was really fucking annoying. And adorable. And charming. And all the things I'm not supposed to be feeling for my best friend's little sister. Any minute now, she's going to show up, and we're going to head to a cabin together where we'll be all alone for over twenty-four hours.

It's going to be fucking torture.

It's dark outside by the time I see headlights pull into my driveway. Maggie parks her car beside my already load-ed pickup packed with snowboarding gear, snacks, booze— all the main supplies you need for a weekend of snowboard-ing. I was able to borrow my sister's snowboarding gear for Maggie so we won't have to bother with a rental.

I hear Maggie dragging her suitcase up the stairs and make my way to the front door, opening it just as she lifts her hand to knock. Her dark hair is wild as it sticks out from her red stocking cap and her blue eyes are wide and frantic. "Sorry, I'm so late. I swear I think Miles and Kate had sex before they left because they disappeared into his bedroom for a much longer time than necessary to pack a few things for a weekend with her parents. I had to fake a cold because Miles wanted me to come with them, and then my mom called, convinced I'm having some sort of mental breakdown because I'm staying in Boulder for a few weeks, so I had to talk her off the ledge, and then the roads are slick from the snow, so I had to be really careful driving up your winding road, and holy cow, it's scary driving around here in the dark, and the sandwiches I picked up for us are prob-ably cold, but I'm lucky I got here, so please don't expect me to look decent."

She sucks in a huge gulp of air because I'm pretty sure that entire monologue just broke some sort of record for most words spoken in a run-on sentence.

My gaze drops down her body, taking in her snow boots, leggings, and red wool coat. "You look great," I reply with a shrug.

And just like that, her eyes soften, and she gets a sweet, sort of shy smile on her face. "Thanks."

She bites her lip, and I have to look away because it makes me want to kiss it. I take her suitcase out of her hand and carry it down the steps to load into the back of my pickup.

"Is this all you have?" I ask, glancing over at her car.

"Yes, my snowsuit is crammed in my suitcase." She looks at all the supplies. "Holy cow, you packed a lot of stuff. I should pay you for some of this."

"Don't worry about it," I reply, slamming the tailgate closed.

"No really, I see snacks here. I didn't even think to pack snacks. And is that Chardonnay? That's my favorite! I can't stand beer. And firewood? I should pay you for this. I should pay you for all of this actually. You're really the one helping me out here, Sam. I'm sure snowboarding lessons aren't cheap."

She's spinning out again, so I place my hands on her shoulders and stare down at her for a quiet moment. When she stops fretting, I reply slowly, "Seriously, Maggie, don't worry about it. I don't want your money." *I just want you,* my inner voice whispers like a two-timing whore.

She looks up at me, blinking in an adorably young and innocent way. It takes all my strength not to lean in and crush my lips to hers. Why is she so kissable tonight? Was it because I felt like she was flirting with me at Tire Depot earlier this week? If I knew bouncing around with my niece was a way to get girls to look at me the way Maggie is looking at me, I would have played that card a long time ago. Or maybe it was our text messages. I'm not a big texter, normally, but with the way she continually set me up to flirt right back, I just couldn't help myself.

Jesus hell, if Maggie and I were in a different time, in a different place, with different names…she would be under me by now, crying out my name and begging me to make her come.

But this isn't a different time or place. We aren't different people. This is Miles's little sister. And I'm just here to help her out for the weekend. Nothing more.

After we finish loading the truck, we head west toward Eldora Mountain Resort. The drive is quiet as we eat our cold sandwiches and I focus on the snow-covered roads. Luckily, it's only a thirty-minute drive from my place, and my vehicle has four-wheel drive. This fresh snow will make for some epic snowboarding powder tomorrow.

When we arrive, we have to stop at the front desk of the main resort to get the keys for the ski in, ski out chalet. After another short ride up the mountain, I pull up to the back end of a small red cedar cabin that's a good deal off the beaten path. We hop out and make our way up to the back door that's lined with twinkle lights, and I fumble with putting the key in the lock.

"Holy heck, it's freezing out here!" Maggie states excitedly with a kid-in-a-candy-store smile.

"Should have worn your snowsuit there, sparky," I jest and then push the door open while flicking on the lights. I step back to follow Maggie through the doorway and down a short hallway that leads into the kitchen. It's small and rustic with knotty wood cabinets and a granite slab island that separates the kitchen from the living area. The living room has an oversized plaid couch with a gray furry rug resting right in front of a brick fireplace.

"I'll get a fire going," I state, striding over to the stack of chopped wood on the built-in shelves along the wall.

Maggie continues flipping on the lights, taking in the small but cozy cabin. She turns to head down the hallway as I light the Firestarter in the hearth. When the fire is going, I hear Maggie call out my name.

I head toward her and find Maggie standing in the middle of the bedroom at the end of the hall. Looking at me sheepishly, she states, "Only one bedroom."

"Oh." I reach my hand up to rub the back of my neck. "I guess I never thought to ask how big the place was. It's no problem. I'll sleep on the couch."

"No, you won't!" Maggie replies, her eyes wide with surprise. "You'll take the bedroom."

"Not gonna happen." I laugh and head back down the hall to start unloading the truck.

"Yes, it is," Maggie chirps, following me closely through the kitchen and back out into the snowy cold. "Look at all this stuff you packed for us. You even brought me your sister's snowboarding gear."

"It was no big deal," I state, grabbing some bags and heading back inside.

Maggie grabs a few and follows. "All of this is a big deal, Sam."

I drop the bags in the kitchen and turn to head back out to the truck again, but she stands her ground in the hallway, refusing to let me pass.

"Maggie, let me through. There are still a couple of things I need to grab."

I move to walk past her, and she presses her hands into my abs and pushes me back. "Not until you agree to take the bedroom."

"Maggie, I'm not that kind of guy," I reply, dropping my gaze to where her hands are still on my stomach.

She immediately rips her hands away, embarrassed to be caught touching me. "Well, I'm not that kind of girl."

I exhale heavily. "I go camping with Miles all the time, and we sleep on the ground. Trust me, that couch is probably nicer than my bed!"

"It is not. I've seen your bed," she barks, crossing her arms and staring back at me.

I step back, my brows furrowing at that response. "When did you see my bed?"

Her face goes white, her blue eyes wide and panicky. "Never mind. Just…when I was using your bathroom," she stammers. "You won't take my money, so you at least have to take the bed. You're the one who raced up that silo like an Olympian, so I'm afraid I must insist." She braces her hands on the hallway. It's so cute that she thinks she can form an immovable barrier between me and the rest of our gear outside.

I prop my hands on my hips as I try to stare her into silent submission.

It doesn't work.

"You know I can pick you up and move you, right? I've done it before."

Her eyes narrow in challenge. "But you won't."

Oh, but I'd like to. Instead, I pull my lips into my mouth, rubbing them together in frustration before finally shaking my head. "Fine, I'll take the bedroom."

She squeals in victory, and her arms wrap tightly around my waist for a quick hug. I stare up at the ceiling, doing my best to ignore the fact that her celebratory hugs are making me wonder what she looks like naked.

We head back outside and unload the rest of our gear, then get to work unpacking and putting everything where it belongs. I begrudgingly plop my duffle bag on the bedroom floor and come striding out to find Maggie standing in front of the back door slider off the living room. She's turned off all the lights in the great room to get a better view of the outdoors, so all that glows in the small space is the crackling fire inside the hearth.

I take a moment, not to check out the view of the mountains, but to appreciate the sight of Maggie with her back turned. Her long, dark hair hangs down her back, and my eyes fall to the curve of her supple ass on full display in her tight leggings. Her feet are bare and dainty looking as her toes wiggle into the gray fur rug. I have a strange desire to touch them, rub them, feel some sort of skin-on-skin contact with her again because it's been too long since I've touched her lips. Her gray knit sweater hangs off one shoulder, and I reflexively lick my lips at the idea of touching them to her flesh right by her black bra strap.

Goddamn, she's sexy. Even when she's not even trying to be.

"Some view," I state, stepping up beside her and shoving my hands into my pockets. Sweeping views of mountains paint the far distance, and a hot tub is nestled at the end of the property. Beyond that are the snowy ski hills with rows of bright lights illuminating everything. The lifts are full of boarders and skiers alike, all out late enjoying the fresh powder.

"Have you skied out here before?" Maggie asks, peering over at me.

I nod. "Yes, a lot actually."

I look over and see her shaking her head at me. "Is there anything you haven't done?"

I chuckle and raise my eyebrows. "I've never sat in a hot spring, to be honest, so if we find that, it'll be a new experience for me as well."

Maggie's eyes light up. "That's right. Where is it? I only saw the hot tub out there."

I point at a small wooden bridge to the left that disappears into the woods on the east side of the house. Dimly lit with snow-covered outdoor lanterns, it leads back into this apparent oasis. "I was reading the cabin's note in the kitchen, and it said it's just down that way. Totally private, I guess. We're supposed to call security if we catch anyone else in it."

"Awesome," Maggie replies with a wide-eyed look of excitement. "Let's go."

"Now?" I ask, amazed that she's up for it already.

"Yes, now! Let's put on our swimsuits, pour some of that wine you packed, and go check it out!"

"Okay," I reply, trying to hide my pleased smile from her because I can feel her staring at me. "Let's do it."

Moments later, I'm trying to keep my tongue in my mouth as I walk into the kitchen to find Maggie in nothing but a little black bikini. And I mean...*little*. If her brother caught her wearing that, he'd freak the fuck out.

She's on her tiptoes trying to reach something on the top shelf so instead of staring at her ass and legs like a pervert, I walk over and reach above her, murmuring on top of her head. "What are you wanting?"

She inhales sharply and falls back into me, her nearly bare body brushing up against my bare chest. I'm standing over her in just a pair of plaid board shorts, and she licks her lips as she stares unabashedly at my chest and abs.

"Maggie." I get her attention with my hand still reaching up high. "What did you want from up here?"

"Oh!" she exclaims and closes her slack jaw. "The stemless wineglasses up there."

I pull them down and hand them over to her, enjoying the fact she still hasn't looked at my face once. "Here you go," I state, and finally, she looks up at me with flushed cheeks, biting that lip like it's her last meal.

"Thanks," she replies and turns to open the bottle of white wine I brought with the corkscrew opener she must have found.

She pours two glasses and takes a big drink before

handing my glass to me. She steels herself before turning around to face me with a bright, toothy smile. "Ready?"

"Always," I reply. We slip our feet into our snow boots, grab our towels, and throw on our coats, then make our way out the back door toward the snow-covered bridge.

We're both shivering like crazy by the time we get over the bridge. We hurriedly follow the lighted path around several trees, and off into the distance, I think I hear the sound of running water. When we finally reach our destination, I completely forget about how cold it is outside because I'm walking into another universe.

The trees suddenly part to reveal a clearing with a stunning rock garden full of large boulders all topped with big piles of powder on them while running water flows below them all around. Pillars with glowing lanterns illuminate the jagged terrain for us. I catch a glimpse of the running waterfall nearby that has frozen edges with steam billowing up in the middle. Off to the side, a few more lights are positioned around an outline of a large rock bowl that runs off over the top into the shallower area.

Maggie and I make our way over there, both of us stunned into silence as we look inside and admire the steaming crystal clear water.

"This is insane," Maggie states softly, bending over and dipping her hand into the water. "It's actually hot."

I chuckle at that comment but can't really fault her for being shocked. I'm amazed myself. "It's a crazy anomaly of nature for sure."

"Let's get in!" she replies excitedly as she hands me her

wineglass and quickly yanks off her coat and boots. I have no choice but to watch every part of her stunning body as she gingerly steps into the water. "Holy heck, it's super hot!"

She squeals as she sinks down into the knee-high water, stretching her legs out in front of her so the water laps up around her breasts. When she finds a comfortable place on the rocky bottom, she reaches out for the wineglasses next. I hand them over and repeat her actions, feeling her eyes on me the entire time as I step in and sink down into the steaming water. It feels fucking life changing.

Maggie hands me my glass and beams over at me. "Incredible, right?"

I look around at the snow falling off the trees in the distance and relish in the sound of the waterfall nearby. It's all fucking magical, and I'm not a guy who uses the word magical to describe things, but hell if it doesn't fit. "This is maybe the best thing I've ever experienced in my entire life."

Maggie's smile turns affectionate as she's clearly touched by that remark. She lifts her glass to mine. "I'm happy to be experiencing it with you then, Sam."

We clink our glasses together and both take a drink, the cool white wine warming my throat as the hot spring warms all my other parts. Maggie's sparkling blue eyes glow in the dim lanterns, and I can't help but think this has to be one of the most bizarre situations I've ever found myself in. A couple of weeks ago, I was hyper-focused on Tire Depot and working with my uncle on my new business plans. Now, I'm in a hot spring with a beautiful woman I cannot touch.

Life is perfectly imperfect sometimes.

"What are your future plans, Sam?"

"Besides taking over Tire Depot?" I ask, taking a sip of my drink. "That's pretty much it."

"Do you have any goals with the business?"

"Yes, definitely. I have hopes to expand the shop with your brother to include classic car restoration. Miles is crazy talented with classics."

"Oh my god, that would be his dream job," Maggie states with wide eyes. "He and my grandpa were always talking cars."

I nod and smile. "Yeah, I've seen your grandpa's truck. It's a thing of beauty. It makes sense that Miles got it when he passed away."

Maggie smiles and waves her hands in the water. "They were really close. Miles would do anything for Grandpa."

I nod thoughtfully. "I'm close with my mom like that. If I can make Tire Depot into all that I think it could be, I hope to be able to pay off the rest of her mortgage so she can retire early. Anything to get her off those hospital floors. She's a great nurse, but she works too hard."

Maggie's eyes are wide and challenging as she says, "You are a total momma's boy."

"No, I'm not," I reply with a sheepish smile and then instantly want to change the focus off me. "So where are you at with your career aspirations?"

She purses her lips together and shrugs. "I guess I'm currently a drifter until things change."

My brows lift knowingly "You mean until you marry an NFL quarterback."

"I'm not marrying him for his money," she snaps and flicks a bit of water at my chest while mumbling under her breath, "Technically, I'm not marrying him at all at this point."

"But that's the end goal, right?" I ask, tilting my head to watch her reaction carefully. "That's what you're working so hard for?"

She shrugs and nods, seemingly ashamed by her response.

I turn and prop my elbow on the rock so I can face her, then ask her the question that's been niggling at me for a while now. "What's the appeal of your ex anyway? Tell me about him."

Maggie slips down into the water farther, sipping her wine and resting her head back on a rock. She takes a deep breath before replying. "Well, he's tall, dark, and handsome…that doesn't hurt. He's talented and extremely passionate about what he does."

"Which is football?"

"Yes, football," she replies with an annoyed frown. "Aren't you passionate about what you do?"

"Am I passionate about tires?" I respond with a laugh. "No, Maggie. I'm not passionate about tires."

"Well, then what are you passionate about?" she asks, taking another sip of wine.

"People," I reply simply, the answer rolling off my tongue like a reflex. "I care about the people in my life…my family, my friends, my employees…especially my employees. I mean, I genuinely like knowing what's going on with their families. I want them to know that their home lives are bigger than the bottom line and being their boss isn't about making more money than them. It's about being the support system they need to not only survive but to also be happy. That's what I'm passionate about. Tires are just what brings it all together."

Maggie stares back at me, clearly startled by my long-winded answer, but her brows furrow as she churns something over in her mind.

"Why do you have that look on your face?" I ask, staring at her curiously.

Maggie gazes back at me with wide, wondering eyes. Her voice is quiet in the dark as she responds. "You're passionate about people but not long-term relationships?"

My head pulls back, this question catching me completely off guard. "What makes you say I'm not passionate about relationships?"

"Kate," Maggie answers with a small shrug of her shoulders.

I inhale and exhale slowly, feeling annoyed that things are being said to Maggie about me behind my back. Not that I blame Kate—she's only relaying the truth—but I guess I'd rather Maggie hear it from me.

"Look, I don't begrudge you for going after your relationship or for chasing after what you think is your happy ending. I respect it and am fucking impressed by it enough to help you out. I just know that it's not what I want for my life. I didn't grow up with a perfect family like you and Miles. Mine is far from perfect. And I know myself well enough to know that I'm better off making Tire Depot my passion...not some girl."

"Some girl," Maggie repeats with a laugh, circling her hand on the surface of the water slowly. "It's not some girl, Sam. It's *the* girl. If you met *the* girl, you would be singing a very different tune."

I shake my head. "So you're saying you are one hundred percent certain that your football player is *the* guy?"

Maggie stops waving her hands around the water, and her brows knit together deep in thought. Her hesitation has me shocked. I would have thought she'd blurt out a resounding yes, but she's actually thinking it over, which seems... mature. "I'm not one hundred percent certain, no. But I'm certain I want to try to win him back so I can find out."

"No matter what it takes."

"No matter what it takes," she confirms and then squints her eyes shut. "Crap...I forgot my phone."

"Have someone you need to call right now?"

"No...I just...need a picture of me in this hot spring to send to Sterling."

I have to fight back the urge to roll my eyes. Maggie has moments of maturity, moments when she's wise beyond her years, but then she slips right back into that twenty-two-year-old college grad who has no clue what to do without a plan in front of her.

"Maggie," I state, my voice deep in warning. "Stop worrying about Sterling and live in this moment. We are in the middle of a hot spring, surrounded by rocks and mountains and snow and nature and...*life*. Your ex should be the last thing on your mind. You should be taking this all in."

"I am taking it all in," she snaps back defensively.

"But are you? Are you really?" I stare deep into her eyes, not in judgment but in understanding. "I know you have a plan, but sometimes plans need to be forgotten so you don't miss out on life."

"Life? Like right now? With you?" she says the words slowly like each one is a sweet she's tasting for the first time.

"Hell, maybe," I reply, my voice growing deeper from the darkened look in her eye. "You seem busy living for a fictional future. Maybe it's time to stop turning the pages for a bit."

The corners of her lips twitch as she watches me for a breath. Her tongue darts out to wet her lips as she pulls her bottom one in with her teeth. She turns around to prop her arms on the rocks, her eyes taking in the scenery all around us. She exhales heavily and then turns to sit on her knees in front of me.

My eyes take in that luscious body of hers, curvy in all the right places and smooth like velvet. Leaning in until her face is only inches from mine, she says, "Kiss me, Sam."

"What?" I ask with a laugh and pull away from her, assuming this must be her idea of a joke.

She bites her lip and narrows her eyes with determination. "Kiss me."

"What are you doing?" I shift nervously in the water to put more space between us. I swear to God, the temperature of the water has just risen ten degrees.

Lifting her shoulders, she replies, "I'm living life in the moment."

"But you want your ex back." A fact she shouldn't need to be reminded of.

"I do…someday." Her eyes wander down to my chest. "But he's not here tonight. And you're a short-term kind of guy, and I'm a temporarily single girl. So why don't we live in the moment right now…together?"

"You don't want this," I reply with a shake of the head, gulping down the contents of my glass in one swig. I set it down and hoist myself up on the edge of the rocks, needing some cool air to clear my head.

"I think I do," she replies, lifting her brows at me. "I know I do. I've wanted it since the day we met."

"Bullshit."

"It's true. Why do you think I threw myself at you in your fishing hut, Sam?"

My body roars to life at that memory, of her body close to mine, of feeling her in my arms and tasting her perfect lips. Maggie could kiss. Even in her haste, she knew how to kiss.

Maggie moves closer to me like a tentative cub tracking its first prey. She kneels between my legs, and I tense when she runs her hands up the outside of my calves. "You're a good guy, Sam. You may not be a long-term kind of guy, but that's not what I'm looking for from you anyway."

Her hands roll over my quads, shooting a zinger right up my groin to my cock. I reach down and grip her hands harshly to stop their movement. "What are you looking for exactly, Maggie? Be very fucking specific."

Her long black lashes are wet from the steam as she

looks up at me and quirks her brow as she replies. "I'm asking for no-strings fucking."

"Jesus Christ," I growl and have to force myself to look away from her. She looks way too fucking hot right now in that little black bikini, her breasts pressing together from the position of her hands on my thighs, and her blue eyes wide and innocent. My dick develops its own heartbeat as it presses into my board shorts.

How did this evening turn into Maggie seducing me? I'm fucking nine years older than her, for God's sake. I should be the one seducing her. But all of a sudden, she's the alluring bait dangling right in front of me, and I'm a fish who hasn't eaten in weeks.

I look at her with pleading eyes. "Your brother will kill me."

She smiles a sexy smile, that dimple in her cheek ever present. "Miles doesn't need to know about my sex life."

I close my eyes, my head falling back as I look up into the stars and grapple with my conscience. I know I'm already lying to Miles, but it's one thing to secretly help his sister out, and it's another to secretly fuck her. "What if this gets complicated, Maggie?" I ask the sky.

"You mean, what if I fall for you?"

I look back down at her as she takes the words right out of my head.

"I won't," she assures, her voice firm and steady. "I'm a very focused person when I want to be, Sam. And when I have an end goal in sight, nothing gets in my way."

I tilt my head curiously because damnit, I think she's

right. From the second I met Maggie, she's been focused, headstrong, and fully committed to her goals. Hell, the girl was going to go silo ice climbing all on her own with a bunch of granola-eating potheads she'd just met.

In the beginning, I thought it was naïvety. Now, I think Maggie Hudson might actually be fucking fierce.

Inching a bit closer, she states in a deep, sultry voice, "Let's consider this a short-term plan that could be another great adventure."

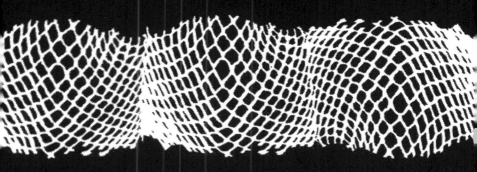

CHAPTER 11

Lure The Best

Maggie

It's not the wine that has me propositioning Sam. It's him. Every second I spend with him, he gets hotter and hotter and hotter. From punching that asshole at Marv's Bait and Tackle to telling me he's passionate about his employees, he's just so much...*man*. And it doesn't help that Kate's urging to make this trip about more than just getting Sterling back is echoing in my mind over and flipping over again.

I glance down and can see the outline of Sam's erection in his board shorts. It's thick and long and pressing against the thin fabric like an animal that wants to be freed. He clearly wants this too, so what are we waiting for?

Sam takes a deep, cleansing breath and releases my hands that he had pinned to his thighs. The act is seemingly innocent, but it feels like a resounding yes as I watch his entire body go taut with anticipation. I stand between his legs, and his eyes heat as they trail down my body.

He lifts his chin to look up at me as he splays his rough hands around my waist, then over my butt and to the backs of my legs. In one quick move, he spreads me so I'm sitting astride him, and when his hard-on nudges my center, I have to bite back a moan threatening to crawl up my throat.

Something tells me that having sex with Sam will be a night and day difference from Sterling. Sam stokes the flames as he palms my ass and rocks me on his lap before running his hands up my sides. His thumbs steal under the fabric of my bathing suit top, and I arch into his touch just as his thumbs brush over my nipples.

"This is your last chance to get out, sparky," he states again, his voice deep with obvious lust.

Is he crazy? His hands feel like freedom, and his dick feels like a mountain I can't wait to climb. I don't want anything to stop. I want it to go faster! Especially when he stares at my hardened nipples and bites his flipping lip!

"I want you, Sam," I pant and then move in to press my lips to him.

He pulls back quickly, preventing my mouth from touching his. Shaking his head from side to side, he says, "You kissed me first last time. Now it's my turn."

In one athletic maneuver, he stands, holding me up like I weigh nothing, and places me on the rock where he was just sitting. These rocks aren't exactly comfortable, but I'm too busy listening to my roaring libido to care about comfort.

Kneeling between my legs, he leans in close to my mouth to whisper, "But I'm not going to kiss you here."

I stare down at his beautiful mouth, my own hanging open like a dog after a run. He brushes his nose softly along my cheek, nuzzling all the way down my neck and causing a riot of goose bumps to erupt all over my body, and not just from the cool air around us.

Because it's not cold right now. It's steaming hot, and I want nothing more than to be slick and sweaty with Sam O'Connor. He begins a trail of featherlight kisses down my neck, over the swells of my breasts, and to my belly just below my navel.

"I'm going to kiss you down here," he husks against the mound of my pussy.

I cry out loudly because I can't remember the last time a man kissed me down there. Not properly anyway. My high school boyfriend was the only one, and that idiot never knew what he was doing. Sadly, Sterling never wanted to. He says it's not his thing, and God, I've yearned for it like crazy.

"Oh my god," I cry when Sam's fingers slip past the fabric of my suit bottoms and brush along my slit. He pushes his thumb deep inside me while his forefinger teases my clit. I feel a sudden rush of pressure down below, and I worry I'm going to have a weird female premature orgasm.

"Is this where you like me, sparky?" he asks, watching my body twitch as he adjusts his hand and pushes two long fingers inside me.

I groan out a frustrated sound from both his use of that

nickname and because I'm scared he's not going to do what I really want him to do. "Don't call me sparky," I state because I can't say what I really want to say.

He chuckles and drops a chaste kiss on my inner thigh. "Why not?"

My eyes lock on his. "Because when you first called me that, it was not one of my favorite moments."

His eyes twinkle with mirth. "That's too bad because it was one of mine."

I smile at that response, but my amusement is completely cut off when he unceremoniously buries his face between my legs. His right hand holds my bikini bottoms to the side as his left hand grips my other thigh to spread me wide. He flattens his tongue on my sex and licks me from back to front in one long, luxurious sweep, stopping at my clit to suck fiercely.

A cry rips its way out of my throat as my hand combs into his hair, fisting it anxiously as my body struggles with sensory overload. The air is too cold, the water is too hot, and Sam's mouth is unrelenting. He seems encouraged by my hair pulling and quickly moves to hook my right leg up on his shoulder so he can grab my lower back and pull me against his face even deeper. He continues to tongue lash me over and over with a variety of lips, nips, and sucks that feel like a goddamn nightmare and dream all rolled into one. The pressure in my lower belly is so intense, I feel like I'm going to split right up the middle.

My hips develop a mind of their own as they buck forward, riding his face like a prized bronc at a rodeo.

Everything he is doing is too much, yet somehow not enough. I'm losing my mind as the desire to feel his tongue thrust deeper overwhelms me.

Sam utters a low, satisfying moan when he feels my legs begin to tense up, and the sound only pushes me higher. My body locks up, preparing for the explosion that's sure to come. Sam must know what's about to happen because when he starts rapid-fire flicks across my clit, he forces an orgasm so strong, my screams are probably heard on the other side of the mountain.

In the background, I think Sam moves from between my legs, but my eyes are so starry-eyed, I can't see anything. I can't feel anything either. My body is like numb Jell-O as I attempt to catch my breath and re-center myself back on this planet.

I finally turn my eyes to Sam. He's moved back into the hot spring and is staring at me like I'm some work of art on a wall he's admiring. The heat and energy in his eyes are everything I want more of. More hotness, more adventure… more Sam.

I shake my head at him in amazement. "I don't know why I'm surprised to discover you're good at that because you're good at basically everything."

Sam's lips twitch with amusement as he rubs his hands over his face and through his short hair. "I'm a man of many talents."

My brows arch curiously at that. "Apparently."

"But you know what, sparky? Somehow I don't think you're as innocent as you look."

He eyes me with a sexy smolder that brings a smile to my face. "Let's put our talents to the test," I state, moving down into the water and making my way toward him.

Sam's face falls, and he draws back from me with a somber look on his face. "We have a slight problem."

"What?"

He clears his throat. "I didn't bring any condoms."

"Oh…shit."

"Yeah." He exhales heavily and ruffles the water beading in his hair. "And with all the snow that came down tonight, I think I'll probably need to wait until daylight to run to town and get them."

"Tomorrow?" I ask with a pout, and then my gaze drops down to Sam's groin under the water. The groin that I felt the full thickness of only moments ago when I was on his lap. The groin that is probably in some serious need of release.

I swallow nervously, my body tensing up as Sam watches me curiously. I know what he wants me to do right now. I know what every man in America would want done in this situation.

But I can't.

Just the idea of it makes my entire body prickle with anxiety, and before I can change the subject, a flashback hits me hard and fast.

Sterling and I had been together about a month when it happened. It was homecoming week, and Sterling had just quarterbacked an incredible game. We were at a party celebrating, and I was more tipsy than I cared to admit when I tried to impress Sterling by yanking him into the bathroom for a quickie. One second, we're kissing, and then the next, he's pushing my head down toward his dick. I was totally okay with this, so I licked my lips and eagerly got to work. But just as I was getting into it, Sterling grabbed my hair and thrust his dick so deep into my throat, I gagged. He didn't seem to notice my reaction and kept pushing himself down my throat over and over again. Tears pricked my eyes as my nails clawed into his hips in a silent plea to calm the fuck down. But he didn't notice. He just kept thrusting and thrusting until finally…

I vomited.

Like…on his dick.

Well, maybe not exactly on his dick, more so on his lap because I managed to extract my mouth from his dick just as another retch reared its ugly head.

Only this wasn't a dry heave.

It was a sputtering spray of the jungle juice I'd been drinking like Gatorade.

Sterling freaked out and nearly tossed me to the ground in his attempt to get away from my upchuck. I was frozen on my knees, head hanging down with puke in my hair as I tried to catch my breath.

It. Was. Mortifying.

I thought for sure he was going to dump me. I thought for sure I'd humiliated myself beyond repair to the man I wanted to marry and that my life was over.

But Sterling didn't dump me. He actually apologized for being overeager and handed me a random toothbrush from the cupboard.

Sam's eyes are on me with a curiosity that I don't want to address. It's one thing to puke on your boyfriend's dick, but it's another thing to puke on a fuck buddy. Not to mention, something tells me Sam is used to experienced women.

"Uhhh, let's head back, shall we?" I state, my voice high pitched and clipped as I quickly stand in the hot spring, my sex drive shriveled up like an old lady after that walk down memory lane. "It's getting late, and we have a big day of snowboarding tomorrow."

"Oookay," Sam replies slowly, his brow furrowed in confusion.

I quickly slide my wet feet into my boots and don't even bother toweling off before grabbing my coat and hustling my ass back down the path to the cabin and away from Sam's very likely throat-choking dick.

The next day, I wake up prepared to talk it out with Sam. I should apologize for my behavior so the day isn't full of awkwardness or resentment...but I don't get the chance.

"Hi," I state sleepily as I pad my way into the kitchen where I find Sam frying bacon and eggs at the stove.

"Morning!" he says cheerily and looks over to eye my plaid pajamas before returning his attention back to the stove.

I take in his gray lounge pants and a white T-shirt that

hugs his very large arms nicely. "You're up early."

He nods knowingly. "Early bird catches the worm. Plus, we'll want to get going early today before it gets busy. It's easier to teach without a bunch of teenage assholes swinging by and spraying us all day."

"Spraying us?" I ask with a frown.

With a half-smile, he says, "Yeah, they ski really fast straight at you and then stop and kick their heels out, resulting in a spray of snow. They always do it to newbies."

"What dicks," I reply with a huff.

Sam just shakes his head. "Yeah, but it's all a part of the fun, though."

I nod and stare at Sam, waiting for him to show any signs of weirdness about the abrupt end to our evening. Surely he's annoyed, right? I rushed back to the cabin so fast, I was changed and pretending to sleep on the couch before he even walked in the door. That had to frustrate him, right?

"How'd you sleep last night?" he asks while scooping the food onto a couple of plates.

"Great!" I exclaim a bit too forcefully. "That couch is really comfortable."

He turns to eye me for a second before flipping the last few pieces of bacon. "Maybe we can trade tonight."

"Forget it."

He turns to look straight at me, sighing in exasperation. "You're very stubborn, you know that?"

"My brother reminds me almost daily," I reply, nabbing the piece of bacon he's just set on a towel. Taking a deep breath, I add, "Hey, sorry I got kind of weird last night."

He shakes his head and replies, "It's okay, Maggie. I figured you changed your mind, and I'm all right with it. It's probably for the best."

My eyes fly wide. "Changed my mind about what?"

"About us hooking up or whatever. It's no big deal."

"I didn't change my mind," I exclaim, grabbing his meaty bicep so he turns to look at me.

His brow is furrowed as he stares down at my lips. "You didn't?"

"No! What would make you think that?"

"Because you basically ran away from me in the hot springs last night. I might not be the most intuitive guy, but I am perceptive, and regret was written all over your face."

My eyes slam shut in horror as I realize that Sam interpreted my mental breakdown completely wrong last night. "It wasn't you...it was me."

He huffs out a laugh. "Got it."

"No...oh my god, I'm horrible at this." I release his arm to hoist myself up on the kitchen counter as I attempt to form my words so I don't sound like a total headache. "I had a bad experience going down on a guy once. So bad, I never want to do it again, and I was worried that's what you were expecting last night since we didn't have condoms."

Sam's jaw drops. "You thought I wanted you to suck my cock?"

I shrug, flushing with embarrassment and feeling a little turned on at his casual use of such a dirty word. "Well, yeah. I mean, you'd just gone down on me, and I could tell your dick was like…majorly hard." My face flames with heat as I stutter out, "Returning the favor would have been the appropriate thing to do."

"Jesus Christ, Maggie…you're really fucking nuts sometimes, you know that?" Sam barks, his tone gruff with chastisement.

"What?" I exclaim in confusion.

"Only assholes expect reciprocation. Men expect orgasms. You orgasmed, and that was my goal. End of story. What kind of douchebags have you dated anyway?"

My entire body recoils with mortification. If I told Sam that my bad experience was with Sterling, he'd never agree to keep helping me win him back. "I don't know…one time a guy just got too excited I guess and he sort of gagged me until I threw up."

Sam's eyes close in anger at my words. "Goddamnit, I want to punch him."

"You don't even know him."

"I still want to punch him." Sam shakes his head sadly and reaches out to shut off the stove burners. He moves closer to me, and I flinch a little as he slides his hands up my legs, positioning himself between them. "I feel like I shouldn't be teaching you how to snowboard. I should be teaching you how to know your worth."

"What?" I ask, my eyes looking all over his rugged features for some sense of what he's talking about.

"Maggie, you are smart, sweet, stubborn, and hilarious without even trying to be. You need to realize that a guy who doesn't treat you right doesn't deserve to be around you. Sex isn't about being equal. It's about being generous."

"You didn't say beautiful," I blurt, my mouth speaking before my brain can stop it.

"What?"

I shrug. "You didn't say beautiful. Most guys lead with that."

Sam tilts his head and stares at me for a long moment. "If that's all you're worried about, then you need me even more than I thought." He grabs my face in his hands and stares so deeply into my eyes, I find myself holding my breath for what might come next. "Your beauty is genetics, Maggie. You did nothing to earn it. All that other stuff I said is because you're a badass."

Belly flips. Loads and loads of belly flips are happening inside me right now along with butterflies and dizziness and all those girlie feelings a girl feels when a guy doesn't just call you beautiful, but so much more.

"Thank you," I manage to squeak out because those words might just be the best thing a guy has ever said to me.

"Don't mention it," he replies with a shrug and releases my face to tend to the food again. "But just in case you need to hear it, you are the kind of beautiful that is unforgettable."

My eyes tingle at his words because even though they are spoken so casually, they aren't casual. Hardly anything Sam says is just words. I reach out and wrap my hand around Sam's bicep, pull him toward me, and whisper into his ear, "You should still run to town for those condoms."

He pulls back with that adorable shy smile that makes me weak in the knees. "Whatever you say, sparky."

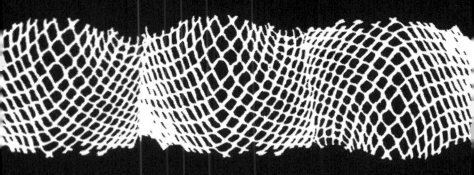

CHAPTER 12

I Always Carry A Stiff Rod

Sam

Maggie is a terrible snowboarder. Like…honestly the fucking worst I've ever seen. I remember my sisters learning how to board—who I don't consider the least bit athletic—and Maggie is still worse than all of them. She gets sprayed by asshole teenagers all damn day. And it's hilarious because every time it happens, she calls them little twerps, and they flip her off.

"You're only encouraging them," I state with a laugh as I lift my goggles up to the top of my head and watch as the pack of boys takes off down the hill, laughing so hard, they can barely stand on their boards.

"I don't care!" Maggie exclaims, her ass planted almost permanently on the ground as she flings her goggles off to wipe the snow off the front of them. Her blue eyes are like fire as she glares up at me. "They're little shits! I wasn't that horrible when I was a teenager."

I do my best to conceal my amusement as I reply. "I know, but now you've made a game out of it for them."

She shakes her head, and I unbuckle one of my feet to skate over and help her back up. We've been on the bunny hill all damn day, and she still hasn't even mastered one-foot riding. My calves are killing me from toe sliding in front of her because when she picks up speed, she can't stop herself. I have to give it to her, though. She isn't giving up.

"Remember to dig the heel of your free foot in to slow yourself down. You get going too fast, and that's why we keep crashing and burning."

"Actually, I have a better idea," She waggles her brows at me, a mischievous glint to her eye that has me somewhat terrified of what's to come.

Fifteen minutes later, Maggie is on her butt again, and I'm on my knees beside her. My eyes land on the pack of little assholes that have been tormenting us all day, and a wide smile spreads across my face. "Okay, I see them now. They're coming."

Maggie's eyes light up as she falls backward onto her back in a dramatic fashion with two snowballs clutched tightly in her hands. "Bring your A game, Sam. These little shits need to pay."

I can't help but laugh because of how seriously she's taking all this. I look up and see the four kids approach as predictable as snow on mountaintops.

When they're headed straight for us, chins dropped with determination, I shout, "Now!"

Maggie leaps up, turns on her knees, and the two of us begin hurling snowballs at the four of them. And not just any snowballs...ice snowballs. The kind that fucking hurt. We have at least fifty perfectly sculpted death balls stashed behind her tipped board, and the boys crash into each other as they get pelted over and over again.

I quickly unclip my boots and grab more snowballs, continuing the assault as the four of them do their best to regain their balance and bail the hell out of here. When they start boarding down the hill away from us, Maggie yells to their backs, "Go home and cry to your mommies, you little shits!"

I laugh hard at her serious expression and then throw my arm around her in camaraderie. Maggie smiles and offers me her hand for a high five.

When we've both stopped laughing, she drops to the ground again. "I think it's time to call it quits, Sam. How about some hot chocolate?"

"Sounds good."

We make our way slowly down the hill and back to our cabin at last. The sun is setting over the mountains as I make my way out to the back of the property to enjoy the view. In my opinion, nothing is better than a mountain sunset.

"Oh my heck, it's stunning out here!" Maggie exclaims, her feet crunching in the snow as she makes her way over to me holding two steaming mugs.

She's ditched her snowsuit and is dressed in a pair of

gray leggings, a sweater, and a thermal vest. In her little snow boots, she looks like she could actually be a ski bunny, but the reality of today has me knowing otherwise. She hands over a steaming mug of hot chocolate, and I take a small sip.

"Is this spiked?" I ask, feeling a faint burn down my throat.

She nods with a grin. "I found some Baileys in the cupboard. They won't miss a couple of shots."

I take another fortifying sip, the sweet liquid warming my insides as Maggie positions herself beside me to enjoy the sunset. Breathing a heavy sigh, she states sadly, "I'm afraid snowboarding isn't in my future, Sam."

I have to bite back my laughter because she's asserting it as if I didn't know. "Yeah, sparky...I have to say you weren't exactly a natural out there today."

She giggles around a sip. "But I tried. You can't say I didn't try."

"You tried like hell," I confirm. "Honestly, I can't believe you wanted to go back out after lunch. I thought for sure you were going to quit on me."

"I'm no quitter!" She furrows her brow seriously, and I can't help but think of the fact that she's most likely applying that same logic to her ex as well. "But maybe I should have quit earlier because my muscles are killing me."

She moves to rub her shoulder, and I look past her at the hot tub nearby. "You know what feels great after a long day on the snow?"

She looks over her shoulder at where I'm looking and

nods. "Good idea! I'll go get my suit and some towels." She turns to walk away but halts in her tracks when I call out her name.

"Maggie." She looks over her shoulder at me. "I thought you were looking for adventure."

"I am," she replies with a frown.

I move past her, walking backward toward the hot tub to open the lid. Setting my mug down, I dip my hand in to test the temperature and then fling some water at her. "Then break some rules with me."

In one swift motion, I tug my shirt off over my head and smile broadly at Maggie's shocked expression. Her eyes fall to my chest, and I have to admit, I get a deep satisfaction over seeing a young, beautiful woman like her staring at me. I undo my boots and kick them off to the side and move to my jeans next.

"You're nuts!" Maggie exclaims, turning around just as I push my pants and boxers down to the ground. "And apparently not at all shy."

I hop over the edge of the hot tub and sink down into the warmth, letting the water soothe my sore muscles. It may not be the hot spring, but with this kind of view, I'm not mad at it.

I head over to the control panel and turn on the jets, then sit back in a corner spot and let the firm stream pound into my back muscles. Groaning loudly, I say, "It feels really good, sparky."

Maggie turns to look back at me, her cheeks red and not just from the cold. She walks over and looks down into the water, dipping her finger in gingerly.

"Why are you acting all shy now?" I ask because her demeanor last night was anything but shy.

"I'm not," she replies like a reflex. Her eyes cast off into the distance for a moment as if she's thinking seriously about something.

I move closer to her. "Last night you propositioned me, this morning you told me to get condoms...and now tonight, you're being shy? What gives?"

She bites her lip, her brows furrowed deep in thought as she stares down at me with an expression I can't quite place. She's most likely wondering how she can snap photos of herself naked in a hot tub and send them to her ex to make him jealous. Even though she forgot about her phone for a minute last night, today, I've caught her snapping selfies when she thought I wasn't looking. I never called her out on it because it was the gut-check moment I needed to realize that even after I said all those things to Maggie in the kitchen, she's no different than any other girl I've hooked up with before. She is temporary and fleeting, and all I want is to see her naked with me in this hot tub.

Without warning, I bolt over the edge of the hot tub and grab Maggie around the waist. Her hot chocolate goes falling to the snowy ground as I lift her over the side and into the steaming water still wearing her clothes and boots.

"You dick!" she cries and bats me away as she grapples to get her feet under her in the water. "What the heck do you think you're doing?"

"Getting you out of your head!" I reply with a smile,

and splash some water at her.

"I was going to get in…I was just going to go get us towels first."

She splashes me back, and I can't help but laugh at her angry little face. She looks like a wet puppy pouting in a bathtub as her clothes cling uncomfortably to her body. She manages to slip out of her now-soaked puffy vest and flings it over the edge.

"God, I still have my boots on," she groans and reaches underwater to pull them off. She gets a hold of one, brings it to the surface, and dumps the water out right in front of my face. "These boots were expensive," she states, glaring daggers at me.

"They'll survive," I reply, spreading my arms out wide on the sides of the hot tub to enjoy the show of her removing her clothing.

My amusement is immediately halted when Maggie glares straight at me, stands up, and peels her drenched shirt over her head to reveal her petite breasts covered in a black lace bra. She flings the wet fabric over the edge and locks eyes with me.

And just like that, she doesn't look like an insecure twentysomething anymore. She doesn't look like a drowning puppy. She has that same look of determination she had with me last night in the hot spring. Her hand goes to her back to unclasp her bra, and when it falls off her shoulders, she chucks it right at my face.

I'm pretty sure I have to roll my tongue back into my mouth as I get a glimpse of her perfect pink nipples through her bra that's now draped over my face. I quickly peel the barrier of fabric preventing me from fully ogling Maggie, but she slips down into the protection of the bubbles from the jets before I get another glimpse.

She ditches her bottoms next, and now we are a couple of bobbing heads in a hot tub on the top of a mountain as the winter sun casts golden sparkles all over the snow.

"I can't believe you spilled my hot chocolate," she pouts, and it's so cute, I get a little hard.

I reach over and grab mine that's resting safely on the far edge of the tub. "You can have mine."

She glares at my outstretched hand but takes the drink anyway. When our fingers brush during the pass, a frisson of electricity shoots all the way up my arm. The spark makes me wish my fingers were brushing another part of Maggie altogether.

"I don't have that many clothes here with me, you know."

My eyes dance with mirth. "You have your snowsuit." Her jaw juts out angrily, but before she freaks out on me again, I add, "And if you need clothes, you can borrow some of mine."

She sets her mug down and swims over to the edge of the hot tub to watch the sun as it begins to disappear behind the mountains. I join her and absorb the scenery in comfortable silence as the orange sky turns pink and violet, and darkness begins to fall.

"This does feel pretty good," Maggie states, turning around so the jets hit her back muscles.

"I tried to tell you," I reply with a half-smile.

She exhales and lays her head back on the headrest. "Is this the kind of stuff you did growing up?"

"Get naked in hot tubs with girls? Yes," I deadpan, my eyes glancing down at the swells of her breasts sticking out above the water.

She gives me a side-eye with a playful smirk. "I just mean, go on ski trips and hang out in cabins. I don't know... you just seem so at ease with everything. Snowmobiling, climbing, snowboarding. You take risks like it's just a normal day. You make it all look so easy."

I shrug dismissively and spread my arms out on the edges of the hot tub. "Growing up in Boulder makes it easy, I guess. My buddies and I taught ourselves to climb and board. And I'm a gearhead, so I've always played with motorized toys."

Maggie bites her lip, failing to hide a mischievous smirk on her face.

"I didn't say battery-operated toys," I state knowingly. "Jesus, get your mind out of the gutter."

"What?" she replies with a laugh. "I didn't say anything! It's not my fault you can read my mind!"

I shake my head at her, blown away that a girl this beautiful can actually be this fun. Most of the girls I meet are either one or the other...never both. "You keep surprising me, sparky."

"How so?" she asks, sliding deeper into the water.

"Last night was a surprise. Today was a surprise. Hell, watching you make it to the top of that silo was a surprise.

You're pretty amazing when you put your mind to it."

She blushes under my compliments, and I feel genuine affection for her that I know I shouldn't be feeling. This is casual. Nothing more. "So what's your ex think of all your adventures so far?" I ask, trying to give myself a much-needed gut check. "You've achieved a lot in only a few weeks, I'd say. Is everything going according to plan?"

Maggie's expression changes before my eyes from happy and carefree to confused and somewhat troubled. "I've been texting him some pictures here and there, and I think he's impressed."

"Does he not say it?" I ask, my brow furrowed.

She shrugs. "He seems genuinely surprised by all I've been up to on my winter break, but he doesn't necessarily say he's impressed. Maybe I'm downplaying it too much, though? I've been trying to play it off like I've wanted to do this kind of stuff for years."

"But you haven't?" I ask, feeling confused.

"God, no!" she replies with a laugh. "You saw me on that bunny hill today. I am terrible at sports!"

"But you still have fun doing it?" I ask because she doesn't seem miserable when she's doing any of it. So either she's a great actress or she's just so hyper-focused on her goal, she is willing herself to have fun.

"I'm having more fun than I would have expected, I guess," she answers with a thoughtful expression on her face. "But I think that's mostly because of you. You're so easy to get along with, Sam. And you're a fun teacher. I get why you and Miles are so close."

The mention of her brother brings a stiffness to my posture that wasn't there before. Probably because I'm currently butt ass naked in a hot tub with his sister, and she's just reminded me of that fact. But hell, she's a grown-ass woman, and I'm a grown-ass man. I know this is getting more complicated than either of us originally expected, but Maggie is clearly still focused on her ex, and I'd be an idiot not to jump at a chance with a girl like Maggie.

"Why does Miles think you're staying in Boulder for so long anyhow?" I ask, resting my head back on the hot tub and running my hand through the cold beads of water in my beard.

Maggie gets a pained expression before replying. "Well, I told him once Sterling gets drafted, I don't know where we'll end up, and this is probably the last bit of free time I'll have before we move away together. When I told him I wanted some quality time before all of that, he ate it up like complimentary cookies."

I grimace because I can just see Miles believing all that. "Yeah, he's pretty gullible, I'm afraid."

"I know, and believe me, I feel horrible for lying to his face like that, but I keep telling myself that none of this will matter once Sterling and I get back together."

"And you're still sure that's what you want?" I ask because honestly, I keep hoping that she'll eventually realize how crazy this plan is and wise up and let it all go.

She nods earnestly. "I'm positive that Sterling is it for me. I've never fallen so hard and so fast for a guy. And my parents were the same way when they met in college, and they've been married forever now."

"But why don't you just tell your family what happened? Surely, it's not that big of a deal for a couple to go through a breakup and then get back together."

Maggie shakes her head. "You remember Miles's ex-girl-friend, Jocelyn, right?"

I get a cold shiver up my neck at the mention of that piece of work, and my upper lip curls. "Oh, I remember."

"Exactly," Maggie states with wide eyes. "She was awful, and she broke Miles's heart over and over again. They broke up and got back together so many times that they were worse than Kourtney Kardashian and Scott Disick. It was so bad it even bothered our grandfather. Now Miles is finally with someone wonderful like Kate, and I don't want to put this strain on my family again."

"But Joce was a bitch," I state as flashbacks of the drama that woman brought into our lives replays in the back of my mind. "Sorry to be the one to say it, but it's true. If Sterling is as great of a guy as you say he is, then your family won't care."

Maggie shakes her head. "No, I refuse to put them through this because in a few weeks or a few months, we'll be back together and it won't matter. I want them to love Sterling. I don't want them to associate him with Jocelyn's behavior in any way, shape, or form. And I especially don't want to rock the boat when everyone is so happy."

I exhale heavily because she's putting a lot of pressure on herself to fix this without anyone knowing, and that's not my idea of family. "Look, Maggie…you can do what you want, but I have three older sisters, and I'm telling you…I'd rather be there for them through all their imperfect moments than be subjected to bullshit perfect ones."

Maggie looks at me with pleading eyes that I don't think I could ever say no to. "I get that, Sam. But this is my problem. My mess. And this is how I'm dealing with it."

I slump back into the jets and press my lips together to stop from saying anything more. I'm doing my part by making sure she's safe. It's not my job to strong-arm her down a path. I'm just being a friend.

Maggie takes in my defeated posture and floats closer to me with a wicked look in her eyes. "Look at it this way…if I wasn't like this, then you and I wouldn't be naked in a hot tub together right now."

She waggles her eyebrows at me and sits up on her knees so her wet, bare breasts are on full display. I have to look away when my dick grows hard under the water. "You're fucking evil."

Maggie giggles. "But I use my powers for good."

Without pause, I reach out and wrap my hand around her wrist to yank her toward me. She splashes up onto my lap, and those perfect breasts brush against my chest as her hip slides over my cock. Being this close to her naked body and not touching her for this long was the act of a saint… and right now, I want to be a sinner. I slide my palm along her hip as she brings her hand to my jaw and stares at my lips with an unmistakable hunger.

Before she can beat me to the punch, I lean in and take her lips with mine. She tastes of chocolate and Baileys, and her lips are so soft, I want to feel them on every inch of my body. Her posture relaxes in my arms as she eagerly meets the demanding thrust of my tongue with her own. I groan my appreciation into her mouth and slide my hand around to palm her ass into me.

She twists in my lap, shifting to straddle me, and a shiver rushes up through my body when my dick nudges her center.

"Maggie," I husk against her lips, our breaths mixing in ragged succession. "If we don't get out of this hot tub, that condom run I did this morning will be for nothing."

"Sam," she groans her little noise of disapproval and rubs herself greedily on my cock with small thrusts of her pelvis. "I don't want to get out."

I dip my hand under the water to rub my thumb over her clit. She gasps a throaty sound right in my ear, her hands gripping my head like a life raft in the middle of a storm. I make the decision to make her come right here with my fingers, but my mind is ripped out of this Maggie-trance when I hear the faint sound of laughter coming from much too close to us.

I grab Maggie's arms and push her off to the side just in time to see a group of young teenagers running away from the hot tub.

"Hey!" I call out, unceremoniously pulling my cock away from Maggie's thighs. "This is private property. What the fuck are you doing here?"

The boys stop and wave something at me that I can't quite make out in the dark. I hear Maggie gasp from beside me and turn to look at her in question.

"They took our clothes!" she exclaims and moves to a standing position. "Hey, you little shits!"

The boys howl with laughter, and I quickly grab Maggie by the shoulders and shove her back down into the water. "Maggie, you're fucking naked."

"Shit," she growls, clearly forgetting herself. "It's the same little pricks from the ski hill. I'm gonna call the cops on you!" she shouts, little veins popping out on her neck.

"Go for it!" one of the boys shouts back. "I'm sure they'd love to see your hot titties too!"

I make a move to jump out of the hot tub and go after them, but Maggie wraps her hands around my arm and pulls me back into the water.

"What are you doing?" She laughs as they go sprinting off into the woods. "You're going to chase them through the snowy woods with your dick hanging out?"

I shrug, feeling annoyed that those little shits got the last word. "I could have caught them."

"And then what?" Maggie's face is bright with amusement. "Were you going to spray them with snow?"

"I don't know!" I exclaim in frustration, swinging my hand angrily into the water. "I hadn't thought it through."

Her laughter bubbles over, and my own mood lifts at the sight of her. "This is all your fault, you know," I grumble, failing to scowl like I really want to.

"My fault?" She giggles, clutching her belly and wiping tears from her eyes.

"Yes!" I exclaim with my chin cocked. "You totally

egged them on with the snowballs today."

"You helped me make those snowballs!"

Her laughter is infectious, causing me to smile. "You're a bad influence on me. I was a badass until you came along. No way those little dicks ever would have fucked with me if it weren't for you."

"As if," she replies with an eye roll and then looks back at the house. "But I think we better make a run for the house before they come back and try to lock us out of our own cabin."

Even though I don't want to get out, I groan and shake my head because I know she's fucking right. We were having a good time until those little pricks ruined everything.

"C'mon, old man," Maggie states excitedly and then stands to throw her leg over the side of the hot tub. "I'll race you!"

She takes off butt ass naked, prancing through the snow like Tinker Bell. I hop out, then close the hot tub lid before I hustle after her. I catch up just as she reaches the slider, and we both fall into the safety of the warm cabin.

Maggie rushes down the hall for the bathroom. "I'll get us towels...put more wood on the fire!"

A moment later, she reappears with a fluffy white towel wrapped around her body and tosses one to me. I quickly cinch it around my waist, and we both huddle in front of the fire to warm our frosty limbs from our little snow streaking we just did.

"Oh my god, my feet are freezing!" Maggie exclaims, her entire body taut with shivers as she stretches her feet out in front of her.

"You know what warms you up the quickest?" I ask, turning so my back is to the fire. I reach down and pull her foot onto my lap to rub the pads of her cold feet.

"What?" she asks, biting her lip and watching me curiously.

"Skin-on-skin contact." I waggle my brows at her mischievously.

"Oh my god, shut up!" She yanks her foot from my lap and attempts to shove me away from her.

I catch her wrist in my hand and connect our lips in a hard, chaste kiss. She freezes in surprise, her eyes fierce with shock before she lowers her gaze to my mouth. Suddenly, as if a starting gun went off, Maggie grabs my face and slams her lips to mine. She's frantic and needy and like a coiled spring as she rises up onto her knees and slips her tongue deep into my mouth. I rise up to meet her, my tongue doing its best to search and possess every part of her with hard, hungry kisses.

My hands move from her cheeks to the towel wrapped tightly around her chest. With one rough tug, it slips open and pools on the floor. I pull back from her lips to stare down at her body, my chest heaving with desire as I take in her completely naked form illuminated by the golden flames of the fire. Hardened nipples on teardrop breasts point straight at me as I lower my head and pull one into my mouth.

She tastes like chlorine and flesh and sex all rolled into one as my hands reach up to cup her breasts. She moans loudly when I suck hard on her nipple, her fingers slicing through the strands of hair on my head. I trail kisses over to the breast in my other hand and pay homage to that nipple as well. Maggie growls and grabs my face to pull me back up to her lips again. Her hands fumble at my waist and finally free my towel. When she grips my length in her palm, I pull away from her mouth and groan.

We both look down at her dainty, feminine hand fisting my undainty shaft and stroking it in long, languid movements. "Jesus," she husks, staring hard at me. "You're big."

"Music to a man's ears," I murmur with a laugh, dropping a kiss to her wet hair and lifting her chin so she looks at me. "Are you sure you want to do this?"

She nods eagerly. "Uh, your dick is in my hand…that's usually a good sign."

I drop a chaste kiss on her smart mouth, and in one swift move, I'm up on my feet and striding into the bedroom where I left the condoms.

When I return to the living room, Maggie is still kneeling completely naked on the gray fur rug. In front of a roaring fire, she looks like every man's fucking fantasy. Her dark hair is wet and slicked back. Her face is free of makeup, her eyes are bright and wide with arousal, and her naked body is begging for my hands to touch it.

I lower myself in front of her, her eyes on the condom in my hands. "Sit back, Maggie. Spread your legs."

She does as she's told, opening herself to me and giving me a beautiful view of that pussy I tasted last night. There's a thin line of hair she leaves in the center, and I have to stop myself from bending down and tasting her again. Instead, I slide my fingers over her clit, causing her chest to shudder with surprise. I slide two fingers deep inside her, noticing how wet she is already. I pull them out to circle around her tight bundle of nerves, and she moans my name.

"Oh my god, Sam." Her hips thrust upward to take my fingers deep inside again. "Oh my god."

I continue fingering her, feeling her body tremble with desire from just my fingers. My free hand drops down and fists my cock, stroking it slowly while she writhes on the rug. When she opens her eyes and sees me gripping myself, her gaze alights with a yearning I cannot ignore.

I push a third finger into her, and her fingers dig into the rug as she cries out loudly, "I need more."

"You still want more, sparky?" I ask, moving in and out of her in slow, smooth motions.

"Yes, I want you!" she cries, her climax already building as her pussy tighten around my digits.

"You want my cock?" I ask because her voice is so sexy right now, I want to hear it over and over again.

She lifts her head and pins me with a look. "I want your cock."

With a small smile, I pull my fingers out and move to roll the condom over my straining erection. She watches with fascination as I center myself between her legs and push the head of my cock inside her.

"Do it," she begs, her breath stuttering with need.

So in one fluid motion, I thrust into her hard and fast. She cries out at my invasion, the tightness overwhelming as

193

I press my forehead to her chest and wince with pleasure. Slowly, I begin moving in and out, taking her deep and pulling out so that just my tip rests inside, then plunging back in again.

Her hands rake up my back, scoring my flesh with her nails as she urges me to go faster. I press a bruising kiss on her mouth and rock into her, my hips jerking in a rhythmic motion as her legs wrap around my sides and she angles herself up to meet my thrusts.

Watching Maggie glow in the warm light is stunning. Her skin covered in a thin sheet of sweat as her cries grow louder and louder. As her climax nears, she transforms before my very eyes from a beautiful girl to a stunning woman embracing her body's pleasure. It's a glorious sight.

I dip my head to her shoulder and nibble kisses along her clavicle, needing to taste her, needing my tongue to sweep over every luscious part of her body as she cries out my name over and over.

Suddenly, she tightens around me, her legs squeezing my sides so unforgivingly, I'm barely able to move. She locks eyes with me and opens her mouth with a cry, and I swear the sexy look on her face alone pulls my orgasm right out of me.

My vision blurs as I come inside her and feel her sex pulsing all around me. We're both panting and soaked with sweat from the way-too-hot fire that it takes every muscle in my body to pull out of her and roll onto my back.

"Holy shit," she says with a heavy breath.

"Yeah." I exhale heavily, my brain barely able to form

coherent sentences.

"That was…unexpected."

I look over and see her frowning up at the ceiling, her mind clearly working a lot harder than mine at the moment. "Unexpected bad? Or unexpected good?"

"Good," she replies, but she still has that frowny face, so I don't really feel any better. "I mean…you have quite a rod."

I turn my head and blink rapidly at her in confusion.

She looks back at me and shrugs. "I've been holding that fishing pun for a while now."

The words then click into place, and I bust out laughing because as far as comments after sex go, that one is definitely a first. With a huge smile on my face, I stand and grab a blanket off the back of the couch to drape over her. Her dimple crease becomes visible as she stares up at me, pleased with her little joke.

"I'm just going to go take care of this."

I gesture to the condom, and she stares at it with great interest as I turn and make my way to the bathroom to clean up. Slipping into the bedroom, I throw on a pair of shorts and grab a T-shirt for Maggie to wear to bed since she mentioned not having many clothes for this weekend. By the time I come back out into the living room, she is fast asleep, curled up in front of the fire like a little cat.

With a smile, I watch her for a moment, enjoying how peaceful she looks. The girl has to be tired after a full day of snowboarding…badly. I'm wiped too, as a matter of fact. Feeling chivalrous, I bend down to pick her up, cradling her limp body in my arms as I carry her down the hall and into the darkened bedroom. I lay her down on the bed, tucking her feet under the blankets and pulling them up all around her.

She begins shifting and groans, "Nooo, I said I'm taking the couch."

She tries to sit up, and I gently push her back down. "Don't be stubborn. You're taking the bed."

I attempt to cover her up again, and she grabs my hand. "If I have to sleep in here, then so do you."

She slides over to the middle of the bed and tries to pull me down with her. "I don't sleep with women, Maggie. That's part of the short-term kind of guy rules."

She grumbles sleepily. "You don't snowboard with women either. Shut up and snuggle with me, Sam. Just until I fall back asleep."

I shake my head even though she's facing away from me. If I crawl into that bed with her, I know I won't get out.

When I don't crawl in, she sits up, and says, "Fine, I'm going to the couch then."

With a growl of frustration, I push her back into bed and crawl in behind her. "You're really fucking manipulative, you know that?"

She purrs like a cat. "It's part of my charm."

She tosses the blankets over me and nuzzles her bare ass into my groin. It's been only a few minutes since we had sex, and already, the inklings of a round two are stirring inside me. She grabs my hand and tucks it into her chest, hugging it like a damn stuffed animal.

"Skin to skin, remember?" Maggie states sleepily as she

presses her back into my chest. "Just go to sleep, Sam. This is not a big deal."

I can't help but lay my head on the pillow in defeat. This pillow feels really good. And as much as I'd love to try to stay awake and sneak out, it's been a long-ass day, and this bed feels like heaven. I yawn and twist my hand around to cup her bare breast.

When she tenses beneath my embrace, I whisper into her ear, "Skin to skin, remember?"

And the last sound I remember before drifting off to sleep is Maggie's adorable giggle.

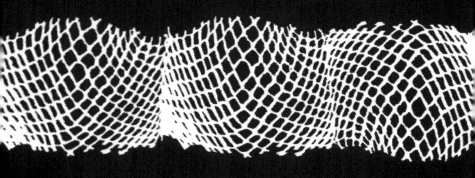

CHAPTER 13

I Fish…Therefore I Lie

Maggie

The next day, I wake to find Sam completely wrapped around me. One of his arms is tucked under my head, serving as my pillow, while the other is wrapped tightly around my waist. It's not a bad way to wake up. He's like a cozy body pillow that's warm and weighted and custom fit just for me.

Last night was completely unexpected. I imagined Sam would be good at sex, but I didn't think he'd be *that* good. It was such a night and day difference from Sterling that I find myself not believing that it all happened the way I remember. Like, was it really that good? Or was it just because it was in the heat of the moment in front of a fire? Or was it because I'm in Boulder and the air is thinner up here so everything feels fluffier? I can't discern whether last night was truly that much better than every other sexual experience I've had or if I'm just dreaming.

I bet if I had sex with Sam right now, it would be more average. The daylight's streaming in through the blinds, and we both have morning breath. It would be totally basic. *And honestly, it'd make me feel better about my life if it was basic.*

Biting my lip, I slowly roll over to face Sam, ignoring the screaming muscles in my legs to admire his red-tinted beard. It's longer now, turning into more of a beard than just stubble. His mouth is hanging open as he breathes deeply. The blankets are shoved down past his waist, so I have a nice view of his chest and arms, that thick muscle that stretches from his shoulder to his neck. He's pretty hot actually.

Slowly, I reach out and trail a finger along his collarbone and down his arm that's still draped over my waist. I slip inside his embrace to touch his belly and then just brush past his groin all casual like.

His groin that is Rock. Fucking. Hard.

My fingers venture farther and gently wrap around his length over his jersey shorts. He groans, and I freeze in his arms as he rolls onto his back. Biting back a giggle, I touch him again, stroking him over the fabric, and since he doesn't seem to be waking up, I delicately pull down the waistband of his shorts and gasp when his bare penis bobs out and points up toward his navel. I stare at his beautifully veined cock for a long moment, and a fleeting desire to wrap my lips around it comes over me.

But I know how badly that could turn out. So, so bad.

Then again, he is asleep. If I ever wanted to try it again, now would be the time. And honestly, if I want to impress Sterling with how much I've changed, maybe learning how to suck cock properly isn't a bad idea.

I lick my lips and shift up onto my knees, sitting back on my heels and tucking my hair behind my ears like I'm prepping for a test. I reach down and fist his erection in my hand, staring up at his face to see if his eyes open. When they don't, I lower my head and gently press my lips to the tip of his dick.

I run my tongue along the soft skin of his shaft from root to the tip. Sam shifts suddenly and expels a deep, gruff moan. I look up, and he still seems dead to the world, but his penis is most definitely alive. Alive and throbbing.

I open my mouth and take him as far back into my throat as I can. When I pull back, the sucking noise is loud in the room, but the sound just encourages me more, so I open my mouth and do it again, enjoying the feel of his slick cock along my tongue. My eager rhythm causes my hair to fall in a sheet around my face, and suddenly, hands are in my hair. I look up to see Sam's amused eyes on me as he gently gathers my hair into a ponytail and holds it back for me.

"Morning," he husks with a lazy smile.

I flinch at being caught in action and wipe my lower lip before sitting up and replying stupidly, "Um…morning."

His smile widens. "Breakfast is self-serve today?"

I slap my hands over my face in mortification. Mumbling against my palms, I reply, "I was testing a theory…for science."

Sam sits up on his elbows, his eyes alight with amusement as he gazes down at my naked body. "Which is?"

I shrug. "I just…wanted to see if it was as good as last night."

He nods thoughtfully and then lies back, propping his hand under his head as he stares up at the ceiling "Well please, don't let me interrupt a scientific experiment. Pretend I'm not even here."

I laugh at that response but then glance down at his throbbing cock again. "Okay, I'll try it but just don't move too much."

"You got it, sparky." He winks, and it's so sweet that I feel brave enough to try it again.

With a small grin, I lean down and take him in my mouth again, this time a lot less gently since I'm no longer worried about waking him. I work him over in quick succession, and the noises in the room are so loud I would be embarrassed if he wasn't moaning his appreciation. Sam does that hair holding thing again, but this time, his other hand runs up and down my spine in slow, soft strokes. It feels kind of wonderful.

His dick suddenly feels like it's even harder in my mouth, and before I'm able to finish him off, he grabs me under the arms and pulls me away from his dick. "What are you doing?" I ask, staring down at him as he reaches for a condom on the nightstand.

"I'm not coming down your throat, Maggie," he states, his voice gruff with arousal as he rolls the condom on in record speed.

"Why not? I thought this was for science!"

He shakes his head. "Baby steps, okay? Right now, I'm dying for you to ride my cock."

Well, okay. In a hurry, I throw a leg over his groin and position his tip against my slit. "How's this?" I ask as I sink down on top of him.

His head falls back into the pillow, and he lets out a deep groan. "Oh fuck yes, just like that."

I balance my hands on his chest and swirl my hips over him, feeling his entire body hard and tight beneath mine. Reaching up to cup my breasts, he stares straight into my eyes as he manhandles them with his rough palms, rolling my nipples between his finger and thumb. I cry out at the sensation overload, my body mindlessly rocking faster on top of him.

Sam sits up, brushing his lips with mine. A gentle caress at first, but I pull his face back to me for something deeper, something more. A stir of pleasure grows inside me as I suck his tongue and continue moving. Sam braces himself on the bed and thrusts up into me so perfectly, causing my orgasm to hit fast and hard.

Soon, I forget where I am or what I was trying to figure out in the first place, and I lose myself in the delirious climax that's like sparklers shooting off inside all my extremities. Sam's guttural tone is deep and wet in my ear as he falls back against the bed and attempts to catch his breath.

I slip off him, lying back on his arm and staring up at the ceiling with him. "Did you figure out what you were trying to figure out...for science, I mean?" he asks, his voice ragged.

I nod slowly, my mind spinning with this new information. "I'm afraid I did."

"And what was your conclusion?" he asks, pulling off the condom and knotting it like a pro before tossing it into a tissue.

I exhale heavily and pull the sheet up over my chest before turning on my side to face him. He mirrors my position.

I pick at the edge of the sheet when I state, "I wanted to see if sex would be any different with you this morning than it was last night."

"Different how?" he asks, tipping his finger under my chin so I'm forced to look at him.

My brows rise in surrender. "Like...less incredible."

He frowns at that. "Why would you want it to be less incredible?"

"I don't...I just, when I compare it to what I've had, I think that maybe perhaps I've been missing something."

Sam does that adorable shy smile thing again, the one that makes me want to kiss his face off. Except for this time, it's a bit more smug than usual. I roll my eyes and shift to the other side of the bed.

"What?" he exclaims, moving in behind me. "I can't help but be a little arrogant. You're madly in love with this quarterback, and you basically just told me I'm better at sex than he is."

"I didn't say those words!" I exclaim, my body going

stiff with annoyance. "Would you just shut up? I don't think we have to talk about this, all right?"

"Okay, okay," he says but then moves in to whisper in my ear. "But I think it'd be a good idea if we do some more experiments in the shower…for the good of science."

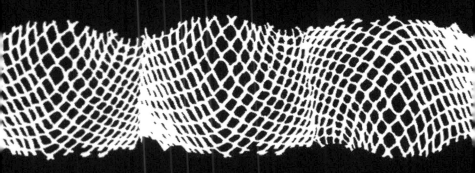

CHAPTER 14

I'm A Man Of Few Words—Let's Fish

Sam

Sparky: So is it just me or does this week feel super flipping boring?

I grab my phone and move from the Tire Depot front counter to the display of chrome rims before I reply.

Me: It's not just you.

Sparky: I keep thinking about this weekend.

Me: Me too.

Sparky: And I'm not thinking about the snowboarding.

The smile on my face is embarrassing.

Me: What are you thinking about? Specifically.

Sparky: About how you had to help me off the toilet because my legs felt like Jell-O.

Me: God, that was really hot.

Sparky: I know, right?

Me: What else are you thinking about?

Sparky: Are you trying to get me to sext with you right now?

Me: Sparky, I'm a gentleman. I would never do that. What are you wearing?

Sparky: That's a sext! You're at work right now, pervy old man.

Me: It's not a sext. It's for science.

Sparky: What kind of science?

Me: I'm trying to determine if I'm psychic or not. See, I think you're wearing that hot pink bra you had on under that snowsuit the first time we met. And I think that's all you're wearing.

Sparky: You're so wrong, it's comical.

Me: If you tell me you're wearing granny panties, I'll still be turned on.

Sparky: OMG, you should be embarrassed.

Me: Yet…I'm not.

There's a short pause.

Sparky: What are you wearing?

Me: There's my spark plug from the weekend.

Sparky: I'll tell you mine if you tell me yours. ☺

"Sammy, can you come in here please?" Uncle Terry hollers from the back office so loudly my heart jumps into my throat.

I send a quick 'got to go' text to Maggie and make my way into his office, feeling like a kid who just got his hand caught in the cookie jar.

When I step in through the door, I look around and see that the office looks completely different from how it looked this morning. "Where's all your stuff?" I ask, glancing around at all the empty walls that were completely covered last week.

"Have a seat," he says, gesturing to one of the chairs in front of him.

Even though I do as he asks, I'm frowning the entire time. I presented him my proposal two days ago, and he's been quiet around me ever since. But Uncle Terry has always been a man of few words. Sometimes, it's hard to believe he's my dad's brother because they are two completely different guys. Where my dad was unreliable and impulsive, Terry is steadfast and responsible. He may be a little quiet and closed off, but he's always there for me when I need him.

"Sammy, I'm heading out today." Terry sits back in his chair and folds his fingers over his belly.

I nod reflexively. "That's no problem. I can close up the shop if you need to duck out early."

Terry leans across his desk and purses his lips. "No, I'm really heading out today, Sammy. I'm going to finish the day out and then I'm hitting the road. I won't be coming back for a while."

"What?" I ask, my voice rising in pitch. "What are you talking about? We were supposed to have the next six months together."

He shakes his head. "I looked over that business

proposal of yours with my financial advisor, and we are both seriously impressed. It's well thought out with contingencies and troubleshooting options. It's so great that I'm going to take my Tire Depot money that you've been paying me for years and become one of the silent investors you need to make it work."

"Are you kidding me?" I ask, standing up and forking my fingers through my hair. "Are you messing with me, Terry?"

He shakes his head. "Not when it comes to business, Sammy. This idea to expand and use Miles's knowledge with classic cars is going to be incredible. I can't wait to see it all come together."

My smile is huge as I sit back down and take a deep breath. "So why are you leaving today, though? This proposal is a five-year plan."

"You don't need me anymore, Sammy." He shrugs and gets a proud, fatherly look about him. "The student has surpassed the teacher in every damn way possible. Hell, you've been running this place for the past year as it is. You don't need some old guy hanging around and holding you back."

"You don't hold me back, Terry," I state, my brow furrowing as I lean in and make direct eye contact. "You hold me up."

Moisture shines in his eyes, and with a gruff, throaty noise, he presses his hands to his desk and stands up to walk over to me. I stand to meet him, and he cups my face in a tight grip, his eyes severe on mine as he says, "You hold yourself up, Sammy. And you hold up everyone around you."

I shake my head, my voice thick with emotion. "What if I'm not ready for you to go?"

He exhales through his nose and pats my cheek. "I'm not leaving you for good, pal, all right? I'm a phone call away, and if you need me to come back, I'll drop everything and do it. You know I will."

I nod and look down, unable to meet his eyes because I'm overwhelmed at what this day has turned into. I'm excited that this is finally happening, but it's the end of an era with my uncle, whom I've grown very close to.

"You're hearing me, right?" he husks, dipping his head down to catch my downcast eyes. "I'm not leaving you. You're my family—and nothing changes that."

He pins me with a look that says so many things we rarely talk about. Things about my own dad and everything that happened in the past. "I got it, Uncle Terry."

"I'm not your father," he states for good measure, shocking me by even mentioning him at this moment. "But you need to know that I'm really fucking proud of you."

I take a deep breath in and exhale before replying. "Thank you, Terry. Seriously. You've set me up for life, and I'll never forget it."

"Nonsense. You set yourself up." He pulls me in for a back-slapping hug, and when things get too emotional, he releases me with a shove and makes his way out of the office. "You should take the rest of the day off because this office is yours starting tomorrow, and bosses rarely get a day off."

With those parting words, he walks out, closing the

door behind him as he goes. I turn around in a circle, taking the space in. It's nothing special. Chipped sheetrock in desperate need of paint. A cheap, veneer-topped desk that's seen better days, and an old sofa and coffee table that haven't been replaced since the nineties. It's basic as fuck.

And it's all mine.

I thrust my fists into the air and do a seriously unmanly victory dance because goddamnit, I'm really doing this. I'm turning Tire Depot into Miles's and my dream job. I'm going to get to work with my best friend for the rest of my life. It always seemed like a pipe dream to do all this, and now it's a reality.

When I twirl around for a third time, a pair of pale blue eyes halt me in my tracks. "Fuck, Maggie, what are you doing here?" I sputter, awkwardly moving my hands around to find a more manly position that doesn't resemble jazz hands.

Maggie's eyes are glowing with amusement as she clutches a bag to her chest. "Sorry, the guys said I could come on back. I should have figured you were busy when you said you had to go." She bites her lip to stop herself from laughing, and I want to fucking die.

I grip the back of my neck and flex my bicep in the most douchebaggiest of ways, but it's all I can think about when I'm this mortified. "This isn't what it looks like."

She steps in, not even trying to hide her smile anymore. "It looked like you were dancing in here all by yourself."

I blink rapidly at her. "I guess it's exactly what it looks like." I roll my eyes and gesture toward the door. "I just got some really exciting news, and I guess I was freaking out about it."

"What news?" she asks, closing the door and giving me her undivided attention.

"My uncle just basically handed Tire Depot over to me."

"Wow!" she exclaims, tucking the small paper bag she has under her arm and walking over to me for a hug. "Congratulations, Sam. That is so exciting!"

I inhale her flowery scent as her free hand tightens around my neck. She feels just as good in my arms today as she did this weekend when I held her in that shower. Plus, she still hasn't told me what she's wearing.

I pull back and smile awkwardly. "I mean, he didn't just give it to me. I've been buying him out. And it's just a tire store, but it's exciting. I've been working for this for a long time."

"It's not just a tire store," she retorts, giving me a playful shove. "It's Tire Depot, home of the famous erotic romance novelist, Mercedes Lee Loveletter!"

Her use of Kate's pen name has me throwing my head back in laughter. "Damn right. I forgot we're basically famous in the romance reader world."

"Your cookies and exceptional service are famous," Maggie replies, bobbing her head from side to side and offering her own little victory dance that makes me laugh.

"So what are you doing here anyway?" I ask, releasing her from the comfort of my arms. "Did you come to tell me in person what you were wearing?"

Maggie's cheeks flush as she holds up a to-go bag. "I was

in line for sandwiches when you were texting me. It's been a few days since I saw you, and since I'm now "*feeling better,*" she says with finger quotes, "I decided to bring you some lunch as a thank you for taking such good care of me this weekend."

She shows me the logo on the side of the Yellow Deli sandwich bag, and I lift my brows in appreciation. "Hey, I'm just glad you're feeling better," I reply with a playful waggle of my brows. "It was a lot of work taking care of you."

"Thank you so much for your sacrifice." She giggles, tipping her chin up with a smile so adorable that I can't help but lower my head and taste it. My tongue feels like it's operating on muscle memory as it instantly slips past her lips and tangles with hers, massaging it in sexy, unhindered strokes. The sandwich bag is smashed between our chests as my hands glide around her waist and pull her body tightly against mine. She moans her appreciation, and I'd be lying if I didn't admit to thinking about how easy it would be to fuck her on this empty desk right here, right now and find out what color bra she has on with my own damn eyes.

A familiar voice suddenly booms down the hallway. "Sam, you son of a bitch!"

Maggie and I shoot apart like a couple of teenagers caught by their parents just as Miles bursts through the door with a big, dopey smile on his face. His eyes land on Maggie and then his brow crinkles in confusion. "Meg, what are you doing here?"

Maggie's eyes nearly bug out of her head as she rush-es over and thrusts the food sack into her brother's unsuspecting hands. "I brought you guys sandwiches."

"You did? Score!" Miles takes the bag and moves past Maggie over to the empty chair in front of my desk. I discreetly find my way to the other side of the desk to conceal the situation that happened to pop up while Maggie and I were kissing.

Maggie grips the doorknob and barks out in clipped tones, "It was a thank you for Sam bringing me soup this weekend." Her voice sounds like a fucking robot, and I try to smile at her to get her to relax a little.

"Aw, Megs, that's nice of you!" Miles replies with a hearty thumbs up. "But you really didn't have to. I just found out this fucker is my official boss now, so he can afford to buy his own damn lunch."

I narrow my eyes at my supposed best friend. "Since I'm your boss now, does that mean I get to pick which sandwich I want?" My tone is flat because, in the back of my mind, I'm thinking about how much I'd rather be eating this food with Maggie instead of her brother.

"No way, man," Miles replies with a wink and begins digging into the bag. "But that doesn't mean we're not celebrating tomorrow night after you finish your first official day flying solo!"

"Yeah? What'd you have in mind?" I ask, rubbing the back of my neck awkwardly because I'd already been brainstorming of ways to see Maggie all week long.

"You, Me, Kate, and Megs. Pearl Street pub crawl. We need to celebrate this momentous achievement for you."

"Sounds fun!" Maggie exclaims and then flicks an

awkward wave in our direction. "I'd better be going. See you tomorrow, Sam!"

"Thanks for the sandwich, Maggie," I state, wistfully checking her ass out as she walks away.

When I look at my best friend in front of me, who literally has yellow mustard on his chin, my boner from earlier slinks away in defeat. We eat our sandwiches and map out our plans for tomorrow night, but as soon as Miles leaves my office, I realize that I can't wait until tomorrow to see Maggie. I bust out my phone and shoot her a text.

Me: Have your snowsuit with you?

Sparky: Is this more sexting? Cuz I gotta say, I think you're bad at it.

Me: Mind out of the gutter, Sparky. Answer the question.

Sparky: Yes, the snowsuit is in my trunk...why?

Me: I'm taking the afternoon off. Meet me at Marv's in twenty minutes.

A huge smile is stuck on my face as I head out to Marv's, which could be flipping Disney World based on how happy I feel right now. But fucking hell, today has been a great day, and I want to embrace it. I'm taking over Tire Depot, my plans to expand with Miles by my side are moving forward, and I get a rare Thursday afternoon off to go ice fishing. Life is fucking good.

When I walk into Marv's Bait and Tackle, Maggie is already inside, decked out in her adorable red and white snowsuit and hunched over a tank of minnows as she has Marv in complete stitches. Honestly, I didn't even know Marv knew how to laugh. I sort of just figured his face was stuck in a permanent wrinkly scowl, but Maggie chatting his ear off clearly indicates otherwise.

As I walk toward her, I have flashbacks of the first time I saw her in here and how out of place she seemed then. Now, she looks like one of the guys…with a really hot ass and sexy long dark hair sticking out from her stocking cap.

When I move to stand beside Maggie, Marv is positively howling with laughter. It's a strange smoker's chortle that makes me worry about how many years he has left on this earth.

"You say they ran off with your clothes?" he sputters, coughing out a wet noise from his throat around his barks of laughter.

"They sure did! We had to run all the way back into our cabin in the buff!" Maggie exclaims and then turns to acknowledge me. "Hi, Sam! I was just telling Marv about our fun weekend."

"Oh, I'm glad you're telling him only the good stuff," I deadpan, narrowing my eyes at her.

Maggie purses her lips together. "Well, I could tell him about your big rod instead?"

"That's enough for today, sparky!" I wrap my arm around her head so I can cover her mouth with my palm. I lean over the counter, and say casually, "Talk to me, Marv. Where are we fishing at today, and what kind of bait do you think will get the job done?"

Marv gets to work helping me, but I swear to fuck, his eyes have a twinkle in them as he scoops up some minnows into a tub and hands them over to Maggie. Minutes later, Maggie and I are in my truck and driving out toward a secluded spot called Fawn Lake.

"No snowmobile this time?" she asks from the passenger seat as she adjusts her seat belt.

"Nah, I didn't want to waste time running all the way home first."

She shakes her head sadly. "That's a shame. I thought maybe you'd let me drive this time."

"Did you now?" I give her the side-eye with a mischievous glint. "Is that to get a picture for your ex or just for fun?" I blurt out the last question without thinking and instantly wish I could take it back.

Why am I bringing that fucker up in the first place? I shouldn't give a shit about him because Maggie and I aren't long term. Yes, I'm doing something different with her than I've ever done with any girl, but that doesn't change the fact that we're temporary. Like a catch and release.

Her brow furrows, and I think my comment may have hurt her feelings when she turns to look out the window. "Not everything is about Sterling."

I feel bad for zapping our happy mood, so I reach over and squeeze her thigh playfully. "I think Marv might have a sled. If you keep sweet-talking him the way you were, I'm sure he'd take you for a spin."

"Maybe I will," she chirps and turns to stick her tongue out at me. "If I become buddies with him, then I won't need you anymore, that's for sure."

I laugh at that response. "I know he's a better fisherman, but I'm afraid I can't report back on his big rod."

She giggles, and the mood goes right back to easy and fun. A few minutes later, we pull up to the lake and make quick work of setting up the fishing hut. Maggie remembers a lot of the setup instructions from the previous two times, so it goes really smoothly. Once we step inside, I fire up the propane heater before helping Maggie bait her hook.

A comfortable silence falls over us as we bounce our rigs in the augered holes, and I can't help but think about how easy it is to fish with Maggie. I've gone all these years without ever taking another person ice fishing with me because of the memories I had with my dad. But then Maggie barreled into my life, and everything feels different now. Less ominous and heavy. Lighter and brighter even. If it weren't for her, I'd probably still be a lonely fisherman out here thinking about shit from my past that doesn't mean a damn thing about my future.

"So are you ready to be the real boss tomorrow then?" Maggie asks, breaking our silence as she glances down at the video monitor that's illuminating the water below.

I shrug my shoulders dismissively. "My uncle Terry seems to think I'm ready, so I guess so."

"Are you pretty close to your uncle?" she asks, turning to look at me with wide, curious eyes.

"Yeah, we're close," I reply and have immediate flash-backs of him helping me out when I was a teenager. "I've worked for him forever. Honestly, if it weren't for him, I would probably be walking a very different path in my life."

"How so?" Maggie asks, still watching me thoughtfully.

I exhale heavily at how loaded that simple question is. But somehow sharing it with Maggie doesn't seem as stressful as it is to share with anyone else, so I clear my throat and reply. "I used to get in a lot of fights when I was in high school, and my mom never really knew what to do with me. She was good with the girls, but with me, she'd always just cry. I'd feel bad for letting her down, but then the next day, someone would say something and set me off again." I swallow a knot forming in my throat over that memory. "But then Uncle Terry stepped in and helped get my head on straight. He hired me to work at Tire Depot after school, and he hung this boxing bag up in the shop and taught me how to box out my aggression there instead of on some random asshole's face."

Maggie chuckles softly. "That seems wise…and also explains why that guy went down so hard at Marv's that first day."

I wince at that reminder. "Yeah, that's the first time I've punched a guy in years, but that asshole had it coming with those disgusting comments. I don't even feel bad about it because it felt really fucking good."

She giggles, and I can't help but laugh along with her. "But as a kid, I needed somewhere to my direct my anger. I was young and full of hormones…always on the verge of snapping at the stupidest shit."

"Why was that, do you think? Was having three older sisters driving you crazy?" She watches me expectantly, having no idea how deep of a question she just asked.

To be fair, not many people do. Not even Miles. My childhood is not something I share with people. But for some reason, Maggie feels like a safe space. Like this weird in-between person who doesn't truly exist in my real world because everything we do together is a secret. And when I stare into her lake blue eyes, I see something that makes me want to share. Something deep and meaningful. Something not casual.

I clear my throat and stare down at my hands squeezing tightly around my fishing pole. "Um, I don't think I ever told you, but it was actually my dad who taught me how to ice fish."

Maggie tilts her head curiously at my change in direction. "Oh, that's cool. You haven't mentioned your dad before."

I swallow slowly as an old ache builds in my chest. It feels like a heavy boot pushing down on me that I want to shove off my body. "Yeah…it was about the only cool thing he ever did with me."

Maggie absorbs that statement for a few seconds before asking, "Where does he live?"

"Fuck, who knows," I reply with a self-deprecating huff. I stretch my legs out around the ice hole and shake my head from side to side. "He skipped out on us when I was fourteen. He's got mental issues, and…well, my childhood with him wasn't easy."

Maggie moves closer, her eyes trained on me with a seriousness that makes me anxious. "What kind of mental issues?"

Memories begin flooding back into my mind's eye, causing me to flinch because I haven't thought about my dad in months. Even when my mom asked me if I went ice fishing with him a couple of weeks ago, I let it go in one ear and out the other. But something about seeing someone else's reaction to your truth brings back all the old feelings that live dormant inside you.

"He has bipolar disorder, which isn't a problem when he's taking care of himself, but he would go off his meds a lot and get manic. It was always really fucking scary. Fishing was the one thing that would sort of re-center him. Ice fishing more than anything, though. I think it's because it's contained, you know? When we were in the hut, it was like he could finally quiet his mind.

"When I was a teenager, he started going off his meds a lot more. And then one day, he just completely disappeared on us. My mom had the cops searching for him everywhere. And when they finally found him, he was living with this other family that he'd been lying to us about for years."

"Oh my god," Maggie groans, and I look over to see the pain on her face. It's a familiar look. One that I remember seeing as a teenager when word spread around Boulder that our dad had abandoned us.

"Apparently, he had another wife and child in a town about two hours away who knew nothing about us or the fact that he was already married. It was a mess."

"What an ass," Maggie says, her upper lip curled with disdain.

I nod in agreement because it's true. I'm well past ever

defending anything my father did. "He tried to blame his disorder on a lot of his choices, but that was bullshit too. He was just a bad guy. He even stole money from Tire Depot, which he built from the ground up with my uncle Terry."

Maggie goes silent for a moment as the heaviness of everything sinks in. "Where is he now?"

"With that other woman still," I reply with a shrug. "Last I heard, they moved to Nevada."

"So you guys don't ever see him?" She looks so young and sad as she asks that question. As if she can't fathom a life with a deadbeat dad. And I'm glad she can't. I hope she never loses that innocence about her. It reminds me that there are still good people left in this world.

"Sometimes when he's off his meds, he shows up, says he misses us and wants to meet his grandkids. My sisters refuse him, and I always end up having to throw him out of my mom's house. It's a fucking mess. Everyone hates him for choosing the other family. I just don't give a shit about him anymore."

"I don't blame you," Maggie says, mindlessly reeling in her line.

"My uncle is the kind of guy I want to be. If he hadn't taken me under his wing, I don't know where I'd be right now. I am who I am because of him."

The backs of my eyes burn with unshed tears as the weight of that statement sinks in. To think about how my uncle had to be so angry with his own brother yet still embrace his brother's son the way he did is a remarkable thing. And the fact he trusts me with a business he started with my father, who not only abandoned his wife and kids but also his brother and business partner...a lot of trust is between us. Trust that I don't take for granted.

"I can't imagine how that would feel as a kid," Maggie says gravely. "To be ice fishing with your dad one day, and the next day, he's gone for good. My brain can't even comprehend how someone could leave their family like that."

I nod in agreement. "Honestly though, I don't even try to understand it all anymore. Now that I'm older, I'm just over it. I refuse to give headspace to someone who can hurt me that deeply ever again."

I feel Maggie's eyes on me when she asks, "Do you think that's why you don't do long-term relationships?"

I jerk my head back in surprise at her change in direction. "No," I reply instantly, and she raises her eyebrows. "No," I confirm and then exhale heavily because I feel like she's trying to look right through me. "When I was younger, I was really freaked out that I was like my dad, so I avoided relationships like the plague. But now that I'm older, and I know I don't have the disorder, I just like my life the way it is. Everything I do is on my terms."

She shakes her head from side to side. "I don't know, Sam. If these past few weeks have taught me anything, it's that I want someone special to bait my hook for me, you know?"

"Thankfully, I can bait my own hook," I grumble, looking down at our poles in the water. "We're two very different people, sparky."

She presses her lips together and shrugs. "I don't think we are. Your passion is people, and that can extend far beyond family and your employees." Maggie's eyes are sparkling as she turns to look at me. "You have a big heart, Sam, and I think you'd be surprised at how wonderful it feels to give it away to someone extraordinary."

I can't help but smile at her optimism. She's perched on that stool, looking adorable with a fishing pole in her hand and speaking passionately about her grandiose ideas of love—it's certainly never a conversation I've had while ice fishing.

Yet somehow, she's inserted herself into a part of my soul that not many people have. The fact that I'm hanging out with her after we've had sex is already very telling. But it's not just the sex that draws me back to Maggie. It's her open optimism. I think it's starting to rub off on me. Maybe her romantic ideals aren't as naïve as I once thought. Maybe my future could look different if I wanted it to.

The next few hours are full of less deep talking and more deep fishing. A school of fish shows up, and it's a flurry of catch and release for the entire afternoon. It's a good thing this excursion is a secret because this is the kind of fishing day that your friends wouldn't believe anyway.

When we're tired out for the day, we tear down and hop back into my truck to make our way back to Marv's. I pause before backing out of my parking spot because something has been on the tip of my tongue all afternoon, and this might be the only time I have the guts to actually say it.

"Thanks for coming with me today," I say stupidly because that is so not what I was going to say.

"Anytime!" she beams, her dark hair framing her

beautiful face like a picture. "I feel like ice fishing might actually be the only adventurous thing I don't suck at."

I chuckle and run my hand through my beard nervously. "Listen, though…um…I've never talked to Miles about my dad stuff. I mean, he knows my dad ditched our family for another family, but he doesn't know all the mental stuff. So if we could keep that between us, that would be great."

Maggie's eyes warm with affection as she reaches out to touch my hand resting on the bench between us. "Sam, you can trust me."

I exhale the weight on my shoulders. "I think I was just feeling sentimental today. My uncle's been my rock…with him leaving, it all just kind of drudged up old memories."

"I get it," she says, lacing her fingers with mine and offering me a soft smile of reassurance. "I'm honored you shared all that with me."

I lick my lips because I'm still not saying what I want to say, and I feel like a fucking pansy because of it. Instead, I stare down at our clasped hands. Holding hands with a girl seems so simple and basic. Like something anyone can do. But the view of her delicate fingers tangled with mine feels important and maybe even a little extraordinary. My eyes move up to look into Maggie's, and something grows inside my chest as she stares back at me with so much openness and vulnerability. It's overpowering.

I swallow hard. "Maggie, my dad is the only other person I've ever gone ice fishing with."

"What do you mean?" she asks, her brows knitting together.

My heart thunders in my chest when I reply "I mean... I've never gone ice fishing with anyone else since he left seventeen years ago. Not even Miles."

Silence falls over us as she takes in my words. I'm not even sure what they mean exactly or why I was so desperate to tell her, but I just felt like I needed her to know. Ice fishing is so simple, but it means a lot to me. And having her fish with me means something to me as well.

"Why me?" she asks, her voice quiet and her eyes glossy as they connect with mine. Letting out a half-assed laugh, she adds, "Because I was so needy that day?"

I stare back at her, my body tense as I reply. "Actually, I think at that moment, I was the one who needed you."

Maggie's brows pinch together, and I suddenly feel too far away from her. I slide over from behind the wheel to sit in the middle spot closer to her. "I feel like I saw something in you that day at Marv's that I lost in myself after my dad left." I reach out and brush the backs of my fingers down her cheek. "A spark."

She smiles a small, almost invisible smile, but that crease in her cheeks shows up, and it makes her whole face light up. "That's why you call me sparky."

I nod slowly. "For years, I started fights, seeking out thrills and taking up dangerous hobbies. I was an adventurist, but I never truly took any chances." I take a deep breath. "I took a chance on you because that spark you have is something I want back."

Maggie inhales sharply, her smile completely vanishing as she reaches out and cups my cheek. "I promise you, Sam, your spark is alive and well."

I shake my head, refusing to believe her words because I know I'm different. I know I'm closed off. I can feel it when I'm with my family and watching Miles with Kate. There's an innocence they all have that I don't give purchase to in my heart.

Maggie shifts beside me, and in one swift move, she unbuckles her seat belt and crawls up onto my lap with one leg propped on either side of me. She runs her hands along the side of my face, and I turn into her touch, brushing my lips against her palm to feel the warmth of her embrace. To feel her skin against my lips. The touch sends shivers all the way down my spine, and I swear my heart expands inside my chest.

"Your spark is right here," she states firmly before leaning in and kissing me.

Her kiss is gentle at first—tender and reassuring—but it's not enough. I want to consume her right now. I want to taste her spark and steal some of it for myself so I can always have a piece of her with me long after our crazy ride ends.

I spread her lips with my tongue and thrust into her sweet, gentle mouth while sliding my hands up her back and clutching her firmly to me. A frenzy stirs inside me because I feel like no matter how hard I try, I can't get her close enough. Our mouths meld together in perfect harmony, but it's still not enough. I want her clothes off now. I want this snowsuit burned, and her body laid out bare for me to devour.

She pulls away for a breath, her hands falling from my face to the zipper on her chest, clearly having the same needs as mine at this moment. She unzips her snowsuit to reveal that same hot pink bra she had on the first time we fished together. I smile and thank fuck I didn't know she was wearing nothing under this suit before now, or I would have thought of nothing else all afternoon.

It's all too perfect. She's too perfect.

I take a brief second to glance out all the windows and ensure we're still the only vehicle around. When the coast is clear, I bury my face in her breasts, rubbing my stubbled jaw against her soft skin, the desire to mark her strong as I reach back and unclasp her bra. Her giggles bounce off the walls of my truck as I free the offensive fabric and toss it away with a grunt.

Grabbing her hips, I turn us so she's laid out on the bench below me with her legs wrapped tightly around my waist. Dropping a soft kiss to her lips, I murmur, "You know this means I'm going to show you my big rod, right?"

She bursts out laughing, and that spark inside me returns with a vengeance. And it's all because of this girl who I think I could be falling for hook, line, and sinker.

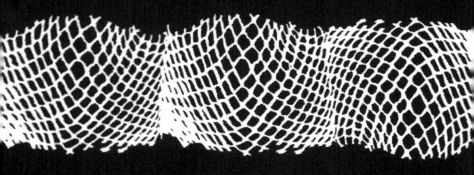

CHAPTER 15

Tall Fish Tales Told Here

Maggie

After hooking up with Sam in his truck, my mind is consumed with how it's possible that sex with him has been exceptional every damn time. I thought our weekend away was a fluke, and it only felt good because it was like vacation sex. Vacation sex is always the best sex because you're on vacation. But then you get back to the real world, and the sex becomes completely ordinary again.

But with Sam, it didn't.

What happened in his truck yesterday was *Titanic*-epic sex. We were Jack and Rose, steaming up the windows and putting finger smears all over the fogged-up glass for over an hour. I never knew I was capable of multiple orgasms, let alone multiple orgasms inside the cab of a truck.

The sex was so amazing that I've been pouting about it ever since because all I can think about is the fact that these orgasms have an end date. And then, I'll likely be having sex with Sterling for the rest of my life. Sterling will be the last dick I ever have!

I mean, don't get me wrong, he's not bad at sex. I orgasm half the time. He just seems to lack any creativity. His go-to technique is to jackhammer any chance he gets. Sam is very different. He reads my body and speeds up and slows down at the most delicious times. And his occasional dirty talk doesn't hurt either.

I'm just finishing my makeup for our big pub crawl tonight when Kate comes striding into my room. She looks me up and down, and a huge smile spreads across her face. "Holy shit, you look fucking hot."

My jaw drops, and I quickly look down at my fitted burgundy sweater dress and black plaid tights. "What? Does it look like I'm trying too hard?"

"It looks like you're dressing for a guy," Kate says, waggling her eyebrows and flopping down on the bed.

"Well, I didn't exactly pack a month's worth of clothes. I never really planned to stay in Boulder this long." I glance around my brother's spare bedroom that I've basically made my own home. "Are you guys getting sick of me here?"

Kate shakes her head adamantly. "No way! You're an easy house guest, and you cook...I'd sister wife you if it wasn't for the fact that you're related to my man friend, and incest is illegal and stuff."

I cringe at that response, but I'm not at all surprised

anymore by the crazy stuff that comes out of Kate's mouth. She is always saying something inappropriate that makes my brother smile like I've never seen him smile. Her perverseness is weirdly heartwarming.

"Yeah, no sister wife for me, thanks. I have man problems to worry about. I don't need to add girl problems to the mix."

Kate sits up on her knees, her curly red hair cascading around her shoulders. "So come on. I haven't had any alone time with you all week. How was last weekend? Tell me everything!" She mimes the act of eating popcorn out of a bowl in anticipation for what she thinks is going to be some epic storytelling.

She's going to be disappointed. "I'm telling you nothing," I reply and reach out to dump out her bowl of fake popcorn.

"Why not?" she groans and tosses fake kernels at my face. "It was my quick thinking that got you a weekend alone with Sam Bam Thank You Ma'am anyway."

I roll my eyes and bite my lip at that very apt description of him.

"Oh my god, Meg, you're blushing!" Kate exclaims with wide eyes. "Look at you! Completely blotchy! It must have been amazing!"

I roll my eyes and flop down on the bed beside her. "It was very enlightening."

Kate nods eagerly. "So you did the deed."

I grimace because I know I'm totally folding under her intense scrutiny. "We fooled around, yes."

"And it was awesome." She squeals with delight and chucks a pillow at me. "I knew Sam was packing some serious wood in there. He walks around way too confidently for a ginger."

I frown at that remark. "Can I ask you something, Kate?"

"Um, duh, ask me anything!" She sits cross-legged and tucks her hair behind her ears, ready for my questions.

Fiddling with the hem of my dress, I ask, "Okay, so in your past...were some guys just way better at sex than others?"

"A resounding yes," she replies instantly.

I look at her through narrowed eyes. "Okay...was there like...a way to fix that?"

"Wait, is Sam bad at sex or Sterling?" Kate asks, her brows furrowed in confusion.

My eyes cast downward as I mumble, "Sterling."

"Yikes," Kate replies, the corners of her lips angling downward with a grimace. "Your future hubby? That's not good."

"But it's not a deal breaker surely," I argue with pleading eyes. "Sex isn't that important. Or surely, he will get better with time. I mean, Sam is older and more experienced than Sterling. That's a big part of it, right?"

Kate chews her lip thoughtfully as though she's trying to find the right words and not just say the first thing that pops into her mind. "I don't know any other way to say this, Meg, so I'm just going to say it. Sex isn't about mechanics or instructions. It isn't about getting better with practice and experience. It's about the connection."

I nod eagerly. "Yes, connection! Sterling and I are so deeply connected."

Kate shakes her head. "I'm not talking about Sterling, babe. I saw you together on Christmas Eve. You guys had been together for several months, right? But it felt like I was looking at two strangers, not two people who couldn't keep their hands off each other. Honestly, I think that's why Miles liked Sterling so much. The guy has zero sexual chemistry. He's like an amoeba or something. Aren't those the single cell animals that just have sex with themselves?"

"Kate," I groan, my fingers combing through my hair in frustration. "My ex-boyfriend is not an asexual amoeba."

Kate shrugs dismissively. "But if the sex isn't great, I'd be worried about your connection."

"That doesn't make any sense," I argue, feeling my blood pressure rise. "I barely know Sam, and we had like mind-blowing, incredible sex."

"Connection isn't about knowing what someone's favorite color is, or how they take their coffee, or even what your future will look like together." Kate balls her hands up into fists and touches her chest. "It's about seeing their soul. Noticing their nonverbal body cues, their noises, having an instinct about who they are and what they need."

A knot forms in my throat at the idea that sex with Sterling might never compare to sex with Sam. And the fact that I hooked up with Sam at all means that for the rest of my life, I will always compare Sterling to Sam. Now I'm in an even more difficult position than I was to begin with!

"Why did you push me into Sam's arms, Kate?" I ask, feeling tears prick the backs of my eyes as panic presses in all around me.

"Whoa, Megan…I didn't push you. I just…thought you might need to give someone else a chance while you were single."

"But I don't want anyone else. I want Sterling!" *Right?* My mind spins over the fact that he's who I'm destined to be with. It was love at first sight. *You don't walk away from the rareness of love at first sight!* my inner psyche exclaims as my anxiety builds into a full-on freak-out.

Kate's eyes go wide, and she looks a little scared of me. I'd be scared of me too. I'm flailing around in Boulder like a fish out of water with no direction in my life. Just mindlessly flopping around, hoping someone picks me up and releases me back into the water. But if they don't hold my tail and release me before I'm ready, I'm freaking dead!

The walls are closing in all around me, and because I don't want to have a complete meltdown in front of my brother's girlfriend, I plaster on a fake smile, and say, "Okay…well, thanks for the talk, Kate. You've given me a lot to think about. I'm going to finish getting ready now!"

Kate freezes, staring at me with guilt-stricken eyes. "Megan, can I give you some advice?"

"No, thank you…I'm all set right now!" I exclaim, trying to ignore the high-pitched hysteria in my voice. I need to get myself back together!

I hop off the bed and make my way over to the door. "I think I'm going to give Sterling a call before we leave, so I'd better hurry and finish getting ready."

Kate rises from the bed and slinks over to me, her eyes piercing through me the entire time. When she reaches me, she leans on the door frame and crosses her arms over her chest. "Meg, c'mon. Just tell me the truth."

"I'm good," I reply and shake my head. "I swear, I'm all good. Thanks for the chat, though."

Finally, she shakes her head slowly and walks out of the room, leaving me alone with this mess I've created my darn self.

My phone call with Sterling goes a direction I never expect- ed it to. He actually propositions me for phone sex—some- thing we've never done before. Like...ever. I mean, we're not even officially back together, so in some ways, I'm slightly offended. But then I wonder why I'm not excited by this prospect. It's a shift in our texting dynamic. Is he finally see- ing me differently now? Less basic?

However, if I am so much less basic, why did the notion of sexting with Sterling horrify me so much? When I did some light sexting with Sam...it was easy and completely natural. It was fun!

What just happened with Sterling was awkward as fuck. So awkward that my response was to blurt out that I was at Taco Bell getting a chalupa and I'd call him later. I hung up like a flipping psychopath just as Miles yelled that it was time for us to go.

Now I'm sandwiched in a truck between my brother and Kate and feeling like a kid forced to go out with her parents when all I want to do is order a chalupa and eat my feelings.

The biggest thing I'm trying to figure out is why Sterling's suggestion didn't excite me as much as it did with Sam. Two weeks ago, I would have killed to have him suggest phone sex with me because surely that's a sign he wants to get back together. Now, it just feels...odd.

I'm no longer able to inwardly freak out about my Sterling call because Miles pulls up in front of our first stop for the night. It's a place called Rayback Collective—an architectural warehouse with food trucks on the outside and a giant community bar that has a stage and lounge areas with loads of tables and couches on the inside.

I follow Miles and Kate inside, where we find Sam sitting at a high-top table in the corner. He's talking to the waitress and butterflies take flight in my belly because he doesn't look like the Sam I'm used to. He's like...sexy Sam—which I didn't even know was a thing.

He's wearing a pair of dark denim jeans with a small tear on the thigh and a pale blue button-down that reveals just a sliver of that sculpted chest I know intimately. With his gelled hair swept off to the side and freshly trimmed beard, he looks so different. He's not the rugged, manly sort of hot that he always is. Tonight, he's...mouth-wateringly hot. I swear I even hear JT singing, *"I'm bringing sexy back"* inside my damn head!

And for some reason, I'm annoyed with how friendly that waitress is. Sam suddenly turns his head, and his eyes find mine as we make our way through the crowd. It isn't until Miles claps him on the back in a bro hug that he finally looks away and acknowledges his best friend.

"How was your first day as the official owner of Tire Depot, asshat?" Miles asks, dropping down onto the stool next to Sam.

"I only thought about firing you nineteen times so, all in all, a great day." Sam stands up to pull the stool out across from him for me to sit on.

Kate's eyes flash curiously at me as I take the seat. She slides in beside me and elbows me with a smirk. I glance over to see if Miles has noticed any of this and exhale with relief when he's busy talking to the waitress.

He looks over at Kate. "You want an IPA, babe?"

"Ha-ha," she replies while rolling her eyes. "I'll have a margarita."

"And I'll have a Coors bottle," Miles adds, then looks at me expectantly.

I bite my lip, unsure why he's staring at me like that. Does he know? Does he suspect something's going on because his best friend just pulled out my stool for me?

"You want Chardonnay?" Sam asks out of nowhere. "They have good wine here."

My head jerks from side to side. "I hate wine."

He frowns back at me, and I internally kick myself because a glass of Chardonnay does sound delicious. The waitress stares impatiently at me to make my decision, so I blurt

236

out the first thing that comes to mind. "I'll have a Guinness." Both Sam's and Miles's faces contort in confusion.

"You hate beer, Megan," Miles states knowingly.

"Not anymore!" I exclaim, feeling my shoulders tense. "Sterling has me converted. He crafts his own beer sometimes." That part is actually true, so I'm grateful that at least one thing coming out of my mouth tonight isn't a total lie.

Miles shrugs, and I can feel Sam staring at me from across the table, but I refuse to look at him. The waitress heads off for our drinks, and the four of us sit there—girls on one side, boys on the other—as though we're on a flipping double date.

Miles and Sam start talking about their classic car expansion plans for Tire Depot when my phone dings inside my purse. When I pull it out, I unlock it and find a text from Sterling.

Sterling: I miss you, baby. I need to see you…soon.

My heart thunders in my chest when Kate leans over. "Who's the text from?" she asks.

I jerk my phone away so she can't see it. "No one," I reply instantly.

She eyes me suspiciously. "Stop lying. It's from *him,* isn't it?"

I roll my eyes, annoyed that she always seems to know everything. Leaning in closely, I whisper, "Yes, it's from Sterling. He says he wants to see me."

Kate's lip curls up in disgust. "Why?"

I shrug. "He said he misses me."

Kate barks out a laugh. "Does he want you back?"

My eyes go wide as I look over to see if Miles and Sam overheard anything. Thankfully, they're still engrossed in shop talk, so I lean in and hiss, "Lower your voice, okay? I don't know what he wants, but I have a feeling that could be it."

Kate averts her eyes to look at Sam. Pointing her finger back and forth between the two of us, she says, "This makes sense to me." Then she points at my phone. "That doesn't make sense to me."

"What are you talking about?" I ask with wide, pleading eyes as I wave my phone at her. "This is what I'm working toward. This is why I've been in Boulder for the past few weeks acting like some sort of woman of the woods."

She takes a long sip of her drink, grabbing an ice cube and crunching it loudly with obvious agitation. At the same time, Sam peers over at me with a tiny hint of a smile that I think is obvious only to me, but I look over to see that Kate witnessed it too.

She leans in and whispers in my ear. "Sexual chemistry with just one look, Meggie-Bear."

"Shut up, Kate," I whisper and resist the urge to push her off her stool.

The drinks arrive, and I nearly gag when I take a sip of the Guinness. It's thick like mud, and I can't believe people actually drink this shit. Sam stares at me over the top of his beer with a furrow to his brow. I'm afraid he's going to call me out on my drink, so out of nowhere, I blurt out, "I don't eat the butt ends of a loaf of bread because when we were kids, Miles told me they were human butts."

Kate sputters out a laugh, spraying her drink all over the table. "Excuse me?" she asks, wiping the dribble off her chin.

"Yep," I confirm with a jerky head nod. "I can't eat them because all I think of are butts. It's illogical because clearly, I know how bread is made and that it in no way requires human flesh as an ingredient, but every time I get a new loaf of bread, the first thing I do is throw away the butt ends so I don't have to look at them."

Miles blinks back at me like I'm a moron, and Sam is trying his hardest not to laugh, which only makes him look even sexier.

Kate is no help as she giggles uncontrollably next to me. "Here Meg, I think you should try this." She slides her drink over to me.

I lean down and take a fortifying sip, hoping like heck it will calm my nerves. Why am I being such a spaz right now? The story of the time I smeared Dippity-do hair gel all over our family dog and told Miles he was really sweaty is on the tip of my tongue…and that's not even a good story!

My eyes connect with Sam, and he seems completely confused by my actions. He can just join the club because I am confused too.

Kate diverts all our attention when she stands up from the table. "Miles, let's go check out that taco truck…I'm starving."

Miles looks over at me. "Do you know what you want yet, Meg?"

I grab the food menu off the table. "Not yet. You guys go ahead, though. This beer is like pudding, so I'm not super hungry."

Miles frowns at that response as he drapes an arm over Kate. "Sam, you coming?"

"I need to look at the menus still," he replies with a half-smile that sends a jolt through my legs. *I really wish he'd stop doing that.*

As soon as they walk away, I exhale heavily and splay my hands out on the table while pressing my forehead to the cool wooden surface.

"You're acting fucking nuts," Sam says, and I see him tip his beer bottle to his lips out of the corner of my eye.

My head pops up. "I'm acting nuts? You're acting nuts!"

"How am I acting nuts?" he asks, jutting his head toward me. "I'm just drinking beer with friends."

"You're acting like a boyfriend!" I exclaim.

"The fuck I am!" The veins on his neck stick out, and oh my heck, even those are sexy. "I don't even know how a boyfriend acts anyway. I'm just…treating you like a human."

"Well, you should be treating me like a stranger." I harrumph and attempt to drink my beer again. The smell alone has me wincing, so I set it back down. "You need to stop being so nice."

"I'm nice to strangers." He shakes his head and turns to look away, a sexy muscle in his jaw ticking with obvious agitation.

My heart pitter-patters at his words because damnit, I bet he is nice to strangers. And I'm over here acting like a jerk. I lean across the table and lower my tone. "I'm sorry, Sam. I don't mean to be a bitch. I'm just nervous being around you and my brother at the same time."

"Well, try to chill," he barks back and takes another drink of his beer.

I cross my arms over my chest, annoyed at his simple demand because he's acting like he's not doing anything wrong in this scenario. "Well, you're not really helping matters, you know."

His brows lift as he points at his chest. "What the hell am I doing wrong?"

I roll my eyes. "Don't do that shy smile thing you do."

"What shy smile thing?"

"You like, look away when you smile sometimes because you don't want people to see. It's really fucking cute, and when you do it, I swoon a little, and I can't swoon in front of my brother."

"You swoon?" he asks, doing that annoying shy smile thing again.

"That!" I state, pointing an accusing finger right at his sexy mouth. "Don't do that. And while we're at it, don't pull your bottom lip into your mouth. It reminds me of Prince Harry at his wedding, and it *does things to me.*" My voice turns low at the end of that sentence like I'm flipping Bane from *Batman*, and Sam can't help but laugh at me. I'd laugh too. I'm acting totally fucking unhinged.

"Well, what about you?" he barks once he's regained control of himself.

My eyes go wide. "What about me?"

"If there are things I can't do, then there are definitely things you can't do."

"Like what?"

"Like…don't ramble." He leans in close, his shirt tight on his biceps as he rests his elbows on the table. "When you ramble, you get this crazed look in your eye that I swear makes your eyes turn even brighter blue. It's distracting."

"Okay, I'll try not to ramble." I shrug.

"And you shouldn't have worn tights." His eyes cut downward, and my thighs instantly clench together.

"What's wrong with my tights?" I ask, lifting my palms.

"They make your legs look really fucking sexy, and I can't stop staring at them, which makes me think of them wrapped around me, which then becomes a serious problem."

I press my hands to the top of the table. "Okay, okay, chill."

"And since ordering for you is apparently too boyfriendy, will you please go up to the bar and get yourself a glass of wine? I can't watch you gag on that Guinness anymore."

"Fine…I'll go." With a huff, I stand, straightening out my dress that's riding up on my tights. Sam's eyes drop to my legs, and he bites his lip. With a sharp intake of breath, I turn on my heel and murmur under my breath, "We are so fucked."

Miles and Kate return at the same time I do, and then Sam and I go our separate ways to get food. Like super separate. I picked the food truck farthest away from his food truck.

Once I've eaten and had a glass of wine, I feel moderately calmer. And thankfully, I manage to keep the embarrassing sweaty dog story in my head for the remainder of our dinner. Once we've all had one more drink, we get up to head down to Pearl Street to the next bar.

I assume I'll be riding with "Mom and Dad" again when suddenly Kate shoves me toward Sam's truck. "Ride with Sam so he doesn't have to ride alone."

Miles nods his agreement, and the two of them take off for their truck without a care in the world while I have to watch Sexy Sam open his truck door for me. I ignore the cute smirk on his face as I hop up into his vehicle, and by the time he gets in and pulls out, I've formulated six different ways I could murder Kate and have it look like an accident.

The silence is heavy as we drive, and all I can think about is the fact that I was laid out completely naked in this spot only twenty-four hours ago. Surely, Sam's thinking about it too because he's gripping the steering wheel so hard his knuckles are white.

I swallow slowly, doing my best to take deep breaths, but eventually, the silence becomes too much to bear. "This is harder than I thought it would be." I expel my words as if I had been holding my breath this entire time.

"Yeah, this kind of sucks," Sam replies, his tone tight and constrained.

"I'm sorry to put you in such an awkward position," I lament because it was my idea to add sex to our little deception in the first place. "It was all pretty innocent until I

243

threw myself at you."

He clears his throat and looks away. "You didn't put me in this situation. I put myself in it."

We drive a little farther until we reach Bohemian Biergarten on Pearl Street. Sam throws the truck in park and turns to face me. His eyes are serious when he says, "We just need to relax and try to have some fun. Your brother is my best friend, and you are his sister, so there's no reason we can't have some drinks together and pretend we haven't seen each other naked."

"Right," I reply, nodding my head earnestly. "Because it's seriously no big deal!"

"Exactly."

"'Cuz you're not a commitment kind of guy, and Miles knows I'd never hook up with someone like you. He's not going to figure it out."

"Right," Sam confirms, a strange look across his face fleeting as he turns away from me and slides out of his truck.

He opens my door for me, and I hold back my comment about this being a boyfriend move because he looks like he's beating himself up about something, and I don't want to add fuel to his fire.

We head inside to the German-style bar that's filled to the brim with people. It's noisy as we make our way past the picnic tables to find Miles and Kate wedged up against the wall sharing a community table with a group of college guys. Sam and I squeeze through everyone and take the last two spaces available directly across from them.

"I ordered us a round!" Miles exclaims with a big smile

as the waitress carries a tray of drinks over everyone's heads. "Meg, I got you wine...I think you're wrong about liking beer."

I force a smile and take the wineglass Miles hands to me. Maybe if I drink enough tonight, this will all seem a lot less difficult. The rest of the drinks are all passed around, and we do a cheers.

"So Megan, is Sterling missing you yet?" Miles shouts over the loud noise of bar, leaning across the table toward me.

"I think so," I reply with a forced smile.

He frowns. "He's back at school now. Surely, he's begging for you to head back to Utah."

"You trying to get rid of me?" I ask and take another drink.

"Hell no! I wish you'd move here." Miles takes a quick drink and adds, "I'm hoping Sterling gets signed by the Broncos so I can see a lot more of you. Denver is so close to Boulder...just an easy train ride away."

I inhale and exhale slowly, trying my hardest not to chug this very generous glass of wine. Miles and I haven't spoken that much about Sterling since I arrived in Boulder, so lying to him hasn't been that difficult...until now.

I decide to tell him the little nugget of truth I received during tonight's phone call. "He said he missed me tonight, so maybe I'll be going back soon. We'll see."

Both Sam's and Kate's eyes bore into me with curiosity, but I do my best not to look at either of their reactions.

Miles nods toward Sam, and states, "You should have

seen our dad when he met Sterling over Christmas break. He was like a kid in a candy store. He always wished I would have played football, so Sterling is like a dream come true future son-in-law for him."

Sam nods slowly and takes a drink of his beer before replying. "I was never one for team sports."

"Me neither, but I love watching!" Miles replies jovially, completely oblivious to Sam's tension. "I'm just glad Megan didn't end up with one of my buddies from back home. They were always giving me shit about how hot you were."

I blanch at that response because just this past summer I saw one of Miles's friends at a college party. They are all several years older than me, so it was odd this particular friend was hanging out at a college party, to begin with, but it must have been destiny because Sterling came out of nowhere and rescued me like my knight in shining armor.

"Your friends are gross," I reply around my wineglass and can feel Sam turn his head to stare right at me.

"Especially this fucker," Miles says, reaching across the table and shoving Sam in the shoulder. "He's going to end up being the Hugh Hefner of Boulder."

"Hugh Hefner was actually a serial monogamist," Kate states, her eyes wide and challenging. "He had three wives and was actually very loyal to his girlfriends. It was always the women who broke his heart."

We all blink at Kate for knowing such details, and then Sam adds, "Well, that's definitely not me."

Miles shakes his head and then looks over at me again. "What are the odds Sterling will end up in Denver, Meg?"

I shrug. "He's done some training camps with their team, which is always promising, but we won't know until the draft."

"We," Sam mutters with a chuckle under his breath. It's soft enough that I'm the only one who can hear him, but Kate must notice his mood change because she's watching him curiously.

Miles is still totally oblivious. "I feel like I didn't get much of a chance to really talk to him at Mom and Dad's," he chimes in. "He should come here and visit sometime, Megs. You think he'd do that?"

I nod instantly. "I think so."

"Cool, I want to get to know him better if you think he's going to propose soon. I need to make sure he's good enough for my baby sister."

"How do you know anyone is good enough?" Sam asks, his eyes narrowing on Miles. "Are you the 'good enough' police?"

Miles raises his chin up. "For my sister, fuck yes, I am."

Sam shrugs. "My sister just got divorced, and I thought that guy was good enough. Clearly, I was wrong. So what magic do you have to tell if someone's an asshole or not?"

Miles takes a moment to stare at his best friend whose entire body is stiff with tension. "I'm sorry to hear about your sister, buddy. That totally sucks. Is it your older one? You had mentioned they were having problems."

I exhale heavily when Miles doesn't seem to understand what Sam is getting at. I'm trying to figure out what Sam is trying to say too. Is he referring to himself, or is he referring to Sterling? Because somehow I don't think he's really considering his sister's situation right now.

"Are you going to work at all, Megan?" Kate asks, chiming in out of nowhere.

"What do you mean?"

She shrugs. "I mean…you're smart as a whip, you graduated early and in the top of your class at Utah, but you're planning to marry a future NFL player, so does that mean you're planning on not working at all?"

My jaw goes taut because Kate's question seems bitchy and judgmental, but she says it with that bright, happy smile of hers. "I'm going to work. Our plan was for me to start job hunting in the spring. I'm just taking some time off before my future really begins."

"Your future with Sterling?" Kate asks, and I see a glint of mischief in her eyes that I don't like.

"Yes, my future with Sterling," I reply through clenched teeth.

"Man, he must be a great lay for you to be basically putting your life on hold for him!" Kate exclaims, slapping her hand on the table.

Miles puts his hands over his ears. "Gross, you're talking about my sister, and I can't hear this!"

Her words sting because she's using stuff I've said to her in confidence against me, and it's not okay. I lean across the table like I'm a boxer standing toe to toe with my opponent. "I know you write erotic romance novels, Kate, but not everything is about sex."

She smiles a fake smile. "Then you need to tell me what

it is about Sterling that's so damn amazing. Because you've been here for weeks, and I have yet to hear one thing to that effect."

I exhale heavily, my nostrils flaring with agitation over how quickly she flipped on me. "You don't have to understand love at first sight, but as a romance novelist, I would have thought you'd respect it."

"I respect and believe in love at first sight!" Kate exclaims, her eyes wide and defiant. Miles looks back and forth between us with a nervous frown, his hands still pressed firmly to his ears when Kate adds, "I just don't respect blind love."

"And you think blind love is what I have with Sterling?" I shriek back at her. "What is blind love anyway?"

Kate tilts her head and eyes me with so much contempt, I want to punch her. "Blind love is being so hyper-focused on a plan and a future and goals and what you think is a perfect life that you stop using your peripheral vision. And let me tell you, Meg…sometimes the stuff in your periphery is where real life is waiting."

She turns her head to the side and yanks Miles's hands off his ears before pulling him in close for a kiss. It's passionate and spiteful and sweet all at the same time. Normally, Miles and Kate's affection makes me feel happy for my big brother. But right now, it just hurts.

Suddenly, I feel claustrophobic, and I move to stand from the table. "This is a pub crawl, not sit, am I right? I think we need to keep it moving!"

Miles pulls away from Kate's lips with a dopey smile

on his face. "Pearl Street Pub?" he asks, his brows lifting excitedly.

"Sure…it's just down around the corner, right?" I ask, pulling my coat on and downing the rest of my wine in one big gulp.

"Let's do it!" Miles cheers, reaching for Kate's jacket and helping her put it on.

Kate watches me nervously as I turn on my heel and take off for the door, desperate for some air. Goddamn her. I thought she was on my side, but the shit she's pulling now is most definitely not Team Maggie!

I wait for everyone to join me outside, and we make our way down the busy sidewalk toward the pub. Kate jogs ahead of Miles and Sam and wraps her arm around mine, causing me to visibly bristle from her touch. I turn to see Miles and Sam a few steps behind before I turn and hiss in Kate's ear, "Let go of me, traitor."

"Megan, don't be mad," she pleads, struggling to keep up with my fast pace.

"Don't be mad?" I shriek and want to shove her off the curb. "Of course, I'm mad. What did you think you were doing in there?"

"Being a big sister," she replies arching her brow at me.

I scoff and roll my eyes. "Big sister, my ass. You're trying to make a fool of me in front of Sam."

Her eyes go wide with shock. "That is not what I'm doing, but the real question should be, why do you care what Sam thinks if he's just fling?"

"He is just casual!" I exclaim and begin walking faster,

causing Kate to stumble in her heels. "I don't need this, Kate. I don't need you against me too."

"No one is against you, Meg!" she exclaims, stopping in her tracks and yanking me around to face her just as we arrive in front of Pearl Street Pub. "We are all on your side, and we all want what's best for you."

"I know what's best for me!" I cry and then an unexpected emotion swells in my chest.

Miles reaches us, concern all over his face. "What's going on?" his deep voice booms.

"Nothing!" I reply and force a smile. "I'm just going to pee my pants." I lie because lying is something I'm apparently very good at—even to myself. Yanking off my coat, I hand it to Miles, and say, "I'm going downstairs to the restroom. Will you get me another glass of wine?"

He nods woodenly, and before he can tell how truly upset I am, I take off down the creaky wooden steps inside the door and head to the bathrooms that I remember from the last time I was here. I reach the single female restroom, thankful there's no line, and burst through the door, heading straight for the sink.

I splay my hands out on the basin, dropping my head forward as I pull in big gulps of air. I just need to get my bearings back because it feels like my entire world is spinning. If that was tough sisterly love from Kate, she could just keep that shit to herself.

Suddenly, the bathroom door opens, and I twirl on my heel ready for round two with Kate, but all the air is sucked from my lungs when I see Sam standing in the doorway. He closes the door behind him and flips the lock.

"Sam, what are you doing here?" I ask, pinching the bridge of my nose and trying to pull myself back together.

"What are *you* doing here, Maggie?" he replies. Taking three strides across the small bathroom, he's standing close enough for me to smell his Irish Spring soap.

"What do you mean? I'm in the women's bathroom."

"No, I mean, what the hell are you actually doing here? In Boulder?" His green eyes bore into mine with so much intensity, I can barely meet his gaze.

"I'm trying to be more adventurous and be the girl Sterling wants," I groan and put my hands on my hips as shame casts all over me. "You were helping me with that, I thought!"

"Stop with the lies then," he says, moving in closer and caging me against the sink with one hand on either side of me.

"What lies? I'm not lying!" I cry, pressing my hands to his chest for some space that he's definitely not giving me.

"You're lying to yourself!" he exclaims, his jaw taut with determination. "That stuff you're saying about Sterling sounds like total bullshit. He is a douchebag, and you're blind to it for some reason. It's what Kate's trying to tell you. Jesus hell, it's what I've been trying to tell you too."

"You've barely said a word about Sterling!"

"I've been trying to show you, sparky!" he growls, the veins in his neck pulsing as he presses in closer to me. His hands move to grip my hips, and he squeezes with an urgency I feel through every inch of my body. "I've been trying to show you that life is a hell of a lot more than just some ridiculous plan."

I swallow slowly as he looms over me in all his statuesque glory. "Well, I think it worked because it appears he wants me back."

"Is that what you want, though?" Sam asks, his eyes pleading as I tilt my chin to look up at him.

"I think so," I reply, but my voice is weak and strangled as if the words are trying to hold themselves inside.

"Stop living your life for him, Maggie. Start living it for yourself."

"Like you're some great example of that!" I argue, thinking back to everything he said to me when we were ice fishing yesterday. "Your family is all you live for. So much so that you refuse to even open your heart to the idea of someone new in your life."

Sam's face contorts as if feeling stung by my statement. "At least the people I live for in my life actually love me back."

As soon as the words come out of his mouth, I can't stop my hand from swinging at his face. The slap is cruel and harsh but no more painful than the words he said to me. The words that speak to that painful part of my soul and scream at me that I'm never enough. I move to swing at him again because everything inside me hurts, but he catches that hand in his fist. I swing my first hand at him again, and he catches that one too. I struggle in his arms as he turns us and pins my wrists against the wall beside my head.

"Maggie, stop," he pleads, his voice pained by my struggle.

"You're a fucking asshole, Sam!" I cry, trying and failing to free myself from his grip.

"I know," he says with a sigh. "But I can't hear you lie about that fucking ex of yours anymore."

"You're lying too!" I bellow into his face, my voice deep with the emotion exploding inside me. "We're both lying. We're fucking trapped in this stupid plan of mine, and it's exhausting because my heart is being pulled in so many different directions. I don't know what to do."

"What's your heart saying you want right now?" he asks, his grip loosening on my wrists.

I drop my head back against the wall. "I wish I knew."

"You do know, Maggie. Just say it." His fingers lace between mine, no longer pinning me to the wall but holding my hands in a firm embrace.

I stare down at his chest, my jaw clenched in frustration because none of this is making any sense anymore. None. My heart knows what I need, but what I want is a very different thing. And what if what I want doesn't want me back?

I move my eyes upward and utter one single, solitary word. "You."

Sam's eyes fall to my lips, and in two heartbeats, his mouth crashes into mine as he releases my hands and wraps his arms tightly around my waist. His tongue is demanding as it sweeps through my lips, parting them with a savage growl that I feel all the way through my core.

I whimper as he lifts me into his arms, and my legs grip his waist as he moves me from the wall to the top of the sink. His tongue continues to devour me as his hands move all over, touching and rubbing and kneading me in the most indelicate of places.

"Fucking tights," he growls against my lips as his hand steals up my dress and pushes past the waistband to discover just how turned on I am right now. He groans with need as my slickness overwhelms both of us. "If you want me to stop...you're going to need to say it."

"Don't stop," I cry, my heart thundering wildly in my chest. "Don't stop."

In a rush, he yanks me off the sink and drops down to yank my tights off my hips. He fumbles hurriedly with my ankle boots, and when I'm bare from the waist down, he pulls a leg up to his shoulder and kisses me right where I need him most.

I cry out loudly, the noise of the bar upstairs noticeable but doing nothing to quiet me from the overwhelming sensations of Sam's mouth on my sex. He sucks me hard and sharp into his mouth, and I cry out, my back arching as my heel digs into his shoulder blade. He assault is so aggressive, my orgasm detonates without warning.

My legs feel like Jell-O as he stands up, and I shakily reach for his belt, our hands colliding as we push his pants and boxers down only far enough to free his throbbing cock. I grab his shaft and sit back on the sink to guide him inside me.

"Fuck, I don't have a condom," he growls, his tip pressing into my wetness and feeling like everything I want for the rest of my life.

"I don't care," I cry and then reach around to grab his

buttocks. "I'm on the pill, and I don't care."

His eyes lock on mine in shock as I pull him into me. *All of him.*

"Fuck, Maggie," he cries, his voice guttural as he sinks to the hilt and stills. He leans in to caress my lips with his, and then he traces a path down my neck before hunching over to bite my nipple through my dress.

"Sam!" I cry in shock, and then he jerks his head up and rocks his hips into me in one smooth thrust. He's slow and steady at first, his eyes enjoying the sight of me leaning back, his body on sensory overload as we both embrace the skin-on-skin contact.

As his pace quickens, one of my arms is braced on his shoulder and the other is braced on the mirror behind me. He smoothly stokes the orgasm I had earlier like a fire of embers in need of a little puff of oxygen. And when the flames finally take flight inside me, he speeds up his motions, thrusting into me in perfect progression.

Our eyes remain locked on each other. Every movement feeling right and perfect. Connected. Sam and I are connected, not just sexually but emotionally as well. He knows what I need and gives it to me without even asking.

My orgasm is on the precipice, and I nod once at him. Without a word, he moves faster inside me, hurrying his own release so we can come together this time. And all of it—the bareness, the connection, the emotions of the evening—feels completely overwhelming. As though I need them to stop and never stop all at the same time.

I cry out when everything inside me tenses and releases.

I sit up to bury my face in his neck as the climax shoots through me with no mercy. Seconds later, Sam groans a deep, vibrating sound, and then I feel himself let go inside me.

Our breaths are ragged and loud in the quiet of the bathroom as he trembles in my arms, his forehead slick with sweat, and my dress rucked up between us. With a quiet exhale, he pulls out of me, and I can feel his seed dripping between my legs.

He pulls his pants up and grabs some tissues on the counter, gently swiping between my legs until I'm no longer drenched. His face looks troubled as he bites his lip and throws the paper away.

"I'm sorry, Maggie."

"What are you sorry for?" I ask, lowering myself off the sink and watching him in confusion.

"That should have never happened."

I huff out an arguing laugh. "I'm pretty sure I made it happen."

He swallows as if there's a knife down his throat. "I know, but it really shouldn't have happened."

A horrifying thought crosses my mind. "Are you trying to tell me you're not clean or something?"

His face falls. "What? Fuck no. I'm clean. Maggie, I'm fucking clean." He takes a step toward me and grabs my face in his hands. "I swear to fuck I'm clean."

"Then why do you look completely freaked out right now?" I ask, my eyes dancing all over his features.

He inhales through his nose, and I can hear a

shuddering in his chest as he leans in and kisses me on the forehead. "Because you're killing me."

"What?" I ask, yanking out of his hands with annoyance. "What is that supposed to mean?"

He closes his eyes and shakes his head. "I need to go. I'm going to tell Miles I'm not feeling well. I can't be around you and him at the same time. Not anymore."

"Not anymore?" I ask, reaching down and grabbing my tights from off the floor. "What are you talking about? What's changed, Sam?"

He moves to the door and stares back at me with a grave look on his face. "Everything."

And without another word, he leaves me in the women's restroom of Pearl Street Pub more confused than ever before.

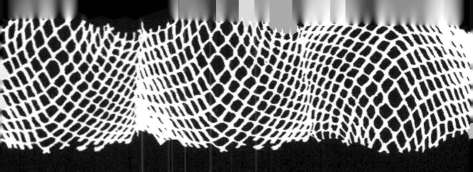

CHAPTER 16

Well, This Day Was A Waste of Bait

Sam

Monday morning comes, and Miles comes striding into my office bright-eyed and bushy-tailed. "Hey man, feeling better?" he asks, dropping into the seat on the other side of my desk.

I push a hand through my hair and try to play it cool. "Yeah, sorry I bailed Friday night. One of those food trucks didn't agree with my stomach." I lie, which honestly should feel like second nature by now.

"That's all right. Megan was in a mood for the rest of the night anyway, so our pub crawl turned into a pub fail, and we called it early as well."

I nod and wince as I think about the million different times I wanted to text Maggie over the weekend but then couldn't bring myself to do it. Regardless of what happened Friday night, she's still after her ex, and I'm still who I am. And now that I've taken over the business, it's definitely not the time for distractions.

"Did you think Meg was okay Friday night? She seemed kind of weird," Miles states, propping his boots up on the edge of my desk and biting into a cookie he brought in from the comfort center.

"How so?" I ask, my arms tensing.

"Just like...emotional. I tried to get Kate to give me some dirt because she clearly knows something, but she's a locked vault."

I shrug my shoulders slowly. "I don't know, man."

"I sort of worry if something might be going on with her and Sterling."

"Like what?" I ask, wishing like fuck she would just come clean and tell Miles that she and Sterling broke up.

"I don't know...it just seems weird she's hanging out in Boulder and not going back to Utah to be closer to him. She says she's madly in love with him, but her love doesn't look like mine and Kate's."

I nod thoughtfully at that. "I don't think anybody's love could possibly look like yours and Kate's. You guys have like...unicorn shittin' rainbows love that makes mere mortals feel inferior."

Miles laughs at that apt description and then shrugs dismissively. "I just worry about her. She's such a hopeless romantic, and sometimes I think she needs to let things progress more naturally."

There is nothing natural about Maggie Hudson's ideas about love. "I'm not much help in that department I'm afraid," I reply.

Miles looks at me seriously for a moment, his eyes blinking slowly as he takes me in. "Are you okay?"

"Yeah, I told you I was feeling better."

"No, I mean…are you good? You seem sort of off too. I would think you'd be on top of the world since Terry gave you the keys to the castle, but oddly, you don't seem that into it."

"I'm into it," I snap back, my shoulders tensing. "I mean, it's a tire shop. I'm as into a tire shop as I can be."

Miles nods thoughtfully, clearly not satisfied with that response. "Listen, I don't know a lot about your family stuff, and I don't need to know because best friends are best friends without any requirements. But I know that this tire shop started off as your dad's, and maybe it feels a little weird to be sitting in his chair now."

"This was Terry's chair," I correct, my hands balling into sweaty fists.

"You know what I mean." Miles sits on the edge of his seat, propping his arms on the desk. "Look, Sam, you and I are close, but I know there's a wall between us. There always has been. I opened up to you about my ex drama like crazy, but you've never opened up to me."

"That's because I don't have ex drama," I argue, feeling my muscles grow tenser the deeper this conversation gets.

"I know, but you still have drama. And don't act like you don't. I know you have plans to help your mom retire

261

in two years and that you're constantly helping your sisters out. Now you have Tire Depot to run. That's a lot of responsibility, Sam. And I get that sharing isn't something all guys do, but I hope you know that I'm always here for you. I'm ride or die, man."

Miles's words stun me into silence. His blue eyes wide and open as if he's trying to convey his love for me with just one meaningful look. It hurts. Everything he said hurts because I don't deserve it. Not after all the shit I've done behind his back with his sister. I don't regret what we did, but I regret lying to him about it. I may have a wall up, but Miles is still my best friend. I'm ride or die with him too.

"Thanks, man. I'm ride or die too."

He nods and reaches out to bump fists with me. "That's basically your version of I love you, so I'll take it." He stands up to head out the door and back to work, but I stop him before he walks out.

"Miles, do you have time to go get drinks with me tomorrow night? There actually are some things I want to talk to you about."

Miles's eyes light up like a kid on Christmas morning. "Definitely. Let's plan on it."

"Sounds good, man," I reply to his retreating frame while thinking to myself, *I hope you're still ride or die after everything I'm about to tell you.*

I pull out my phone to text Maggie.

Me: We need to talk.
Sparky: Okay…

Me: Can you meet me at Marv's for lunch around noon?
Sparky: Sure, I'll see you soon.

I'm seated in the same booth Maggie and I first sat in, and my palms are slick with sweat as I stare out the window, waiting for her car to pull up. When it finally does, I swear my heart begins racing as I watch her stride into the bait shop in her long red wool coat, wedge boots, and skinny jeans. Her dark hair is straight and loose down her back, and I stare in amazement at her because this is so not who I imagined would have walked into my life a few weeks ago.

She smiles a soft smile as she spots me in the corner and makes her way over. Sliding into the booth, she licks her lips and looks around at all the old guys playing cards. "Maybe I should have brought a deck," she says, her eyes flicking to me nervously.

My eyes blink slowly at her. "I'm afraid I'm not in the mood for games."

She nods and exhales heavily. "I'm sorry, Sam. I'm sorry for so many things."

"Like what exactly?" I ask, pushing my sleeves up so I can brace myself for what's to come.

"For making you lie to my brother. For turning our friendship into a fuck buddy situation—"

"Fuck buddies?" I interrupt, my chest tightening at that crass label. "Is that what you think we are?"

She winces. "I thought so? I don't know. What would you call us?"

"Not that," I reply, turning my head to look away from her as my jaw ticks with frustration. What do I think we are? Definitely not just fuck buddies, that's for damn sure.

"What is it then, Sam? What did you want to talk about?"

I look back at her, inspecting her face just as I did the first time we sat here. She's changed since that day. She still has the same light eyes and dark hair, but her face holds something more to it now than it did when I met her—perhaps an inner strength that she was sorely missing.

I exhale heavily. "I want to come clean to Miles about us."

Maggie's eyes fly wide. "Are you nuts? He's going to murder you!"

I shake my head from side to side. "I don't care. I can't do this to him anymore."

She expels a deep breath, her cheeks puffing out. Clearly, she did not expect this from me today. She shifts forward in her seat and chews her lip thoughtfully. "I mean, I realize that we've taken this as far as it can go, but that doesn't mean Miles needs to know about everything."

I swallow a knot in my throat at her response. "He needs to know."

She blinks rapidly. "But if we tell him about us, then he'll think I cheated on Sterling."

"You didn't cheat because you aren't with Sterling, and your brother deserves to know that as well."

Her face pales. "So you're saying you want to tell him like…everything?"

"Yes."

"Why, Sam? Why the sudden need to be forthcoming about stuff that is none of his business?"

"Because he's my best friend and your brother, Maggie. He cares about both of us, and this fantasy world you're living in where you think he'll hate Sterling for dumping you is just that…a fantasy." I splay my hands out on the table, my heart thudding hard in my chest. "Your fairy tale can't happen like this anyway. It's tainted now."

"You don't know that," Maggie sputters, her eyes wide and defiant as her face flushes with anger. "And besides, I'm not taking relationship advice from you. You're a thirty-one-year-old who's never been in love, let alone had a monogamous relationship. Just because your heart isn't open to love doesn't mean you have to ruin my chance at it."

Her words punch me right in the gut because I don't know for sure that my heart isn't open to love. There's a lot I don't know about myself anymore because this spark plug of a woman barreled into my life and electrified everything I thought I knew. But right now, the most important thing on my mind is a clear conscience.

"My decision to talk to your brother is final." I sit back in the booth and cross my arms over my chest.

Her lips twitch, anger bubbling up through her whole body all the way down to her clenched fists on the table.

"So this is great. Now my entire family will know that I'm a desperate, *basic* loser who went to the most ridiculous extremes to win back a guy who doesn't love me. Thanks for all your help, Sam!"

She moves to stand, and I reach out to grab her wrist, halting her in her tracks. She spins around, hitting me hard with her blue eyes full of pain and embarrassment. But above all...betrayal. She feels betrayed by me, and hell, maybe I deserve it.

"I'm sorry, Maggie," I croak because it's the only thing I can think of to say.

She huffs out a laugh, biting the inside of her cheek as she nods over and over. "It's fine, Sam. It's fine. Tell Miles everything, see if I care." Inhaling deeply, she leans down to add, "But do you know what the worst part of all this is?"

I look up at her silently, waiting on bated breath for her to tell me.

"That a sick, delusional part of me thought you were bringing me out here today to tell me you had feelings for me."

In a huff, she yanks her wrist out of my hand and storms out of Marv's, leaving me completely tangled up like fishline in a tree.

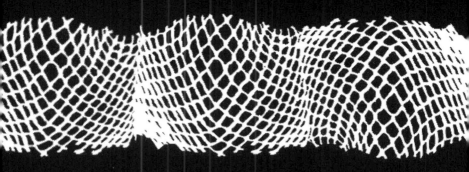

CHAPTER 17

Wishin' I'd Gone Fishin'

Maggie

W hen I was a kid, I was famous for epic tantrums. I remember everyone in my family always feeling so much bigger than me and smarter than me and stronger than me that if I didn't roll around on the floor and make a gigantic scene, they wouldn't even notice me.

My mother said I was melodramatic because I hated change. She told me one time when I cut my Barbie's hair that I immediately started sobbing and begging her to glue it back on even though I was the one who cut it. And apparently, that lovely part of my personality never went away because I still recall bawling on my brother's shoulder when he told me he was moving eight hours away with his girlfriend to Boulder, Colorado. Granted, part of that was because I loathed his girlfriend at the time, but the majority of it was because I hated change.

I still hate change.

Case in point, Sterling dumps me, and I go on a crazy road trip of self-discovery. I guess some things never change.

It's almost dark outside before I pull myself out of my bedroom for the first time in twenty-four hours. I've been hiding in my room like a hermit, terrified Miles is going to come storming in at any minute and disown me for lying to him and screwing around with his best friend. But so far, all is quiet in Boulder. Like the calm before the storm.

I shuffle into the bathroom for a shower that I'm hoping will clear my head, but I know it won't. Right now, I feel like I keep getting hit by one bus, only to get hit by another bus. First with Sterling, then Kate, and now Sam. For a girl who doesn't handle change well, a lot of crap is coming at me way too fast.

The house is quiet when I step out of the bathroom with a towel wrapped around me. Miles and Kate will be home soon after another romantic day together at Tire Depot. Maybe I should throw something together for dinner. It could very well be my last supper with them.

My cell phone rings, and my mom's face illuminates the screen. I swipe to answer it, feeling a homesick knot form in my throat just at the idea of hearing her voice again. "Hey, Mom."

"Hi Maggie, how are you?" she asks, her voice soothing like always.

"I'm good," I lie through my teeth. "How are you?"

"I'm great. I miss you, though. When do you think you're coming back from Boulder? I feel like I haven't seen you in forever."

I sigh heavily. "I'll probably be coming home soon."

"Good. Your father and I aren't ready to be official empty nesters yet."

"How is Dad?" I ask, biting my lip and trying to stop the tears from welling in my eyes.

"He's good. He has that ridiculous flag football league practice tonight. I still can't believe he joined a senior football program. It seems like an oxymoron to me."

I laugh at that. Dad always has loved football. "Mom, tell me how you and Dad met again."

"What?" she asks curiously.

"Tell me the story again."

Laughing softly into the phone, she says, "Well, I was at my first college party with my girlfriends, and this boy kept trying to get me to dance with him all night. I was not interested. He rolled his cigarettes up in his sleeve, and I always thought that was so tacky. But the boy wasn't giving up, and just when I thought I was going to have to leave the party to get away from him, your father stepped right between us, stared that guy in the face, and said, 'Move along, or your next dance will be with my fist.'"

My face spreads into a wide, happy smile. "And then he turned around…"

"Then he turned around, smiled at me, and somehow I knew that I was looking at the man I was going to spend the rest of my life with."

"And Daddy felt the same."

"Your father later told me that when he saw me across the room rejecting that other guy, he knew it was because I hadn't looked his way yet."

"Gosh, this story is the best."

"It really is." My mom laughs. "I never get sick of telling it."

I sniff once into the phone, and croak out, "Do you think that's what Sterling and I have?"

"What do you mean?"

"Do you think we could be just like you and Dad?"

"Honey, I don't know why that would matter. If I've learned anything through my Dirty Birdy's Book Blog, it's that all stories are unique. Beginning to end. Fiction and nonfiction."

"But you and Dad are so happy. Your story makes me believe that what we read in the romance novels can be real life. I would do anything for that kind of book-worthy happiness."

"Happiness shouldn't be forced, dear. It should come naturally. Do you feel happy with Sterling?"

I bite my lip, holding back the tiny sob that wants to tear out of my throat because I have been such an idiot. So blindly stupid that I hate myself at this moment. I open my mouth to pour my heart out, but the doorbell interrupts me.

I look at the front door with a frown. "Hey, someone is at the door, Mom. I better go get it."

"Okay, honey. Call me later, though?"

"I will, Mom. Thanks for the talk."

"Always, Maggie."

I hang up and tighten the towel around my chest and pad over to the front door, expecting it to be some postal delivery, or maybe Kate and Miles forgot their key. When I open it and peek my head around so they can't see I'm in nothing but a towel, my mind can't even accept what's on the other side.

Like, my eyes see it, but my mind doesn't have any physical reaction to it. It just…blankly stares at it with no emotional response whatsoever.

"Baby," Sterling's husky voice says. Pushing the door open all the way, he blasts my nearly naked body with the frigid winter air. He steps inside and closes the door before turning around and eyeing me in my towel. He scoops me up into his arms, and as my feet dangle off the floor, I do everything I can to get my brain to wake up and respond. It's like I'm having an out-of-body experience as I watch myself cringe while my ex-boyfriend hugs me in the foyer of my brother's house.

When he sets me down, I look up at him to make sure it's actually him. Tall, check. Dark, check. Handsome, check. Brown eyes that are just a touch beadier than I remember, check.

"Sterling?" I state his name like a question so I get a verbal confirmation that I'm not in the middle of a nervous breakdown and imagining the postman is my ex.

"Yes, baby. God, I've missed you. What are you wearing?"

I glance down at my towel, pulling out of his arms to tighten it around my chest. "I just got out of the shower."

"It's almost six o' clock, baby. Why aren't you dressed?" he asks, sliding his hands into his pockets and walking farther into the house, inspecting it with an air of entitlement to his posture.

I shake my head, the fog lingering longer than it should as I try to figure out why he keeps calling me baby. "Wait, why are you here? Don't you have school?"

Sterling shrugs his broad shoulders. "School is pretty pointless for me right now since I know I'll be drafted." He smiles a cocky smile, and it feels bizarre. "I'm here because I missed you and I needed to see you."

"Needed to see me?" I repeat, slowly blinking while my mind tries to wrap around the words he's saying. "How did you know where Miles lived?"

"I called your parents," he replies with a proud smirk.

I look down, still shaking my head in shock, and I see his jeans hanging over his shoes. Big, saggy jeans bunched over the top of a pair of expensive sneakers.

"Where's your bedroom?" he asks, staring down at my towel and causing me to cinch it even tighter around me.

"My bedroom?" I stammer while goose bumps crawl over my skin.

He slides his coat off and tosses it on the nearby chair while stalking toward me. "I told you I missed you." He reaches me and slides his hands into my wet hair, pulling me to him while I do my best to suppress the visible cringe taking over my face.

His body feels strange and foreign instead of warmth covering my body. It's worse than a bucket of cold water dumped over my head. "So you came here for…sex?" I blurt out as I push him away.

"No," he replies, having the sense to look slightly wounded. "But I certainly wouldn't say no to a quickie if you were in the mood."

I move out of his reach and shake my head firmly. "No, I'm not in the mood."

Sterling frowns. "What's your deal? I thought you'd be happy to see me."

"I am…I think," I say quietly, trying to gain some clarity back. "I'm just trying to figure out what you're doing here."

Suddenly, I hear the garage door opening, and Sterling and I stare at each other while the voices of Miles and Kate waft up the stairs from the lower level garage.

"Meg, whose car is that outside?" Miles bellows and then strides into the foyer to see Sterling. "Oh hell, Sterling! I didn't know you were here!" Miles reaches out and shakes Sterling's hand, clapping him on the shoulder. "Megan, why didn't you tell me Sterling was coming to Boulder?"

"I just found out," I reply and force a smile as Kate enters the room and stares over at me cautiously.

"Hi there, Sterling," she says a lot less enthusiastically than Miles.

"I was missing my girl, so I just thought I'd surprise her," Sterling says with a smile for me. "You're surprised, aren't you, baby?"

I nod, and Miles hoots with laughter before saying,

"Well, hell, let's go out to dinner then! We need to show Sterling the wonders of Boulder."

Sterling nods slowly while staring at me. "That sounds great actually."

Miles frowns for a moment and then snaps his fingers. "Shoot, I just need to call Sam real quick. I was supposed to meet up with him tonight, but I'm sure he's good with postponing for this occasion."

The blood runs cold in my veins, and I blurt out, "Don't tell Sam that Sterling is here!"

Miles frowns at me. "Why not?"

Nervously biting my lip, I stammer, "Um…he's a big football fan I think, and I don't want him to show up and overwhelm Sterling."

Miles's face twists. "You don't know Sam at all, Megs. He doesn't give two shits about football."

Miles turns and looks down to start tapping out a text to Sam, and everything inside me turns to Jell-O as I debate how the hell I'm going to get through this night in one piece.

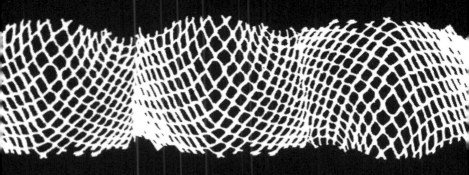

CHAPTER 18

*I've Spent My Whole Life
Fishing In The Wrong Hole*

Sam

After work, I head over to my mom's before I'm supposed to meet up with Miles because she called earlier and said the ceiling below her upstairs bathroom was leaking. It's a reoccurring problem with that shower, and something I've been meaning to replace for a while but just haven't got around to doing. She wanted to hire a plumber to come fix the issue today, but I know it'll only take me ten minutes. It just needs a patch job, and it'll be good as new.

I let myself in the front door using my key. "Hey Mom, where are you?" I holler.

Her voice drifts down from upstairs. "I'm just up here in the bathroom getting stuff out of the way for you to take a look! Come on up!"

I make my way up the stairs, toolbox in hand, and find her arms full in the hallway bathroom. "Hi," she says with a feeble smile. "I was just clearing this stuff out for you. I'm sorry you had to come out here."

"Mom," I scold with a shake of the head but give her a reassuring smile. "It's fine."

She shifts out of my way with various shampoo bottles clutched to her chest and drops them on the vanity counter. I shine my flashlight on the floor of the shower and spot the hairline crack instantly. All it needs is a quick sanding and an application of fiberglass from the repair kit I picked up for a few bucks, and it should be good as new.

I drop down on my hands and knees to get to work as my mom perches on the counter behind me. After no more than a moment of silence, she says out of the blue, "So you haven't been by for Sunday brunch in a couple of weeks. Is everything all right? Is taking over the shop too much for you? I told Terry I didn't want him to rush you."

"No, Mom. The shop is good," I reply as I sand down the fiberglass around the crack. "It's not work. It's…personal stuff." The second the words come out of my mouth, I regret them.

"Personal stuff?" she asks, her voice rising in curiosity. "What kind of personal stuff?"

I roll my eyes and glance over my shoulder at her. My mom has a nose for lies, and if I try to make something up, she'll interrogate me until I'm sweating. "I've been helping this girl with a dumb project. It's basically over now, though."

I finish sanding and sit back on my heels to work on mixing the epoxy gel coat next. I can feel my mother watching me quietly as her mind races with the best way to crack me like the floor of this shower.

"Is this the same girl you took ice fishing?" she asks, hitting the subject right on the nose.

I lift a brow and look back at her. "Yes, and she's Miles's little sister."

"Sammy." She gasps, her blue eyes wide. "Are you *involved* with her...romantically? Does Miles know?"

I shake my head. "He doesn't know. I'm going to tell him tonight." I dip the fiberglass cloth into the mixture and lean back over the floor to spread it along the crack. "Stuff just got too heated. Too stressful. And I hate lying to my friend."

I hear her tsk. "What does the girl say about it? What's her name?"

"Maggie," I reply and reach back for my putty knife to smooth out any air bubbles. "She's not happy. Pretty pissed actually."

Once the patchwork is smooth, I turn and sit on my rear with my back against the wall. Looking up, I take in my mom's reaction as she considers everything I'm sharing.

"What do you think Miles will do?" she asks, her brows knitting together in worry.

"Probably deck me," I reply with a huff. "But I deserve it."

She doesn't like that response one bit as she fiddles with her necklace and stares at the wall with a serious expression.

"Well, what's your end goal then? Are you in love with the girl?"

"Love? No, Mom," I snap and turn to grab the bottle of sealer out of my box. "Why would you think I'm in love with her?"

"Because you're risking a friendship for her."

She shrugs her shoulders as if it's the most obvious thing in the world, and I quickly turn around so she can't see my reaction to that statement. My eyes blink rapidly as her words have an unexpected effect on me. Am I risking my friendship with Miles for Maggie? Surely, I'm not. I don't want to lose Miles, but coming clean seems like the only thing to do at this point. Maggie and I have obviously progressed somewhere past casual, and I can't keep lying to my best friend when I'm falling for his sister.

My heart begins to pound in my chest at that realization, and I turn to lean back on the shower wall and get my fucking shit together. My phone chimes from its spot on the floor, and I glance down to see a text from Miles.

Miles: Hey man, change of plans. Megan's boyfriend just showed up unexpectedly, so can I get a rain check on drinks tonight? Kate and I are going to take them to Rio and introduce them to the two limit margaritas.

My hand tightens around the phone, my eyes losing focus as I absorb the fact that Maggie's ex-boyfriend is here. *Sterling is here? What kind of fucking name is that anyway?*

And seriously, what the actual fuck? It was only days ago when I was inside Maggie making her come, and *now* this fucker decides to show up?

"Who is it?" my mom asks, her voice soft but probing.

"It's Miles," I reply, my hand loosening around my phone. "Maggie's ex just showed up, so he needs to take a rain check on the drinks we were supposed to have tonight."

"Maggie's ex?" Mom asks, her voice rising in pitch. "Is he from Boulder?"

"No," I reply through clenched teeth. "He's from far away." Which means if he's here, Maggie's stupid-ass plan actually worked, and he wants her back.

I stand and begin tossing my tools into my toolbox, throwing them in way faster and noisier than necessary, but damnit, I'm freaking the fuck out right now. Who is this guy to show up at my best friend's house and have dinner with my goddamned people?

Mom slides off the counter and grabs my arm, so I turn my focus to her. "Sammy, what's going on?"

"Nothing, Mom. Leave it alone," I growl. Pulling away from her, I grab my toolbox off the floor to head out the door.

"It's not nothing!" she exclaims and uses all her strength to turn me to look at her. "Talk to me."

Her face is stricken with worry, and instantly, my anger morphs into an apology. "I don't know what to tell you. I'm just pissed off, I guess."

"Because of that text?"

"Yeah, because of that text," I growl and rake my free

hand through my hair. "That ex of hers is an asshole. He broke her damn heart, yet she's obsessed with getting him back. She's going to take him back. I know it."

"And why do you care?" she asks, her hands reaching up to touch my cheeks so I stop darting my gaze all around the small bathroom and look at her.

"Because I care about her," I state without pause.

She nods, her brows pinching together in the middle. "I can see that. Does she care about you?"

I shake my head in frustration because it doesn't fucking matter. "That's not the point, Mom. She's Miles's little sister. I can't go there."

"Of course, you can," she says, slapping my chest with her hands before placing them on her hips. "He loves you, and he loves her. He'll understand it if it's what makes you both happy."

"It's not just that," I state and fight the urge to roll my eyes. "You don't know Maggie, Mom. She's got her mind set on winning her ex back, and she went to great lengths to do it. If he's here, it's game over. She's succeeded in her mission."

Mom pins me with a seriously unimpressed stare. "Are you trying to tell me that after all that horrible brawling you did as a kid, you don't have it in you to fight for this girl?"

I bark out a laugh because getting romance advice from my mother is about as useful as a bucket of frozen minnows. "I don't think Maggie wants me to fight for her."

"It doesn't matter!" Mom argues, whacking me in the stomach. "If you've given your heart to this girl at all, Sammy, that's not something to walk away from."

I exhale heavily because I hate having to explain all of this to my mother, but I know she won't let this go if I don't. "I can't handle being with someone like her, Mom. Maggie is...a lot. She's young and stubborn and way too obsessed with a perfect life and achieving her happily ever after. She wants romance novel shit. I'm not the kind of guy who can give that to her."

"Of course, you can, you fool. Happy endings come in all shapes and sizes."

Mom is not letting this go, and it's killing me because I know that my truest fear is going to hurt her. With a quiet voice, I reply, "I'm not good enough for her, Mom. What if I'm like Dad?"

"Samuel Michael O'Connor!" she exclaims, her voice high and ragged just like it was when I got into trouble as a kid. "I never raised my hand to you during your entire misspent youth, but I swear to God, my palm is itching right now with how badly I want to slap you."

"Mom, jeez!" I exclaim, holding my hand up in defense.

"You are nothing like your father, you hear me?" she hisses, reaching out and shoving me to accentuate her point. "You are kind and good and giving. You take care of this whole family. You always have...even when you were a little terror at sixteen, you still got up early and shoveled the driveway. Your father never did a thing around here. Not even for you kids. The only decent thing he ever did was teach you how to ice fish, and you even have a hang-up over that because you think you have to do it alone to hold on to the one good memory he left you with."

My eyes begin to burn from her words because damnit, they are true. For years, I've gone ice fishing on my own because I didn't want to lessen the one decent memory I have of my father, who, let's face it, is deceased in my family's eyes. I worried that if I brought someone else with me out on the ice, new memories would outshine the old.

Then I met Maggie and, suddenly, without any concrete or tangible reason, I opened myself up to create a new memory.

My mom reaches out and pulls me into a hug that's so tight, I feel the entire weight of her on my neck. "If you found someone you were willing to take ice fishing, then you need to stop bitchin' and start fishin'." A broad smile spreads across my face as she releases me with a smile of her own. "Don't let this girl be the one who got away."

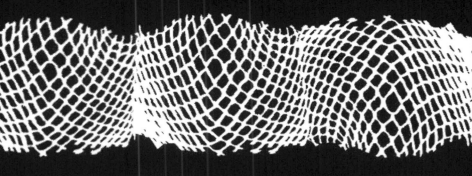

CHAPTER 19

Men And Fish Are Alike... They Both Get Into Trouble When They Open Their Mouths.

Maggie

Not enough Chardonnay exists in Boulder to get me through this dinner. And sadly, we are at a Mexican restaurant, so wine isn't even an option here. On the entire ride to the restaurant, I mentally flip out at the fact Sterling is here in Boulder. This is like all my romance novel fantasies come to life. The hero shows up on the doorstep of the heroine's house after traveling through a plethora of natural disasters to tell the love of his life that he needs her back, and he's been a fool, and he wants to marry her and have a million babies and goats.

Well, maybe not the goats.

But that's the dream, right? Yet the entire time at dinner,

something feels off. Looking at Sterling's face doesn't bring me the same flutters in my stomach it did only weeks ago. Is my heart just still that broken?

Even my brother seems to be struggling to connect to the person I've fantasized about marrying at least fifty different times.

"So Sterling," Miles says, setting down his Corona and leaning across the table at the Mexican restaurant, "how's it feel to know that in just a few months, your entire world is going to change?"

Sterling frowns and sits back, draping an arm across the back of my chair. "Pretty crazy."

Miles blinks, waiting for Sterling to elaborate, but when he realizes he's not going to, he adds, "What team are you hoping for?"

"Not the Broncos," he huffs and takes a drink of his margarita. "I did a training camp here, and the elevation was brutal. And how do you guys handle all this snow all the time? I can't stand it."

My brother's face falls as if Sterling just kicked his favorite puppy. "Well…you get used to it."

"Better you than me," Sterling huffs.

Kate's eyes find mine as she sips her drink, and she offers me a sympathetic smile. I offer one back. I'm still mad at her about Friday night, but she's the only one who truly understands the position I'm in right now, and I need her support.

My brother continues to try his hardest to make small talk when suddenly Sterling's hand slips under the table and grabs my thigh firmly. Something about the way his fingers inch slowly up my tights has me reaching down and squeezing his hand in silent warning. He looks over at me with narrowed eyes while my brother continues to ramble on about the wonders of Colorado and the seasonal changes.

When Sterling's hand touches the hem of my plaid skirt, I lean in and hiss, "Stop."

He half smiles at me, his eyes slightly hooded. "Why?"

"Because we're here with my brother," I grind out and then smile politely at Miles as he asks Kate about the name of some hiking spot they found this past summer.

Sterling harrumphs and yanks his hand away from my leg, visibly annoyed. I lean down and take a large gulp of my very strong margarita. Sterling has always had a thing for public displays of affection, and once upon a time, I enjoyed them with him. What's changed?

"Mind if I join you?" a familiar says from behind me, and I spew part of my drink out all over Sterling's lap.

"Jesus Christ," Sterling says, pushing back away from the table and wiping at his lap where most of my beverage landed. "What the hell, Maggie?"

Ignoring Sterling's fit, I turn around to find Sam standing only a foot away from me, watching the entire scene with great amusement. My eyes fall down his body to see that he's dressed in another one of his hot button-downs, green this time to match his eyes, and a pair of perfectly fitted jeans. He looks at me, and his eyes flash down to my tights and widen ever so slightly before he slaps on a strained smile.

"You okay there, sparky?" Sam asks, leaning in to gently pat me on the back.

Miles chuckles from across the table. "Hey man, what's up?"

Sam smiles over at my brother. "Well, I got your text and then decided I was in the mood for tacos anyway, so I figured I'd stop in and see if I could join you. That is if you guys don't mind a fifth wheel."

"We love all wheels!" Miles says, standing up and walking over to the next table to ask if he can borrow a chair. They nod their agreement, and he twirls the seat around, placing it right on the end, smack dab between Miles and Sterling.

"I'm afraid we haven't met," Sam says, holding his hand out to Sterling.

Sterling takes Sam's hand in his and shakes it firmly. "I'm Sterling, Maggie's boyfriend."

"Boyfriend!" Sam exclaims, his brows raised in surprise as he continues shaking. "You're the football player boyfriend we've all heard so much about? Wow, nice to meet you at last."

Sterling smiles awkwardly at Sam as the two shake hands for much longer than is necessary. "And you are?" Sterling asks finally.

Miles claps his hand on Sam's back. "This is my best friend, Sam. He owns Tire Depot here in town—where I work," he replies.

Sterling lifts his brows. "You're a business owner?"

Sam nods thoughtfully. "Very recently, yes."

Sterling nods but doesn't say anything. Instead, he takes a drink of his margarita and eyes Sam like a rooster who's agitated by the presence of another rooster.

Sam smacks his hand on the table. "So what'd I miss?" he asks.

"Sterling was just telling us how much he hates Colorado," Kate deadpans, then tips her margarita to her lips to polish off the last drink. Her eyes appear slightly glazed, and I'm certain the tequila is currently doing the talking.

Sterling shifts in his chair. "I didn't say I hate Colorado. I just said I would never want to live here."

"That's a shame," Sam replies, shaking his head. "There's so much here to do for the adventuring types. You're pretty adventurous, aren't you, Sterling?"

Sterling nods and stretches his arm around me again.

Sam's eyes fixate on where Sterling's hand lands on my shoulder. "I could tell that about you. You have the confidence of someone who takes a lot of risks. What's the craziest thing you've done recently?" he asks.

Sterling chuckles softly. "You mean besides avoid tackles from three-hundred-pound linemen?"

Miles nods his appreciation of that response—the sweet, oblivious puppy dog he always is.

"Linemen is just work, though," Sam says, propping his elbows on the table. "I'm asking what you do for personal adventure. Something that feeds your soul."

Sterling stares down at the table, his brow crinkling as he attempts to come up with an answer. "I'm afraid nothing comes to mind."

Sam's face bends in confusion. "Nothing? You're from the East Coast, right? Have you ever done some deep sea fishing or water sports? You know…the *basics*."

Sterling shakes his head, clearly not picking up what Sam's putting down.

"Huh," Sam retorts, scratching his jaw. "What about bungee jumping or white water rafting?"

"Nah, man. I haven't done those."

"Rock climbing?"

Sterling shakes his head again.

"Paintball? Surely, you've done paintball. Hell, even twelve-year-old boys do paintball!"

Sterling's eyes light up. "I've done laser tag with my buddies at this indoor facility in my hometown. It gets pretty intense."

Sam's lips turn down as he tries to suppress his amusement. "Sounds badass."

Sterling shifts in his seat, clearly catching on that Sam is messing with him. He narrows his eyes. "What about you?" he asks.

"What do I do for fun?" Sam asks, pointing at his chest with wide, innocent eyes. "Well, in Boulder, it's endless adventures even in the winter. I snowboard. I climb frozen waterfalls. Hell, there are even these ice-covered farm silos that you can scale now that are pretty thrilling. But my true love is ice fishing. I do that any chance I get."

Sterling's brow furrows, and my eyes flash to Sam, who has literally just listed nearly every single thing I've done over the past few weeks and sent a picture of to Sterling. If Sam were sitting closer to me, I would kick his shin under the table.

"So Kate, what book are you working on right now?" I ask, my voice robotic as I try to force the subject change.

"So Sterling, what do you love most about our Maggie?" Sam asks, blatantly ignoring me.

Miles's face turns sharply to Sam this time, clearly taken aback by his buddy's aggressive conversation skills. "Sam, what's going on?"

"Nothing!" Sam replies and exhales heavily. "I guess I'm feeling big brotherly to Maggie here. I want to make sure this guy is good enough for her."

Miles sits up a little taller, his eyes hard on his best friend, but instead of challenging Sam, he turns to Sterling, waiting for his answer.

Sterling leans forward, bracing his elbows on the table as he looks at me and stares at all the features on my face. "Well, she's beautiful. Light eyes and dark hair are so unique, you know?"

Sam's gaze locks on me, and his right eye ticks with annoyance. "That's what you love most about her?" he asks.

I reach over and grab Sterling's arm possessively. "We have a lot in common as well."

Sam's brows lift. "Do tell."

I swallow slowly and flick my eyes to my brother. Miles is starting to figure out that Sam is basically in the middle of some sort of dick measuring contest with my boyfriend. Or ex-boyfriend, I should say. "We both love the movies, and we love to go to parties." I force a smile that Sterling halfheartedly returns. "We have really similar backgrounds growing up. Sterling was a football player. I was a football cheerleader."

"How cute," Sam says, propping his chin on his hand like he's in rapture over this pathetic response I'm muttering like an idiot.

"We love pizza," I add weakly. Sterling bristles beside me, so I quickly blurt out, "And when we met, it was love at first sight, so the rest is history."

Sam sits back in his chair, bringing his ankle up to rest on his knee. "How cute. Both of you couples are so cute. You make me consider actually attempting monogamy."

"Bro, that's awesome!" Miles exclaims, his mood lightening as if he now understands why Sam is acting like such a maniac. "Is this interrogation all because you're falling for that ice fishing hottie you told me about?"

Sam doesn't reply to Miles. Instead, he hits me with a look that's so intense, so telling, so mind-blowingly overwhelming that I can't breathe.

My chair scrapes loudly on the floor as I move to stand. "Would you guys excuse me? I'm just going to hit the bathroom. Too much margarita," I state and wave my hand in front of my face.

I make my way to the long hallway at the back of the restaurant that leads to the bathrooms and a back exit. Feeling claustrophobic, I bypass the ladies' room and burst through the back door, finding myself in the back alley next to a couple of dumpsters and vents blasting out steam of

God only knows what. I inhale the frigid night air into my lungs and begin kicking the packed snow beneath my boots in a childish attempt to relieve some of this anxiety coursing through me.

What is even going on tonight? Why is Sterling here? Why is Sam here? Why is my brother such a sweet idiot, and why hasn't he figured out that I'm a complete fraud? Why is Kate not helping me get out of this freaking mess? This feeling in my chest? This is the reason I don't read novels with love triangles!

I lean against the stone wall and see a figure walking down the alley toward me. At first, I think it could be a murderer, so I turn to head back inside, but then Sam calls out my name. "Maggie!"

My brow furrows. "Sam?" Why are you walking down the alley?"

"I went out the front door so no one would think I followed you to the bathroom."

"You and bathrooms," I murmur, shaking my head.

Sam reaches me finally, cold air puffing out of his mouth as the single blue light in the alley shines down on us like a spotlight. "What are you doing? It's fucking freezing out here."

I cup my hands in front of my mouth and blow hot air into them. "I needed some air. I was being suffocated in there."

He barks out a haughty laugh. "I can see why. What the fuck are you doing here with that guy?"

I cross my arms over my chest defensively. "He just

showed up."

"And just like that, you're taking him back?" he snaps, his eyes wide and accusing. "He's a fucking idiot!"

"You spoke to him for five minutes!" I retort, defending not only myself but also Sterling incidentally.

"Five minutes is all it took," he grinds and stuffs his hands into his pockets, his broad shoulders lifting up to his ears as he attempts not to freeze his ass off out here.

"What are you even doing here, Sam?" I ask, pulling my blazer tighter around myself. "You made it very clear yesterday that you were done with this charade."

"I am."

"Then why are you here?" I ask, my voice echoing down the alley as my emotions begin to bubble to the surface.

"I'm fucking here to save you from yourself apparently," he snaps, his jaw jutting out angrily.

"Why would you think I need saving?"

"Because you're in there acting like a completely different person, Maggie. You're not being yourself. You're being the version you think he wants, and it's stupid. Don't change for a guy. You're not that girl."

"Sam, how well do you even know me?" I ask. I don't even know me anymore, so how the hell could he?

"I know you better than that dimwit in there, that's for fucking sure!" he growls, his voice low.

"Whatever," I snap, shaking my head in disbelief.

This seems to ignite something in Sam as he steps closer to me, his body vibrating with something intense. Something overwhelming and maybe even a little bit scary.

He crosses his arms over his chest. "You like Chardonnay, you hate beer, and you're terrible at fishing jokes."

"What are you doing?" I ask, but he doesn't stop to answer.

"You get a sick thrill out of waking people up. I think you charmed Marv at the bait shop because you felt bad about his first impression of you. You are so stubborn that no matter how bad you are at something, you never give up. You get hot when you're upset. You fucking hate the cold, but you actually do like ice fishing because a heater is involved, and I'm pretty sure you enjoy imagining a world of possibilities for the fish you catch and release."

My breath is stuck in my chest, unable to be released because nothing could have prepared me for this onslaught of words.

Shaking his head, Sam leans toward me to add, "Fuck your ex. I know you. And in the short time I've known you, I have never, not once, not even for a fraction of a second thought you were basic. Crazy? Yes. Delusional? Absolutely. Idealistic to the point of believing in unattainable fairy tales? One hundred fucking percent. But you are so far from basic, Maggie. You're like the great catch of the day that you know could never be topped even if you fished for the rest of your life."

My eyes well with tears because he's saying so much, yet somehow, he's still not saying enough. "What are you getting at with all of this, Sam? What exactly are you trying to tell me?"

"I want you, Maggie," he exclaims, the veins on his neck bulging as he steps right in front of me. "I want you…not as a fuck buddy and not as a secret friend who's helping you with a problem. I want you…for everything."

My icy fingers move up to cover my mouth. "But you don't do relationships."

"For you, I want to try," he states simply, his eyes softening around the edges.

"So just like that, you're ready now?" I ask, throwing my arms out wide. Because it seems too easy. If he was really ready, why didn't he say so at Marv's yesterday? Why did he let me walk out? "It has nothing to do with the fact that Sterling showed up and now you're jealous?"

"Yes, I'm fucking jealous," he growls, his jaw jutting out defiantly. "But it doesn't make any of what I just said less true. I want you!"

"You're going to break my heart," I cry out of nowhere, my mind reeling with a deep, dark, terrifying fear. Losing Sam will be a hundred times worse than losing Sterling. "You're going to break my heart worse than Sterling did."

"Because you care more about me," he retorts, stepping in so close to me, my back is pressed against the cold stone. "Admit it."

I shake my head, crossing my arms over my chest as I look away from him. "You're clueless about how to treat a woman. I mean, look at how you behaved Friday night."

"You said I was acting like a boyfriend that night!"

"That was before you fucked me bareback in a bar bathroom," I yell, my voice coming from the depths of my very soul. "What the hell was that all about?"

He flinches at my crass words and then grinds out through clenched teeth, "That was something only someone you completely trust would be allowed to do. And trust is at the core of relationships, isn't it?" He takes a deep breath and stares right into my eyes. "Maggie, I trust you. You trust me. It may have taken me a minute to work out my feelings for you, but I'm here now."

"Work out your feelings for me?" I huff and flick my hand to push my hair out of my face. "And what did you figure out?"

"I love you, Maggie," he croaks, his eyes haunted with that admission.

I suck in a sharp breath, my eyes blurring because nothing could have prepared me for those words to come out of his mouth. "You love me?"

His hands reach out to cup my face. "Like a fucking great day of fishing I love you," he murmurs against my lips. He presses his hard body flush against mine, and I can feel his heart pounding in his chest.

And in one breath…he's kissing me.

Not just kissing me, though…

Worshiping me.

He parts my lips with his tongue and dives in deep and purposeful with a ferocity to his touch that I've never felt before. He gives me everything he has, and I give it right back because I can't help myself. His lips taste like a confession my soul wants to hear. My hands tighten around his waist, aching for his warmth and affection to be felt over every inch of my body as our tongues dance and our bodies grind into one another.

It's too much and still not enough. It feels like no matter how hard he kisses me, that fear that lives deep in my belly will still be there when he's done. The anxiety of change presses down on me, and I'm being sucked out of the moment like yanking a rip cord during a free fall.

I pull back, my lips raw as I pant out hot breaths of cloudy air. My entire body has seemingly gone numb to the cold in response to this overwhelming declaration. I press a hand to Sam's chest. "This was so not a part of my plan."

"Fuck your plan, sparky," he replies, tilting my chin up so I look at him. "I can't promise you a fairy-tale happily ever after, but I can promise you an adventure that you don't have to fake. Hell, just waking up with you is an adventure."

A tear slips out and freezes halfway down my face. "I need time to process this."

He stiffens, his hands falling away from my face. "Time to process what?"

"All of it," I huff out with a laugh. "You and me. I need to get rid of Sterling and wrap my head around what this all means."

He shakes his head from side to side. "Bullshit."

"What?" I ask as he jerks away from me, putting way too much cold air between us.

"I'm not going to sit here and hope that I'm next in line for you, Maggie," he growls and narrows his eyes at me. "It won't happen."

"What do you mean?" I exclaim, stepping closer to him

with desperation in my eyes. "If you are finally admitting to having feelings for me, why can't you be patient and understanding?"

"Because I'm not the kind of guy who waits in line," he roars, clenching his fists at his sides, his entire body vibrating with a flash of anger that came out of nowhere. He suddenly stalks toward me, backing me up against the wall again and caging me in with his big arms. "I'm the kind of guy who's always in the front, and if you don't see me, then we are wasting our time."

"What the fuck is going on out here?" a voice states from the restaurant doorway.

I look over and see Sterling standing there with the door propped open, his eyes dark with accusation.

Sam exhales, and his lips puff out angrily as he pushes off the wall. "You need to leave," he states in an ominous tone.

"I need to leave?" Sterling barks back, stepping out and letting the door close behind him. "I think you're the one who needs to step away from my girlfriend."

"She's not your fucking girlfriend," Sam growls as he takes a step toward Sterling.

Sterling looks at me, his eyes full of confusion.

"Yeah, I know," Sam answers Sterling's silent question. "I know you had the fucking decency to dump her on Christmas. And I know you called her basic. And I know you're ten times fucking wrong for her. So unless you want my fist in your face, I suggest you leave us the hell alone."

Sterling laughs, stepping right into Sam's space to play

up his two-inch height advantage. "There is no us with you and her. I'm her past and her future, bro. So step the fuck back."

He reaches out and shoves Sam on the shoulder.

Sam laughs with delight. "You do not want to put your hands on me."

"Don't put your hands on my pussy, and we won't have a problem," Sterling retorts and reaches out to push Sam again.

With those words, Sam snaps.

He dodges Sterling's hand that's reaching for his chest, and in a quick maneuver, he manages to hold a foot out and push Sterling in the back, sending him down to the ground with a loud thud. Sterling hops back up on his feet and lunges for Sam with all the athleticism of a quarterback while Sam grabs Sterling like a prepared lineman.

Sterling rears his right hand back and sends it flying into Sam's ribs. Sam winces at the blow, but then he yanks Sterling off his hips, and in a flash, Sam's fist connects with Sterling's face.

The blow throws Sterling into a spinning half circle, and before I can scream, "Watch out," Sterling falls straight back toward the wall, cracking the back of his head on an exhaust pipe.

"Sterling!" I exclaim, rushing over and dropping to my knees beside his limp body on the ground. I carefully lift his head off the ground, and my hand feels instant wetness.

I look up at Sam. "He's bleeding."

"Fuck," Sam growls and rakes his hand through his hair.

Suddenly, Miles bursts through the back door, his eyes hitting Sam, then me, and then Sterling. "What happened?"

"Sterling hit his head on this pipe. We need to call an ambulance."

Kate appears next, and she instantly whips out her phone. "I'm on it."

"Sterling, are you okay?" I ask, my voice thick with anxiety. "How many fingers am I holding up?"

Sterling squints and stares up at me, his eyes glassing over in the blue light from up above.

"Sam, what the fuck happened?" Miles asks.

"I'm sorry," Sam husks, his voice laced with regret. "I'm sorry for everything."

I look up just in time to see Sam turn on his heel and run down the alley, leaving me behind with my brother, his girlfriend, and my bleeding ex-boyfriend.

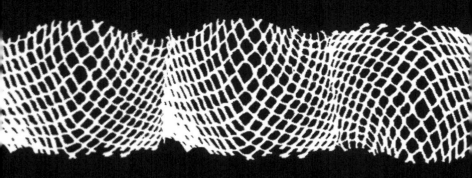

CHAPTER 20

There's A Fine Line Between Fishing... And Standing On The Shore Like An Idiot

Maggie

An hour later, I'm seated in the emergency room waiting area of the Boulder hospital with Kate on one side of me and Miles on the other. I keep looking nervously at my brother whose teeth are probably cracking from how hard he's clenched his jaw since we arrived.

He hasn't said a single word since the ambulance showed up to take Sterling away. And he refuses to even look at me. So basically my brother is a ticking time bomb, and he could detonate at any moment.

Out of the corner of my eye, I see a man in blue scrubs come striding out of the double doors where they took Sterling when we arrived. He looks decidedly grumpy as he grabs a clipboard out of a slot.

"Hello, Dr. Dick," Kate whispers into my ear.

I frown and shake my head at her and then flick my eyes to Miles.

Kate laughs softly. "I'm an erotic romance novelist, Maggie. Everyone is material for my imagination, and Dr. Dick over there might just be my next bestseller," she whispers.

"Why are you calling him Dr. Dick?" I ask, puzzled.

"He looks angry," she says, her eyes squinting at him objectively. "Look at his posture. He's totally closed off and wants nothing to do with people. A male nurse probably just threw himself at him, and he had to reject him, which upset him because he hates communicating, and it's been over a year since he got laid. Plus, you can totally see the outline of his dick in those scrub pants!"

My head turns to gape at her. "Kate!"

Her face twists. "Yeah, you're right. That's a weak plot. I'll workshop it and get back to you."

Suddenly, Dr. Dick calls out, "Maggie Hudson?"

"That's me!" I exclaim, standing up out of my chair.

With a sullen frown, he makes his way over to me. "You came in with Sterling Fitzgibbons?" he asks.

"Yes, I did."

"Okay. He's going to be fine. He just came out of X-ray, and there are no signs of a concussion. We had to give him two stitches."

"Two?" I ask, shocked by that small of a number. "Only two?"

He nods, his expression bored. "Head wounds are notorious for looking a lot worse than they are. Honestly, he could have driven himself in for the stitches."

I exhale heavily and look over at Kate who has her hand clasped tightly over her mouth, completely failing to hide her amusement.

The doctor then adds flatly, "He was crying pretty hard during the stitches, so we gave him some pain medicine that will make him a little loopy. He shouldn't drive himself home."

Kate explodes with snort-filled laughter against her palm, spit flying everywhere as she loses her will to stay cool.

The doctor frowns over at her. "He's completing his discharge papers now and will be out soon."

I press my lips together to keep from laughing and manage to reply. "Okay, thank you, Dr. Dick, I mean, Doctor."

Kate erupts into full-on hysterics as he turns to leave. I shake my head at Kate whose eyes are wet with tears of laughter. Miles is still doing the brooding brother routine, so I feel a little alone with my relief that Sterling is okay.

Regaining her composure, Kate turns to Miles, and says, "Babe, can you go get me a water?"

With a glower, he nods and takes off down the hallway around the corner where we'd spotted the vending machines. I watch him leave, and then groan, "Is Miles ever going to talk to me again?"

She shakes her head sadly. "Mostly likely. But honestly, I can't even tell what exactly he's mad about."

"Me neither," I reply and drop back down in my chair.

Kate sidles up next to me. "He should be mad at Sterling. Good God, the way he was carrying on when the ambulance showed up, I thought for sure he was leaking brain matter."

A burst of manic laughter explodes out of me because holy heck, she's right. What a mess that was. And all just for two stitches?

"My emotions are shot," I say by way of an explanation for my outburst.

Kate turns to face me. "What the heck happened out there anyway? Tell me quick before Miles gets back."

I shrug helplessly. "Sam and I were talking, and Sterling showed up. It got heated, and the next thing I knew, Sterling was bleeding on the ground."

"Some football player," Kate murmurs.

I pin her with a look. "Tonight was all my fault. If I never would've started sleeping with Sam and lying to Miles, none of this would have happened."

"What the fuck?" Miles's voice bellows as he comes around the corner with two bottles of water in hand. "What did you just say, Meg?"

"Miles!" I exclaim, my eyes wide as I stand.

"Did you just say that you fucked Sam? Tell me I heard wrong."

"There's more to it than that—"

He holds his hand with the water bottle out to stop me from speaking. "Wait...wait, wait. Answer me. Did you fuck my best friend?"

I inhale sharply. "Yes."

"That's all I need to hear," he says, shoving the water bottles into Kate's hands and shooting daggers at her. "And you fucking knew?"

Kate winces. "I did, but Miles, Maggie and Sterling were broken up. She was totally single—"

"What?" Miles growls, looking at me with accusing eyes. "When did you break up with Sterling?"

My heart inverts inside my chest as I quietly reply. "He broke up with me on Christmas morning. I was supposed to go visit him, but instead of going to the airport like Mom and Dad thought, I drove to Boulder and checked into a bed and breakfast for a week to get my head on straight. I didn't want to tell you about my breakup."

"So you've been *lying* to me all this time?" he roars, the veins on his neck bulging angrily. "I'm your brother, Maggie. You should have told me."

"I know!" I reply, my voice wobbling at the end. "But I thought Sterling and I would get back together, and I didn't want you to hate him."

"I hate him, all right," he replies, clenching his jaw and exhaling out his nose like a bull ready to charge. "And now I get to hate my best friend...so thanks a fucking lot, Megs." He turns to walk away, and I reach out and grab his arm, trying to drag him back toward me.

"Miles, I'm sorry! Sam and I were just supposed to be casual and fun. It wasn't supposed to get this complicated."

"You're my little sister, and that is my best fucking friend. You both should have known better." He yanks his arm out of my hand and storms out of the ER without looking back.

I look at Kate with wide, terrified eyes. "This is bad."

Kate nods. "Really bad."

Then, to add fuel to the fire, Sterling comes shuffling out of the double doors holding an ice pack to the back of his head. He looks at me with a somber look. "Twelve stitches. Can you believe that?"

My eyes roll so far to the back of my head, I can see the wall behind me. "I have to go, Sterling."

"Go where?" he exclaims.

"I can't be around you anymore," I state honestly because it's about damn time I start being honest for once.

"Maggie," Sterling growls, grabbing my arm and turning me on my heel. "What about us?"

I shake my head, laughter bubbling up inside me because just looking at Sterling as he is right now, I can't believe I ever truly loved him. "Us? You dumped me, Sterling. There is no us. Probably never should have been. I thought I knew what love was, but I was wrong...so wrong about so many things."

I turn to leave with Kate by my side, and I hear Sterling shout behind me. "So you're just leaving me in an emergency room in Boulder? Where the hell am I supposed to go?"

"I'll text you the number to a lovely bed and breakfast," I call over my shoulder. "Tell Claire I said hi!"

Just as we fly through the emergency room doors, we have to jump back out of the way for a stretcher being wheeled in. I glance down at the patient, and the girl looks oddly familiar.

"Lynsey?" Kate asks, her eyes wide and questioning. "Lynsey! Holy shit!"

"Oh my god, Kate. Thank God!" she cries, tears streaming down her face.

"Are you okay?"

"I'm fine," she says pathetically.

"What happened?"

She whimpers as she clutches her hand. "I was on a date, and I cut myself with a steak knife."

"Yikes."

"And I'm having an allergic reaction."

Kate's and my eyes fall to the blotches covering Lynsey's chest in what looks like a really cute first date dress.

"And I twisted my ankle when I tried to run to the bathroom, and I think it might be broken."

Kate shakes her head in disbelief. "Holy shit balls, Lynsey."

"I know. And then my Tinder date just bailed on me."

The paramedic looks up at Kate with sad eyes. "Yeah, we even said he could ride in the ambulance with her, and he passed."

Lynsey lets out another whimper. "I even heard him complaining about picking up the bill."

"What a fucker."

The paramedic agrees.

Kate looks down and grabs her friend's unbandaged hand. "Well, I'm here. I'll stay with you."

Lynsey's eyes fill with grateful tears as Kate turns to look at me. "Your car is here, right Meg? You good to get home?"

"I'm good," I confirm and nod at the paramedic so he can continue through the doors. "Get well soon, Lynsey!"

As they head into the hospital, I hear Kate say, "Oh my god, we are so requesting Dr. Dick!"

And with that, Kate will probably have loads of hot doctor, clumsy girl book ideas floating around in her mind and can hopefully let go of the brother's best friend narrative.

Thank goodness for small favors.

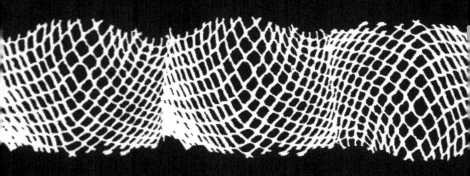

CHAPTER 21

*Fishing Is A Jerk On One End Of The Line
Waiting For A Jerk On The Other End*

Sam

"I can't believe you fucked my sister!" Miles roars as he bursts through my front door.

I knew this was coming when I saw his truck pull in, and now I have to face it. Exhaling heavily, I set the ice pack for my fist down in the sink and walk out to the foyer. "I was going to tell you everything," I say, holding my hands up defensively like a man approaching a bear.

"Oh goodie, just the kind of story I like to hear," Miles snarls back. "One that involves my best friend and my sister fucking betraying me."

I roll my eyes at his dramatics. "We didn't betray you."

He shakes his head, clearly not interested in hearing

what I have to say. "I can't believe you'd risk our friendship for a quick lay! Why her of all people?"

"I didn't know she was your sister at the time, man. We had no clue who the other was. As far as I knew, she was just some girl I ran into at Marv's!"

His face goes white as realization dawns on him. "This is the ice fishing hottie you were telling me about?"

I nod my head.

"The one with the"—he swallows uncomfortably and cups his hands out in front of him—"water balloon tits?"

I wince and nod again.

His hands fly up to scrub over his horrified face. "How could you do this to me, man? How could you play musical beds with my sister just like all your other conquests?"

"She's different, man," I say, taking a step toward him in warning.

"You're damn right she's different!" Miles bellows, his voice shaking with rage. "She's my sister, but apparently, that meant nothing to you because you guys continued to do all this behind my goddamned back."

I exhale heavily and murmur, "Well, I don't think you would have liked me to seduce her in front of your back any fucking better."

Miles turns beet red as though he's about to spout blood from his ears. He steps toe to toe with me, his knuckles cracking at his sides as he prepares to knock me out. And right now, I'd be fine if he did. Oblivion would be better than what I'm feeling.

Instead, he steps back, shakes his head, and looks down

at me as if I'm the dirt on his boots. "It's like you're trying to be like your dad now. He fucked around on your family, so now you're fucking around on mine."

My blood pressure skyrockets. "Come again?"

"Like father, like son," he grinds out, his eyes cold and vapid as they look down at me.

Without hesitation, I bolt for Miles, taking him out at the knees. He crashes to the wooden floor like a goddamned tree, knocking over the coat rack in the entry. "That's below the belt, you fucker."

He struggles out of my grip around his hips, and growls, "How? How is this any lower than you fucking my sister?" With a fast reversal, he attempts to throw me into a full nelson that I twist out of and come over the top of him, catching him in a strong headlock.

I squeeze my arm around his neck, and yell, "Because I'm not just fucking your sister. I'm in love with her, you dick stain."

Miles freezes, no longer fighting my hold on him. "Bullshit," he growls.

"It's the truth," I grind through clenched teeth still holding him tightly. "I've never said those words in my life until now."

With a huff, I release Miles, and he falls backward onto his butt, his legs bent toward me and his eyes hard on mine. "How do you know?"

I swallow slowly, cracking my neck painfully as an ache shoots up from where he cranked on me. With a heavy sigh, I reply, "I miss her when she's not around. I can't stop smiling when I read her texts. The minute something half-way interesting happens to me, she's the first person I want to tell. It's a fucking unicorn shittin' rainbows, man."

He's still out of breath when he looks at me. "A unicorn shittin' rainbows?" he repeats.

I nod somberly. "I wouldn't say it if it wasn't true. And I wouldn't risk our friendship if I didn't want a future with her."

"Jesus, man. You're serious? Like long-term serious?" Miles asks, running a hand through his hair.

"Fuck, I think I'd marry her tomorrow if you weren't such a controlling asshole."

"You'd marry my sister?" Miles asks, his voice taking on a weird, high-pitched tone.

"That's what I said."

"Would I be your best man?"

I look up at him, his eyes full of hope and wonder as I reply stone-cold seriously, "Yes."

In a flash, Miles stands, grabs me up off the floor, and pulls me into a bear hug that crushes all my organs. He slaps my back so hard, I'm certain I'll have Miles-size handprint bruises there tomorrow. He sniffles into my shoulder. "I'm feeling very emotional about this," he murmurs.

"I can tell, big guy," I reply, holding on for dear life.

"Part of me wants to love this, but part of me still wants to murder you a little."

"I get it."

"Mixed emotions are hard."

"Yeah, they are."

311

Miles pulls back, gently wiping at his red eyes. "Does Maggie love you too?"

I shake my head. "I don't know, man. She never said."

Miles blinks nervously at me. "If she doesn't come for you, I'll kill her."

I smile a small smile. "Boy, you really came around quick, didn't ya?"

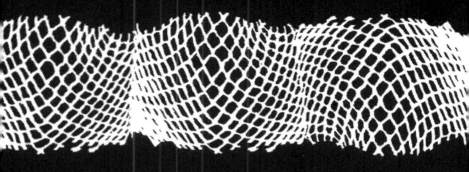

CHAPTER 22

When the Going Gets Tough...
The Tough Go Fishing

Sam

The next day, it takes all of my energy not to text Maggie. After my wrestling match with Miles, he told me Sterling was okay and only needed a couple of stitches, which means I have nothing more to say to Maggie. I've said all I can.

At Tire Depot, Miles tries to talk to me, but I don't want to hear anything his sister has to say from him. If she's back together with Sterling, I need to hear it from her. But she never shows up. She doesn't call or text. Not even a lame fishing joke. So by the end of the day, I decide the best thing for me to do is to go fishing.

It's dark after work, but Marv says there are some good

spots to hit at night where the fish will come to you. I sled out to the lake he recommended and do my best to quiet the raging voice in my head reminding me I screwed everything up for good.

My fishing hut is quiet as I jig my rig by the dim light of my lantern. I keep thinking about what Maggie would be rambling about if she were out here. She'd probably ask about when fish sleep, and where they sleep, and if they sleep with their families, or if they're just swimming along and all of a sudden black out only to wake up the next day and discover they've lost their entire family.

"Get a fucking grip, Sammy," I mumble to myself and then frown when headlights shine along the side of my hut.

I prop my pole in its holder, grab my lantern, and unzip the doorway to see a sled approaching over the ice. I squint through the flurries and see headlights to a sled with two riders on board. The driver looks to be wearing a red and white snowsuit, but it can't be Maggie. There's no way she can drive a snowmobile.

The sled comes straight at me, stopping with a harsh jerk only four feet from my hut. My jaw drops when I see Maggie pull off her helmet and shake out her long, dark hair. "This thing drives like a dream, Marv!" she exclaims and turns around to look at him.

He removes his helmet and looks like he's just shit himself. "That will never happen again, darling," he says softly, his voice trembling with fear.

"What?" Maggie asks, hopping off the bench and holding her helmet under her arm. "I thought I did pretty good for my first time."

Marv's wrinkled eyes go wide. "You said you were an experienced snowmobiler!"

"Welllll." Maggie shoots him a crooked smile. "I should have said I'm an experienced rider. I've never driven before."

Marv presses his hands to his face and shakes his head with exasperation. "I have to go. I need my blood pressure medication." He looks at me with a terrified shake of the head, yanks on his helmet, and takes off faster than I've ever seen an old man drive in my entire life.

Maggie turns to look at me, her face glowing in the light of my lantern as perfect white snowflakes cling to her dark hair.

"Hi!" she says excitedly.

"Um…hi," I reply, still totally fucking confused by her presence out here.

"I was waiting at your house for you, and you never showed, so I checked at Marv's, and he said you were here." She shrugs and smiles awkwardly. "I convinced him to give me a ride out here."

I nod and reply woodenly. "I…um…decided to do some night fishing."

She looks back at my hut with wide eyes. "I didn't know that was a thing."

"It's a thing." I shrug.

She nods and sticks her hands in the pockets of her snowsuit. "So how are you?"

I exhale heavily. "I'm fine. Look, Maggie, we don't have to do this—"

"I wanted to tell you this great fishing story," she says, stepping into the light so I can see the bright blue of her eyes.

She smiles hopefully up at me, and I can't help but smile back. "How do I know if it's true? Fishermen are always telling lies."

She presses her lips together. "Well, this one is a love story, so it has to be true."

I roll my eyes because even after everything that's happened, she still believes in fairy tales. "I'm more of a real-life romance kind of guy," I reply, setting the lantern down on the ice and crossing my arms over my chest.

"Then you're going to like this one," she says, pressing her hands together to begin. "So there's this girl. Let's call her Margaret. She's never fished a day in her life…but one day, in the dead of winter, she hears these guys talking about a famous fish that always gets away. Now Margaret is a determined sort of gal who enjoys a bit of a challenge, so she decides she's going to catch this famous fish and impress her whole family."

"Margaret sounds stubborn," I interrupt.

Maggie tilts her head, snow sticking to the tips of her long eyelashes. "I see it more as tenacious but tomatoe, tomahto. Anyway, she shows up at this bait and tackle shop and upsets everyone because she's running her mouth like a smartass. But this one lonely fisherman…let's call him Sid…takes pity on Margaret and decides to help her out."

She removes her gloves and tucks her hair behind her ears before continuing. "He's a grumpy old fisherman, but magically, the two hit it off and become fast friends in his ice fishing hut. Time flies as they catch small fish after small fish. It's a great time, but of course, Margaret isn't happy because she wants the big fish. The uncatchable catch. The one that always gets away."

"Stubborn," I add again.

"Okay, she's stubborn," Maggie concedes with a wink. "But as the weeks pass, she finds out that Sid doesn't fish with anyone. In fact, she's the first person he's ever even let inside his fishing hut. Margaret is so touched by his kindness, she begins to fall for the grumpy old guy who was kind enough to help her in the beginning."

Maggie steps closer to me, the light from below casting a halo around her head as she places herself right in my space. "But once Margaret stops focusing on impressing her family and accepts what's in her heart, she decides to stop baiting her hook."

I shake my head from side to side. "It's hard to catch a fish without any bait."

She bites her lip. "It's not, though, because Margaret figured out that the biggest catch wasn't in that icy water…it was sitting right beside her all along."

I exhale heavily as Maggie reaches up and cups my face in her hands. I turn and press my lips to her cold palm, and murmur, "Let me guess, Sid is Sam?"

She beams up at me. "Only if Margaret is Sparky."

I nod once, letting the sentiment of that story soothe the ache in my chest. "Are you sure you're done chasing after that big fish?"

She splays her hand on my chest. "I don't even care about the catch. I just care about you. I love you, Sam."

My heart races in my chest as I lean down to kiss this stubborn, amazing girl in the snow, but she stops me just before we connect. "And it wasn't love at first sight either. It was better…it was like a fish you have to be patient to catch because there's no way you're going to let it get away."

"God, these fishing puns are turning me on, sparky," I murmur, and she laughs against my lips. I press my forehead to hers, and add, "You totally caught me hook, line, and sinker."

Maggie

The prospect of ice fishing at night definitely intrigues me, but not as much as the prospect of being horizontal with Sam. We tear down his hut in record time and race back to his house like a couple who have been separated for weeks, not days.

He parks his sled in front of his house, and we clumsily begin kissing in the snow as we make our way up the steps and into his cabin. The blast of warm air after a long ride in the dark is almost as great as the warmth building between my legs.

We strip off our winter layers and are down to our

underwear when Sam picks me up around the waist. My legs squeeze around his hips, pulling him as close as I can as our mouths fuse, and his tongue sweeps in to taste me.

He turns to walk down the hallway and heads straight for his darkened bedroom. A security light from outside shines down on his delicious-looking bed. In another breath, he pulls the covers back, and I'm laid out on the sheets. He slowly removes my panties and bra, flinging them to the floor with his boxers. The bed dips as he positions himself over me, one hand on either side of my face as he looks down at me naked and trembling beneath him.

"This is the first time I've ever done this with someone I love," he says gently, his eyes full of care and concern. "I want to do this right."

I reach up and run my hands through his hair, sweeping down to his jaw as he turns to kiss my palm. "This already feels all kinds of right."

He smiles a satisfied smile, then his face grows serious. "I love you, Maggie."

"I love you too, Sam." I reach down and guide him between my legs. With one firm thrust, he fills me, holding himself for a moment while his lips connect with mine.

His back muscles tense and contract as he moves inside me, my body rolling up to meet his as we gyrate against each other, building in speed as we adjust to each other. The fullness of him inside the tightness of me provides the perfect amount of friction.

He dips his head and pulls my nipple into his mouth hard and sharp. I cry out, my hands running through his hair and pulling on his short strands with delicious agony. "Sam, oh my god," I groan out, my voice deep and overwhelmed as the sensation between my legs rolls through my entire body.

"God, I love your noises," he murmurs, pressing kisses up my neck until he reaches my lips. "I'll never tire of them."

"Don't stop," I groan loudly because his voice and his movement inside me are all adding to the climb. To the delirious state of mind I currently find myself in. "Keep going, Sam."

He thrusts faster, the sounds of our hips slapping together echoing off the walls along with my cries. When he begins to whisper sweet nothings against my skin and then swipes his tongue over my tender, tingling flesh, I feel an unimaginable heaviness flowing between my legs.

"You're so sexy." *Kiss.* "You're so stubborn." *Kiss.* "I'm going to love you forever." That last one brings tears to my eyes as my dreams grow bigger and brighter and more clear than ever before. The dreams I have with this man—this sweet, honest, soulful man who tells me he isn't a fairy tale, but he is real—are incredible dreams, but for once, the reality is so much better than the fairy tale.

"God, I love you," he groans, brushing a kiss along my clavicle.

"More!" I cry, my desire shameless and needy.

"I love you," he whispers against my shoulder. "I love you," he whispers on my neck. "I love you," he whispers in my ear. The tears seeping from my eyes are beautiful and real and wonderful. And when he finishes peppering my entire body with his words, I realize that my dreams were nothing compared to this.

We climax together. At the same time. With the same breath. Our hearts beating as one. I stare up into his eyes and feel as though no two souls could be more connected in the entire world than we are right now.

After we clean up, we return to bed naked and beyond satiated. Sam wraps his arms around me and holds my back to his chest, his breath falling into rhythm with my own.

"I hope you're ready for all of this," I state softly, staring out the windows from where my head is propped on a pillow.

"All of what?" he asks, pressing a kiss to my bare shoulder.

"All of me, all the time," I reply with a sigh. "I'm a lot."

He tightens his grip around me. "I'm aware."

"And you know I like to dream," I reiterate.

His shoulders shake with silent laughter. "Yes, I do, sparky."

With a nod, I turn over to face him, his eyes glowing in the faint light from outside. "But do you realize you got the tamed down, recapped version of Maggie dreams? Full-on girlfriend dreams are a whole other thing to prepare for."

He narrows his eyes on me. "Give me your worst."

My brows lift. "My worst, most delusional, most fanciful dreams that sent the last guy running for the hills?"

He nods stoically and kisses me on the lips quickly. "I can take it. Your crazy dream talk is one of the things I love about you, sparky."

A squeal of excitement shoots through my entire core as I roll onto my back and gaze up at the ceiling. "Oh my heck, you're giving me full rein. I hope you're prepared."

He kisses my shoulder. "Bring it."

I swallow hard and frown as I think for a moment. "Okay, here's the love story of Maggie and Sam. So I'm going to move to Boulder, obviously. You have Tire Depot and plans with Miles to expand the business, and even though I want to strangle Kate a couple of times a day, she's actually one of my favorite people in life...so Boulder is going to be our home."

"I like the start of this," he says, and I can hear the smile in his voice.

"I'm going to meet your mom at Sunday brunch, and she is going to love me."

"Full of yourself, are ya?" he asks, pinning me with surprised eyes.

"Duh!" I exclaim, flicking my hands out in front of me. "She's going to see me as the light to your dark, the sweet to your salty. All my goodness has completely brightened your soul."

"Mmm, I agree," he murmurs, reaching over and squeezing my breast.

I shove him off. "I'm musing here. This is our fairy-tale future, and I can't lose focus."

"Sorry," he says, sliding his hand down to wrap around my waist.

"Your nieces and nephews will love me because I'll read stories to them. But your sisters will be a little hateful because I'm taking you away from them. Eventually, they'll warm to me, especially when we have kids because they'll love seeing their little brother become a daddy."

"Kids?" Sam asks, and I look over to see a surprised look on his face.

"I was thinking two?" I state it in a question but then wave him off because these are my dreams, not his. "However, I could see us having a surprise third baby when our youngest is like ten years old because you're such a horn ball, and you'll refuse to get a vasectomy."

This makes Sam bark out a laugh. "God, your mind is incredible." He pulls me to him and kisses my temple.

"I haven't even gotten to the good part yet," I reply, elbowing him softly. "We're going to have a boat. A pontoon boat for the family where all the grandkids will fit and take the most epic fishing trips ever."

I look over and see warmth and affection in Sam's eyes that nearly takes my breath away. I expected shock and judgment, laughter, and loads of teasing. The worst-case scenario would be fear-stricken regret. What I didn't expect was to be looking into the eyes of a man who's just discovered the meaning of life, and I'm the one who showed it to him.

Without a response, Sam pulls me to him, our naked bodies flush as he kisses me with so much tenderness, my eyes sting behind my closed lids. This is a dream come true reaction. This is the reaction that makes me feel like I really can be my truest self with this man, and he will accept me—crazy, optimistic love stories and all.

We pull apart breathless, and I touch my fingers to his wrist. "How's your pulse? You sure you're not getting cold feet?" I slide my feet over and curl them around his legs.

"I promise you, Maggie. I am toasty warm," he says, his voice low as he hits me with that adorable smile that he fails to hide every single time.

I grin against his lips. "So does this mean I'm not going to wake up tomorrow and find you gone?"

"No way," he replies and gets a serious look on his face. "I love our fictional story, and I hope it comes true."

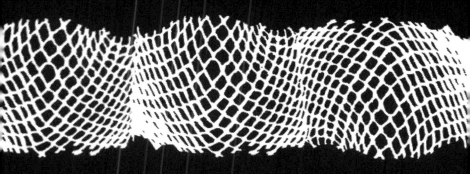

CHAPTER 23

Hook, Line, And Sinker

Sam

A Few Months Later

"Hey, Marv…how does one become a master bait-er?" Maggie asks, pushing her sleeves up before she sweeps a net into a basin of fresh minnows.

I look over at Marv standing beside Maggie behind the live bait counter with a clipboard in his hand. "What's that you're saying?"

Maggie transports the bouncing minnows into her customer's minnow bucket. "I was getting bait for a guy in here the other day, and he said I looked like a great master baiter. I said, I've only been working here a couple of months, and I didn't even know being a master baiter was a thing."

The male customer standing in front of Maggie looks

over at me with wide eyes that I return because seriously… what the hell?

Marv's face twists up in confusion. "I've heard of pro-master fishermen. But not master baiters. Surely, I'm a master baiter. I've been doing it my whole life."

My hand flies up to cover my mouth as a sputter of laughter lands on my palm. The customer crosses his arms to stare at the floor and conceal his reaction to Maggie and Marv's conversation.

"You're clearly a great master baiter," Maggie replies with wide eyes. "But I wonder how much practice it'll take for me to become one?"

Marv removes his ball cap and scratches his head. "I think you've caught on quick here these past few weeks, so hell, I'll give you the promotion right now if you want."

"You will?" Maggie exclaims.

He shrugs, his feeble posture hunching over the countertop. "You pretty much gave yourself a promotion on your first day of work here, darlin', so I don't see the trouble with adding master baiter to it."

Maggie turns to me with a bright, beaming smile. "Did you hear that, Sam? I was just promoted!" She snaps the lid shut on the minnow bucket and sticks a sheet to it. "There you go, sir. Barb will ring you up in the tackle shop."

The guy nods his thanks and turns to leave, offering me a bemused shake of the head as he goes.

Maggie props her elbows on the counter. "Maggie Hudson, Marv's Bait and Tackle marketing director and master baiter. Has a good ring to it, right?"

I can't let this go on any further, right? I have to tell her, don't I? She stands up quickly, bending down to grab her spring jacket. "You ready to head home?"

I nod and pull my lips into my mouth to stop myself from replying, "Come on," because the puns have already gone way too far.

She waves goodbye to Marv and comes around the counter, stretching her hand out to mine. With a smile, I lace my fingers with hers, and we head out to my truck.

It's springtime in Boulder now, which means Maggie and I have been together for a few months. She went back to Utah after the big Sterling mess to tell her parents about their breakup. They were understanding and sympathetic and all the good things a family who truly loves each other would be. Then, without my knowing, she packed up the rest of her stuff and moved in with Miles and Kate so she could start looking for a job around Boulder.

It wasn't something she discussed with me aside from our fictional future musings that one night in bed. She said she wanted to make the decision on her own. She made the mistake of listening to a boyfriend's ideas for her future once, and she wanted to take her own life in her hands this time. She also took it upon herself to become Marv's new permanent employee of the month. They're an odd pairing, but no more crazy than Maggie and me.

"What do you want to do tonight?" Maggie asks, nudging me with her shoulder as I open the truck door for her.

"Drink and have sex," I reply as she hops up into the cab.

"Weird, me too!" she exclaims with wide eyes. "But

before we head to your place, we have to stop to check out this townhouse that Kate called me about. I guess it's the same one that she and her ex bought together. He's selling it, and it's right next door to Lynsey. Lynsey is totally crazy, and I think she'd be a fun neighbor."

I nod and close the door to my truck, walking over to the driver's side with my brow furrowed in thought. The idea of Maggie moving out of Miles's house in Jamestown and closer to me in Boulder is a good thing. I should be happy because it'll make seeing her every day that much easier. But this townhouse idea irritates me.

A short while later, we pull up in front of Kate's old place on the east side of Boulder. I'd been here once before for a party. It's a secluded two-story townhouse with a great view of the Flatirons, but it's no cabin in the woods.

Maggie walks through with the realtor and makes comments about all the rustic finishes and how much she loves the natural lighting. And I can't fault her for it because it's a great space. But it's not with me.

And I would have thought after all that dreaming Maggie did early on, she'd be on the same page as me. Hell, I told Miles I would marry his sister before I even knew she loved me back. I'm all in, no question. So why isn't she pushing for us to move in together?

We end up in the kitchen, and the agent gives us some space to talk it over. Maggie's eyes are wide and excited as she says, "This is perfect. It's a little expensive for me because Marv doesn't pay the greatest, but I could probably find a roommate. I need to make some more friends in

Boulder anyway."

"You don't need more friends," I reply grumpily. "You're with me all the time anyway. And besides, you've been hanging out with Kate, and Lynsey, and their friend, Dean, I thought."

She huffs out a laugh. "I know, but still. It's nice to meet new people."

"If you have a roommate, then they're going to hear everything we do," I reply, feeling the childish pout on my face but not giving a fuck.

She smiles a sexy smile that makes my dick thump with life. "We can do that stuff at your place. I think this space could really work for me. Not too far from Marv's Bait and Tackle either, which is nice."

I pull my lower lip into my mouth, chewing it for a moment before I blurt out, "Or you could move in with me."

Her eyes widen as the corners of her mouth curve up into a smile. "Move in with you?"

I shrug like it's no big deal, which just makes her smile grow even more. "Yeah, that's what I said."

"Do you actually want me to move in with you, Sam?" she asks, crossing her arms under her beautiful water balloon breasts.

I shrug again. "I mean…it makes sense."

She frowns. "That's not very romantic."

"Jesus hell, Maggie," I snap, rolling my eyes. "Not every moment has to be a scene from a romance novel."

"You're right," Maggie says, turning on her heels to take in the kitchen. "That's why I should take this."

"What do you mean?" I bark out, my blood pressure spiking with annoyance.

"Practically speaking, it's probably too soon for us to move in together." She glides her hand along the granite countertop and gives the house one more nod. "And since we're not living in a romance novel, this townhouse is the right choice."

My jaw drops as she turns to walk out of the kitchen and make her way to the front door. Is she seriously turning me down because I didn't ask her romantically enough? With a growl of frustration, I stomp through the house and out the front door to see Maggie on the small front deck.

"What the hell, sparky?"

She turns with wide, innocent eyes. "What?"

"You're telling me no?"

She lifts her brows and shrugs, her lips twisting off to one side, showcasing that adorable dimple of hers.

I press my hand to my forehead. "So wait a second…I love you. You love me. I've heard you dream about our future before. I tell you that you should move in with me, and you decide to buy a townhouse?"

"Sam," Maggie says, walking toward me with a playful glint in eyes. "I know you're real-life romance, and I love you for it. But even real life deserves some moments of romance. When we decide to move in together, it'll be because we're excited about our next great adventure. Not because it makes logical sense." She rises up on her tiptoes and presses a chaste kiss to my lips, then turns and makes her way down the steps toward my truck.

Fucking hell, this woman is infuriating, and maddening, and brilliant, and stubborn, and all of it turns me the fuck on. With a deep breath in, I slap the side railing and jog out after her, moving past her before she reaches my truck. I grab my keys out of my pocket and hold out the one that unlocks my front door. Dropping to my knees in the grass, I outstretch my hands and say, "Megan Allison Hudson, will you do me the honor of moving in with me because I'm so fucking in love with you that I'm starting to believe in the fairy-tale happily ever after."

She laughs at my declaration, her eyes shining with pride as she clutches her hands to her chest. She reaches out and takes my keys. "It took you long enough!"

I press my hands to my thighs and stand, eyeing her skeptically. "Were you really going to buy this house?"

"Of course I was," she snaps back, while fingering my key like it's a diamond ring. "Miles and Kate go at it like rabbits, and no sister should have to hear that."

"Then why wouldn't you just talk to me about moving in to my place?"

Her blue eyes flash with shock. "Are you kidding me? This is your first relationship…I'm not going to be the one scaring you off with big moves here. And it was so cute how you got down on your knees to ask me!" she gushes excitedly, clutching the key to her chest.

I shake my head at her. "But I asked you inside first."

She tips her chin up, a proud smirk playing on her lips. "That's not how I'm going to retell this story to our grandkids."

She winks, and I can't help but smile at her. God, she's cute when she's crazy. I wrap my arms around her waist and pull her in close. "And what were our grandkids names again?"

"Finnigan and Lacey."

I purse my lips and nod. "As long as we can teach them to fish, I like this story."

The End

MORE BOOKS BY
AMY DAWS

The London Lovers:
Becoming Us: Finley's Story Part 1
A Broken Us: Finley's Story Part 2
London Bound: Leslie's Story
Not the One: Reyna's Story

A London Lovers/Harris Brothers Crossover Novel:
Strength: Vi Harris & Hayden's Story

The Harris Brothers Series:
Challenge: Camden's Story
Endurance: Tanner's Story
Keeper: Booker's Story
Surrender & Dominate: Gareth's Duet

Wait With Me: A Tire Shop Rom Com
Next In Line: A Bait Shop Rom Com

Pointe of Breaking: A College Dance Standalone by Amy Daws & Sarah J. Pepper

Chasing Hope: A Mother's *True* Story of Loss, Heartbreak, and the Miracle of Hope

For all retailer purchase links, visit:
www.amydawsauthor.com

ACKNOWLEDGMENTS

Ahhh, my fourteenth book! How crazy is that? This book is especially fun to complete because I've just completed my one-year mark of being a full-time author, and I feel so incredibly grateful to be home for my kid every day after school and still doing my dream job.

I have many people to thank for all their incredible help with bringing this story together. My alpha reader, Jennifer. Girl...thank you so much for hand holding me on this one. I completely love brainstorming and giggling with you! Jane Ashley Converse...you were a clutch girl! Not only did you give me your awesome outdoorsy knowledge but your thoughtful notes were everything I needed!

Beth...oh my sweet Beth. You are my compass of suckage. If you say the book is good, I know it is because you never accept subpar work from me. Thank you! Lydia Rella: My straight shooter! You tell it like it is and I love and need you in my life. You're the Jack to my Rose, and I'll never let go! Franci! Thanks for your mad beta skills and for tolerating my short deadlines!

Thank you to my PAs, Julia and Tiffany, for tolerating my neediness. You girls are superwomen! Thanks to my editor, Jenny Sims, for your awesome attention to detail and super cat speed!

To Brother Joseph Yoder aka my hubby...thanks for not really being my brother but letting me call you that because your Amish beard apparently brings out weird comedy in me. You put the kid to bed, and you don't freak out when I get tunnel vision with every single book, so thank you.

Lorelei...oh sweet Lolo. My six-year-old partner in crime. I finished my book and now we're going to Disney World! (no really, I finished this book within a week of our family vacation to Disney). If that doesn't show you that I love you, then I don't know what will.

And finally, to my six angel babies up above, I wish you were coming with us to Disney, but I promise that my daily smiles will be for you.

MORE ABOUT THE AUTHOR

Amy Daws is an Amazon Top 25 bestselling author of sexy, contemporary romance novels. She enjoys writing love stories that take place in America, as well as across the pond in London; especially about those footy-playing Harris Brothers of hers. When Amy is not writing in a tire shop waiting room, she's watching Gilmore Girls, or singing karaoke in the living room with her daughter while Daddy smiles awkwardly from a distance.

For more of Amy's work, visit: www.amydawsauthor.com

www.facebook.com/amydawsauthor
www.twitter.com/amydawsauthor
instagram.com/amydawsauthor

Chad Hanson
Cabinets
615 - 542 - 7371

762 - 300 - 4475
Precision Home Solutions

Made in the USA
Monee, IL
01 August 2022

10654258R00199